One
Drop

PETER KALU

ANDERSEN PRESS

First published in 2022 by
Andersen Press Limited
20 Vauxhall Bridge Road, London SW1V 2SA, UK
Vijverlaan 48, 3062 HL Rotterdam, Nederland
www.andersenpress.co.uk

2 4 6 8 10 9 7 5 3 1

British Library Cataloguing in Publication Data available.

ISBN 978 1 83913 206 3

Printed and bound in Great Britain
by Clays Ltd, Elcograf S.p.A.

Ruled Britannia

This book is part of a triptych of novels: three separate stories all taking place in the same imagined world. *Three Bullets* by Melvin Burgess, *The Second Coming* by Tariq Mehmood, as well as my own book, *One Drop*, all take place in the UK as it might be in the near future.

Thanks to Tariq and Melvin for the notes, for indulging my late-night agonising, and for the laughs. This worldbuilding has been a four-year rollercoaster journey, and I wouldn't change one bit.

You can find more about the Triptych on our Facebook page
https://www.facebook.com/RuledBritannia/
Or at www.ruledbritannia.net

To Fereshteh.
For everything and all.

1

The Drawbridge

They forced us to the drawbridge, the guards circling tight around us. Low whimpers. Mud. The smell of rot. Pus. Someone retching. A blow from behind. Steel on bone. Dune, close to my side, was a mess: blood still running from the cut in the side of their head where the guards had struggled with the SIM chip so they drilled it in deeper. I knew I had a chip drilled into my skull too, behind the sewn skin flap. All of us did.

The guard by me eased off a little, passing round a cigarette.

I took the chance.

'Hey, Dune.'

Dune looked up. Their eyes blotchy, the flesh around the sockets swollen.

'Hang in there. I got you.'

Dune nodded, took a breath that was a sigh too and their hand reached for my shoulder. Squeezed.

We were huddled together, about forty of us. Outside the Interrogation and Reception centre, facing the drawbridge and the moat. Shouts ahead. A scuffle, then a blur of rags and a woman fell into the mud. She was dragged up by guards and shoved back among us.

In my ear, whispers: 'I want to wake up.'

'You are awake,' I tell Dune.

Dune shivered. They'd slipped their hand into mine and now pressed it hard enough to hurt my knuckles.

A whine of hydraulics, then a shadow in the sky which clanged and spread. The drawbridge was lowering. Its draught flung up smells: burned diesel. Concrete dust. Muck. The vibrations made the moat water churn and spit. Somewhere among all this, the barking of dogs. I was dizzy. For a moment I saw nothing, only a bird wheeling in the white sky.

The bridge clanked level on the concrete lip and the first gate trundled back. Shouts. The bridge juddered as we were escorted onto it, then made to move across. Dune's left foot was dragging and they were making a keening sound like the noise of the wind in the fence. I took Dune's weight on my shoulder. My tongue was swollen. I put a hand up to the painful side of my head and brought my fingers to my eyes. Flakes of dried blood, like rust off an old motorbike wheel.

The second gate drew near. A crane above us shifted. Rain had turned the paper masks of the guards a darker blue and some flung them off. They started pushing us from the round huddle we'd become back into a crocodile line. Handheld scanners read our head SIM chips and the guards shouted out our numbers to each other, pairing us off.

'Number?'

'One.'

'Number?'

'Two.'

Pair.

'Number?'

'Three.'

'Number?'

'Four.'

Pair.

'Number?'

2

We were way down the line. I looked to the ground. The drawbridge's steel. A dragonfly drowning in the sphere of a raindrop. A scanner pressed into my head.

'Number?' the scan guard shouted.

'Twenty-seven!'

Dune was next in line.

'Number?'

'Twenty-nine!'

'No!'

They held Dune's sides and clicked and clicked on the scanner, knocking it into Dune's head. Dune barely flinched. The guard squinted, read off Dune's chip again.

'Number?'

'Twenty-eight!'

Pair.

'Number?'

The count continued till forty-four. Then finally, we were done.

Above us, the crane adjusted. A loudhailer called out: *All Paired. Peace Committee, take over!*

The second gate retracted in another burst of hydraulics. We shuffled into the camp, Dune's breathing heavy. The wind ripping into the rags of our clothes.

A brown-faced man in a silver wig and cassock stepped forward. He was waving a white rag on a stick above his head as he bowed to the guards.

'I am Dolphus of the Peace Committee. We thank you for these new additions. The sky is blue and every day is new.'

I saw the spasm of his head, his rictus grin, as he said, *The sky is blue.*

'And?' a guard said.

'And I have one drop of white blood, and that is the drop I worship.'

The guards retreated. The gate clanged behind them, then, seconds later, there came a backdraught as the drawbridge rose up, trapping us inside.

Dolphus had a team of orderlies and they handed us water in bottles and herded us across grass fields, along tarmac pathways and through a city of tents that had UNHRC lettering on them. We stopped at the largest tent. Inside, at the front of the tent, there was a pull-up banner:

Welcome to
ERAC: Evangelical Realignment Centre
Stay blessed

Inside, other signs were strung up. Rows of wooden benches. Dune was twitching. We shuffled along a bench and sat. At the front, Dolphus started waving jazz hands in the air, pacing and humming. A row of people sat behind him, looking like a starved church choir, their black, brown and white faces circled by bleached white ruffs. They joined in with Dolphus' jazz hands and hums. Slowly the tent went quiet, the hums faded to nothing, and Dolphus started talking, arms high and palms up, like a preacher. I tried to tune in but most of what he said was lost to the pain spreading from my head to my body.

'What fresh hell is this?' muttered Dune. Then, 'Ax, you OK?'

I nodded.

Dolphus' voice rang out across the heaving tent. He'd been talking a while and still had flow.

'. . . so between the fences, the moat, the guard dogs, you can forget about escaping. The SIM chips they have drilled in our heads explode if they are tampered with and can track you day and night, twenty-four-seven. If you try anything, they send in the Scavengers to hunt you down. You don't want to meet the Scavengers.'

I couldn't listen any more. I called out to him from the benches: 'Is this a prison?'

'This is a camp. You are in a scientific experiment. We are here because they want to test these chips in our heads. The chips are designed to make us model citizens in the new world that the Brotherhood of the Blood of Jesus are creating for us. The Bloods are gifting us a new, purer world.'

'What does that mean?' someone else shouted.

'Every night, drones fly over and activate our SIM chips to give us fresh memories and clean our thoughts. Make us all holier.'

Murmurs. Shouts. Dolphus raised his voice in reassurance. 'All *wrong* history will be wiped from your minds. All false thoughts. You will enter a brave new world. I myself am almost there and I can see it. Clean. White. Beautiful. We are blessed.'

The choir behind him began humming and finger-snapping. Dolphus' face went into rapture.

I took in another pull-up banner:

NO-GOOD REBELS
The Pankhursts
Alan Turing
Marilyn Monroe
Amy Winehouse

'Look,' I whispered to Dune, and flicked my eyes at the banner. '*Monroe*. What's she up there for?'

'She was a civil rights sister, back in the day,' mumbled Dune. Then, 'This is freaky, Ax.'

'You can say that again. Totally wack.'

A litter picker was moving robotically around and between the rows. He had been glancing at me since I stood and asked the first question. Now our eyes met. He clenched his fist at his waist. Defiance and challenge flashed across his face. Then he pivoted away and his face was a black mask again.

'The drones will be above tonight and will start their work on you. Stay in your assigned tents. Do not cause trouble. Resistance is harmful. There are shadowy people in the camp. Trouble-causers. They want to fight the Bloods and break out of here. We cannot fight the Bloods, any more than we can stop rain from falling. Or push back the sea. Let's celebrate this new world we are entering, instead of battling it. By joining the winning side, we all become winners. The Bloods' victory is close. They are building a new England, and it will be a shimmering bright thing, a shining city on a hill . . .'

I looked around. Few people outside his choir were listening. We were cold and tired and in pain. We needed clothes to replace our rags. And food. And sleep.

'Today is a special day. You are so lucky. This week, there will be a magnificent parade with top Blood VIPs in attendance . . .'

Dolphus kept on about the parade. I read another of the pull-up banners at the end of a tent walkway.

HEROES
Francis Drake

Sir Walter Raleigh
Edward Colston
William Shakespeare

'. . . remain two to a tent according to your pairings. It is crucial to stay in place overnight. If the night drones find you out of place when they come over for roll call, they will destroy you.'

A stench of sick and stale clothes filled the tent. Along the rows, some sat bolt upright and alert, others were slumped and had their faces buried in their arms, or else had shoved their hands into their mouths. I read another sign.

NO-GOOD NEGROES
Malcolm X
Angela Davis
Martin Luther King Jr

A low moan that may have started with one person but was now a general noise from the benches filled the tent. It was edged with rebellion and fuelled on hunger and pain. Dune began muttering curses. My eyesight was fading, and I didn't know if the fade was caused by the SIM chip or exhaustion.

'It's time to eat!' announced Dolphus with a clap that startled the slumberers.

A cauldron arrived, carried in through a tent flap by two figures in chefs' chequered trousers. They hoiked it onto a metal table.

There was a rumble of tilting benches and a stumble of bodies towards the food. Bowls appeared and the orderlies began ladling it out. Me and Dune forced our way through the scrum and grabbed some. It was hot green slop that smelled of cabbage. We wrestled out of the scrum and sat on a bench to eat. Music tinkled inside the tent. And slogans. Voices of all ages, all joyous.

I love being here.
My mum and dad sent me a letter.
Well done.
I feel good here.
Life's great at camp.
Living here is fun.
Good food, fresh water, nice guards.
Don't be scared. This is beautiful.
The sky is newly blue and I can be reborn too.

We paid the piped-in words no mind. We ate.

Suddenly a red glow lit the tent. Then came a thud. To our left, something wet shot up, hitting the slopes of the tent's peaked ceiling and sliding down its sides. Grey and red, becoming pink where it blended. I looked back and saw a body, blood flowing freely from the side of the now-incomplete head. Screams. Howls.

'I warned you!' Dolphus roared above the din. 'Some fool has tried to remove their head chip! Never try that! Stay calm!'

Peace Committee orderlies rushed to the body and lifted it up.

Memories lurched up. *Mum. Blood. Dad. Blood. The Commander. Blood.* Everything blurred.

When I opened my eyes again, Dune was stroking my face. 'What the fuck,' I whispered to them.

People took their bowls back up and ate. The only sounds were those of spoons on bowls, the push of the wind on canvas, and the slip of the wetness down the tent's sides.

*

They gave us an arrival pack of blankets, tied with string and stuffed with things, and we were sectioned off into groups of eight. Each group had a flunky assigned to it and we had to follow them to the tent zone. Me and Dune trudged on. The pain in my skull was starting to wake up. Every footstep jolted. How the Bloods caught us was still heavy on my mind: Mum's guts on the tarmac. Dad's cry.

The *thunk* of a stave.

I broke from memory. Into this. Here. Now.

The coil-haired flunky escorting us was murmuring something rhymey as he thwacked a stave on his hand. Each thwack made his flunky robes billow.

'Blue eyes dream me away. Pray!'

Dune glanced to me, quizzical. I shrugged.

The paths were concrete, the land level all around. I saw a busted washing machine drum rolling like tumbleweed across low grass, the flattened remains of a military transporter. The nose cone of a fighter jet, its windows gone.

The sun was up. Smoke was blowing from the north from stubble burning somewhere too far off to see. It carried a tarry taste. Over to the east were clusters of bomb-busted low buildings and a long wide stretch of concrete that swirled left. A runway. The smoke thickened, cutting visibility. The grass underfoot was sodden. Still slapping the stave into his outstretched palm, the flunky was onto his next verse.

'White at last, white at last, thank God Almighty, I am white at last!'

In the corner of my eye, I saw a shadowy figure; they had been steadily following us as we walked with the flunky. I turned my

9

head, looked, let them know I saw them. The litter-picker guy. He nodded to me but said nothing.

Shouts ahead. The smoke obscuring everything. We picked up pace.

Cries.

Ahead of us, someone fell under harsh blows. A flunky had her splayed out on the grass. I'd seen her before, in the reception tent. I recognised the pink hair ends. The moon face. The flunky was pressing a scanner to her skull with one hand, pounding her ribs with the butt-end of their stave with the other.

'Number?!'

'Thirty!'

'Number?!'

'Thirty!'

'Number?!'

Dune stumbled to go and help her, but fell. I hauled them up and together we ran to her. Our own flunky called us back. I made five leaps and me and Dune reached her and Dune flung themselves at the flunky and I tried to follow but the pain from my wounds wiped me out. I came round to the sight of scattering feet. Flunkies all about, protecting the one standing over the girl.

'You no-good negroes.'

I got up. Dune clung to the girl with the pink hair. I kneeled down to her. Tears budded in her eyes. I brushed hair from her face.

The shadow man came over and said something to the girl that I couldn't follow because a flaring pain tore through my head, like the SIM chip in my skull was threatening to burst. I waited. The pain dimmed. Then the shadow man was whispering to Dune, '. . .

understand? You did good, but not now.' He was holding Dune, who was on their haunches, blinking back rage and confusion.

The girl stood up.

The flunky we'd wrestled with brushed his robes down. He had his scanner back in his hand and was standing in front of the girl with it once more.

'Number?'

Everyone tensed. The girl had to have clocked the controls on the flunky's scanner because she pointed to it and said to the flunky: 'Run update. Press settings. Then tools. Tools. Then update. OK?'

Somehow, whatever she said got through to the flunky. A glimmer of recognition. He fiddled with the scanner. Then pressed it to her head again.

'Number . . . thirty.'

'Like I said,' said the girl.

'Move now.'

The flunky's gaze landed on the shadow man.

'What are you?'

'I'm a no-good negro.'

The flunky nodded and moved on.

The shadow man whispered to us. 'Get back with your group. Go to your tent and rest up. I'll call. We got business.'

'Why were you following us?'

'Tomorrow we can talk. Now go. Conform. Before they mark you.'

And the shadow man disappeared into smoke.

We rejoined our group of eight waiting by the edge of the path with our own flunky, still murmuring his song about blue eyes.

Minutes later we arrived at the tent field. Row after row of grey, A-frame canvas tents. Numbers on the side. Our flunky assigned the tents by number. Me and Dune were allocated the third tent in the sixteenth row, four back from the main path. The field extended way beyond our pitch. The Bloods had plenty of spare capacity.

When the flunky left, we undid the tent flaps and went in. The air inside was musty, the light dim. Dune took the left side and we unpacked.

'The girl,' Dune said. 'Why did that litter dude say "not now"?'

The question hung in the air.

We were unpacking the bundles. A rough blanket. Inside the blanket, a thin foam mat and a small cube of foam for a pillow. A camping stove and a gas canister the size of your hand. Matches. A tube of cotton wadding. An electric lamp. A pot. A silver foil pack of mixed edible seeds and another of rice grains. Dried noodles. Some flavour sachets. A zippered green pack with a white cross on it. Inside the green pack, antiseptic wipes, a tube of cream, a small plastic bottle of iodine, one bandage roll.

'Yeah. Who was that guy? "We got business."'

We laughed. Even though it pained our heads to do it.

'What was he whispering to you, Dune?'

As I'd held the girl's head in my hands, I'd seen them talking.

'He told me drones will fly over tonight and knock us out, you know, make us fall asleep. Be ready.' Dune was lying on their foam now. 'Lucky us.' Then, 'This is bad, right?'

'Can't be worse than what we went through when the Bloods stopped the car.'

'Don't talk about that.'

12

I rolled out my own foam. Dune had their head propped on an elbow, watching me; they were moody, else the head wound was giving them a headache. A sheen of sweat sat on their forehead.

'Come to Ax, Dune, babes. Your head hurts?'

Dune nodded. They pulled my arms closer around them.

'If I could rewind time,' I said with Dune in my arms, 'I'd have made sure we never took that road. And you wouldn't have been in the car.'

'If they'd known me and you were Resistance, they'd have shot us straight off instead of toying with us.'

'What they did to you, Dune . . .'

'Don't.'

I let Dune roll onto me and their face pressed into mine. They kissed me and then rested their head on my shoulder. Their breathing slowed.

'I don't think they put moisturiser in the Welcome Pack,' Dune murmured after a while.

'Natch. Not even cocoa butter. What we meant to do?'

'The big zit here always erupts and ruins the profile of my chin.'

I smiled to myself. After all the shit we had been through, they obsessed on that. That was Dune.

Outside, children were playing and something about the weird joy in their shouts had us stir, even though we were tired. We peeked our heads out of the flaps. Three kids in busted-up shoes were kicking a can. Another kid was pretend-flying near a tent where a mother cradled a floppy baby, the mother whimpering, an older child leaning into her, crying. Someone walked past, their lips sucking at a scrunched plastic bottle of milky water.

Wind pushed through the camp, making ropes and canvas

groan. It flexed the grass, so it showed silver green then glossy green then back to silver; and the air flow lifted up smells of soil, piss and oil, and made swirling eddies of dust and debris. Then the grass turned to grey and the children vanished and the sunlight dimmed to darkness and heavy grey settled over everything.

'There's no stars up there,' Dune said. We were still at the entrance to the tent.

'There are,' I replied. 'Always. It's just sometimes we can't see them.'

Someone was singing happily in a deep voice not far from us.

> '. . . *this valley of mine!*
> *Oh, Bloods! You're so divine!'*

'What the fuck?' Dune whispered.

I shrugged. 'At least he holds the tune.'

The warbler stopped. Lights began to extinguish from inside tents, cooking stoves *phutted* out all around us, and soon it was if the other tents were no longer there and we were alone in the black. A hum of engines overhead in the air. A klaxon. The drones. Moving overhead. We braced. My skin pricked.

Then I was gone.

2

Mussed Afro

I woke quietly. I was under a coarse blanket. I pulled it back and looked around. I was in a tent that was shaking in the wind. It was ice-cold. *Who am I?* Axel. *Who is this under here with me?* Dune. Dune was asleep next to me, mouth frozen in an angry O.

Noises outside. I untied the tent flaps. Rows and rows of white UNHRC tents. People stumbling around. Small fires beside the tent openings. A standpipe at a crossroads in the rows.

I gathered it in and made sense of it all. We were in a Bloods camp. *Welcome to ERAC: Evangelical Realignment Centre.* I recalled stumbling across the drawbridge. The Peace Committee. The blood and brains in the tent. *Don't mess with the SIM chips.* The pink haired girl. The night drones. *The night drones.* Had they come? Had they messed with my mind? I turned back into the tent, letting Dune snooze on. I fished out the stove and unfolded its legs, screwed the gas container into its belly, then went with a pot to fetch water. My head buzzed, the scalp hairs riffling in some weird reflex and waves of blurred thoughts ran around like the beginnings of a migraine. Everything slipped in and out of focus. Blotches became tents where figures were stirring, weird low clouds became puffs of smoke rising in front of tent openings. Small fires were being lit. Grunts. Hawking. People in underclothes emerging to stretch, scratch, gaze up or down or simply stand outside, twitching. The brain fog lifted.

There was a chicken running around one row of tents and I wondered how it got into the camp. Two children in bobbly orange jumpsuits were playing a dice game on one of the paths. The bigger of them threw two marked stones and hopscotched along a chalk ladder.

> '*TWO!*
> *Nigger, nigger, in the hole,*
> *I rolled two, now you roll!*'

At the standpipe, I waited my turn then filled the pot with water. My mind felt brittle but sharp. A tug on my sleeve. I looked up to see the girl with the moon face. The one who'd been beaten by the flunky. Her grin spread the greening bruises on her face into something resembling beauty. We hugged.

'Hello, you.'

'Hi right back at ya.'

'You OK?' I asked her.

She nodded. She stood waiting with her pot, the toes of her bare feet mashing mud. I had my hiking boots on.

'I'm across the field,' she said, pointing. 'There.'

A man cut into the line before us and plugged his lips to the standpipe tap. His eyes were vacant, his face heavily bearded, shirt tattered and pyjama bottoms caked at the hem with mud. He trembled as he drank. Another joined him in the same clothing. They pushed into each other. Nobody protested. They burped, then trailed away in a stuttered walk. The walking dead.

'How does that happen?' I asked, nodding to the two who had just left. 'Do the head SIM chips cause it?'

She shrugged. 'If the shitty circuits running their scanners is anything to go by, it could be a glitch when the head SIM chips update. Could be deliberate. I guess we'll find out. Anyway, where's your tent? Can I come over?'

'Sure. What's your name?'

'Beta.'

'I'm Ax.'

Beta snuck her hand into mine as we walked back. My other hand was lugging the water.

'I like your hair,' she said.

Last time I'd caught my reflection, it was a muss of Afro, with a slash of angry red skin at the front left, where the SIM chip went in. Mostly, I didn't look.

'Thanks. Grunge look is big in Brixton. You had yours shocking pink, didn't you? Before . . . this.'

'I'll get it back to pink again. Watch me.'

Beta kicked a stone off the path. I squeezed her hand.

We were not far from the tent when a figure came into view on the pathway, trailing a rattling bag. He was swaddled in dark cloaks and had a visor over his face made from a flattened plastic bottle that blurred his features.

He shouted out as he neared. 'Hey, move your filthy black ass out of my path!'

We stepped aside. His rattle-bag was a string sack full of empty gas canisters. He leered at us as he went by.

'Wait there a sec,' I said to Beta when we reached the tent. I ducked inside.

Dune was still laid out on the foam mat, but their knees were twitching up towards their chest, their eyes taking little bites of daylight.

17

When Dune finally sat up, I had the gas stove going outside by the flaps, and Beta was stirring the mixed seeds and rice goop I'd got going in it.

'How you feeling, dude?' I said.

'Like someone's been chewing on my head,' said Dune.

'We're fixing noodles.'

I added the sachets and smelled what bubbled up. Some herb and chilli mix.

'Who's that?' Dune nodded, shuffling to the tent flaps.

'Beta. The one the flunky was whacking with the pole?'

'That happened?'

I looked at Dune. Had the drones affected their memory already? It couldn't be. This was just Dune. They were always like this in the morning.

'Yeah.' I nodded to Beta. 'This is Dune. They. Them. They're always groggy in the morning.'

'Hiya,' said Beta. 'Thanks for trying to help.'

'I did?' said Dune. Their voice was slurred.

Me and Beta exchanged looks.

The noodles tasted good. I shared my bowl with Beta and let Dune have a whole bowl to themselves. The cuts and bruises on Beta's face had purpled up and were oozing a clear liquid. I found the antiseptic cream and spread some over them. Dune was sitting with a gone expression on their face, then their eyelids dropped. Me and Beta talked quietly. She told me how she'd landed here, her voice rising and quickening as the emotion built.

'Blood graffiti got sprayed on the fences near our home. Mum logged on to the Bloods' website and left comments, but she didn't use a VPN.'

'So the Bloods got her IP address?'

'Yes, and they tracked her down, came into the house and . . . shot her. She was in the bath. They used silencers. She didn't know anything. Two Blood youths. The way the bathroom is, she didn't see or hear them. It happened fast. Like ten seconds, all over. They came into my room next. I thought they were joking. But the guns were real.'

'OK. Breathe.'

'They . . . they tied my wrists with cable ties, slapped me around and took me down. Threw me into a lorry with a crowd of others, all tied, and more Blood youths around. Then drove us here. To be *saved*.'

'It's OK.'

Beta was sniffling into my top now.

'I'm all right,' she said.

'You sure?'

Then suddenly she was alert.

'Stay still, Ax, you got something on your shoulder.'

A searing pain.

'I can feel it. What is it?'

'A beetle or something. It's got these little silver jaws and . . .'

'What are you doing?'

A slap on my shoulder blade. Then I felt my shoulder being sucked.

'It's done. The poison's out.'

She showed me the squashed beetle.

'They poisonous?'

Beta finally spat out a pink-white fluid. 'Better safe than sorry,' she said.

19

Dune started shifting, their eyelids fluttering.

We were sitting at the tent's entrance. A chorus of quarrels was coming from nearby tents. Beta brushed herself down, shaking out debris from her ruffled yellow patchwork top and shifting grass off her leggings. A piece of noodle slipped out of one of the ruffles and she picked it up and ate it. She looked up. 'Those noodles, though. What flavour was that?'

'God knows,' I replied.

We smiled. Her hand snuck into mine again.

In sniffles and grunts, Dune was coming round.

'How are you feeling?' I asked.

'My head's killing me and I need to pee. What's the time?'

'It's morning. The drones came last night. We're all just waking up.'

'Where are we? Who's she?'

'I'm Beta. This is a military airbase that the Bloods took over. RAF Alconbury. There was an American bomber fleet here once. You could watch big grey bombers land. Huntingdon Airbase.'

Dune turned to me.

'Ax, who is she?'

'*Beta*. We met her yesterday, remember?'

'Yeah, yeah. Can you two stop niceing each other up?'

I'd been stroking Beta's hair.

'She lost her mum to the Bloods,' I said.

'I'm sorry for your loss,' Dune mumbled. 'This fog in my brain . . .'

'That's because the drones flew over messing with the chips in our heads,' I said to Dune. 'It will clear. Give it a few minutes.'

'We need to work out how to get out of here,' Dune said, then went off to the toilet stall, cursing as only Dune could curse.

A figure in a denim rag dress covered with sewn-on trinkets came stomping past Dune. Her blue-black face shone with happiness as she talked to herself: 'I love my teeth. I love my nails. I love every shiny white piece of me.'

The figure rattled with crosses, bracelets, ankle charms, keyring loops. A dozen metal amulets were tied on a string around her neck. She paused in front of us. I exchanged a glance with Beta, whose face creased into a *what the fuck* frown.

The woman walked on.

Someone else emerged. The litter picker.

'Look who's coming.' I nodded.

'Pharaoh. He was over by my tent last night,' said Beta. 'He knows everything about the camp and the Bloods. I think he's with the Underground. Asked me lots of questions.'

'Like what?'

'What I'm good at. Any training. That kind of thing. You're next. Watch.'

He came wielding his litter picker and a black bag. He saw us together and acted surprised. 'Room for me?' he asked, glancing over his shoulder as he said it.

A smoking quarrel inside a tent somewhere close by had ignited into shouting. Dune was coming back now and drawing close. Pharaoh waited and then the two of them sat down so we were in a circle.

'Welcome to ERAC,' Pharaoh said. 'Stay strong. We will overcome.'

The argument in the tent near us still raged.

'Why are there so many arguments?' Beta asked.

'The head chips. As they take effect, they start rewriting people's memories, their sense of who they are, what they believe in. They drip-feed Blood propaganda till it takes over their minds. Some are more vulnerable than others. These chips can make a Muslim into a Christian. Have Black folk believing they're white. LGBT people declare they're straight. You wake up and somebody you thought you knew, you don't recognise any more. You're going to argue, right? But everybody here is good?'

My eyes flicked over to Dune. We all nodded.

Dune snorted. 'It's a total minstrel show. *Haha, we're in deep shit.*'

'Be patient. The Bloods make out they're all-powerful. But they're going to fall apart eventually. We're going to take the ground from right under their feet.'

'Meanwhile, they're amping the chips in our heads?' I said.

'We have overcome many trials. This is another.'

'So what do we do? How do we break out?' said Dune.

'Dune's right,' I said. 'We got to break out. This is not my idea of fun.'

I looked around.

'The camp is vast,' Beta said.

'Vaster than you know,' replied Pharaoh.

'Are you chipped?' Beta asked him. His hair was all grown out.

'Yes. Everybody in this place is chipped.'

'How come you're not affected then, if you been here longer than us?'

Pharaoh ruffled Beta's hair. 'Good question. This kid, Beta? You know her? She's good with wiring. Aren't you, Beta?'

Beta blushed. 'Electrics,' she said, 'I like wiring stuff.'

'You two saved her from a worse beating. You stepped up.'

'We were in the Resistance,' Dune said proudly. 'If you're Underground, you should sign us up. I'm a crack shot and Ax is a code fiend. We shit hot.'

Pharaoh chuckled. 'And modest with it, right?'

Dune did the Resistance hand sign on their chest.

Pharaoh plucked some grass. 'Some people know all the signs, but they're fakes.'

'You think we're lying?' I said.

'The Underground does checks, is all I'm saying. But you were brave with the flunky. They can get back-up fast.'

'Will you take us?' Dune asked again. 'You *are* the Underground, right? It's you who decides?'

Pharaoh didn't answer. 'Let's see how your brains handle the drones. How are you three feeling? Up there?' Pharaoh tapped his head.

'Good,' said Dune.

I nodded.

Beta squeezed my shoulder. 'Me too.'

'Here's a riddle,' said Pharaoh, 'see how your brains do. If I say hip, you say?'

'Hop!' burst out Dune, beating me to it by a microsecond. Dune's face lit with joy, remembering nightclub vibes.

Pharaoh saw the spark and blew it into a fire: 'Say it loud?'

'We Black and proud!' Me and Dune both landed it, fists punching the air.

'If I were a boy?'

'I swear I'd be a better man!'

'Hey, you Black and beautiful thing?'

'What will the morning bring!'

We laughed. Even as people looked around at us – because in that moment, we didn't care – we were in the club, heaving, rolling.

'I guess the drones ain't got you yet,' said Pharaoh.

There was a lull while we were lost in our clubbing memories.

A man shuffled towards us on the pathway. He was wearing grubby drawstring trousers and a torn, cheesecloth shirt. His hair was tufty short dreads. He had an unkempt, greying beard and his teeth were green. He was singing like he wanted to join in with us.

'Marti, don't let me down!' he sang. His next line was in another tune altogether. 'We are all beautiful people!' He wiggled his hips at the last line, and did a dance kick, some vaguely Northern Soul move.

He stopped and stared at Pharaoh a second. Pharaoh had frozen when the man had sung his first line; now Pharoah gazed at him benignly. The man made a hesitant fist, then shuffled on.

'Who he?' asked Dune. 'I mean, like, the way he stared at you?'

'Just another lost soul,' said Pharaoh. 'Calling for their child. Pay him no mind.'

We went back into our silence.

'What are the piles of stones for?' asked Beta eventually. A series of stones heaped in mounds stood at intervals on every pathway, like weird monuments.

'In case of Scavengers.'

'And they are?' she quizzed.

'More Bloods shitfuckery. Zombie humans. Wiped to zero by their chips and reprogrammed to work for the Bloods as human soldier drones. They have body armour. Batons. They live outside camp in barracks and come inside in packs to do arrests, searches, stuff like that. If you see them, you will know them.'

There was a shout.

'Pharaoh!' A figure came limping towards us. 'Pharaoh! You've got to come!'

3

The Shaft

Dressed in a baggy maroon hoodie and torn white tennis shorts, she came squelching through a stretch of muddy grass. She fell, picked herself up, tumbled again, scrambled onto concrete, kept going and reached us as we were moving towards her. Her legs shook.

Pharaoh held her shoulder and steadied her. 'Hey, hey. Something wrong?'

'She's felled down it!'

'Who?'

'A little one. The big hole. She drowning!'

'Down a shaft?'

'Yes.'

'Let's go.'

We hesitated. Pharaoh didn't. 'You three, come with me.'

We followed the hoodie woman in a scramble south-eastward. Tent after tent came alive at the noise and people tagged on. It was a strange-looking crowd, clothed in rock band T-shirts, clubber jeans, blankets, leggings, overcoats, pyjamas, head wraps, makeshift helmets. The bandaged, the bruised, the chattering, the tranced, the mumbling.

Others simply gawped from their tent openings or offered jeers.

I saw the robes of two flunkies cutting in among the crowd.

We crossed a length of busted runway, weaving between concrete rubble and twisted steel rods that poked at the sky. The hoodie woman stumbled again. Pharaoh picked her up and held her by the waist. We made it over to a stretch of concrete where a ring of people had linked arms to make a barrier around something. At Pharaoh's nod, they let us through.

A woman, wailing.

'Her aunty,' someone said.

The aunty fell into Pharaoh. 'I turned and she'd gone.'

'How old?' quizzed Pharaoh.

'One. Nearly two.'

'How d'you know she's down there?'

'She called my name.'

'Directly from there?'

'Yes.'

'You not heard her since?'

'No.'

'OK.'

Pharaoh stared at the hole. 'It's a ventilation shaft.'

'What for?'

A big youth had pushed through the circle and stood next to Pharaoh.

'Not now,' Pharaoh said to him.

'But if it's a methane vent, there's gas, and anyone going down could be knocked out,' the big youth said. 'Or it could ignite.'

'All right, this is Horse, everybody,' said Pharaoh. 'Horse helps. He's always keen to help, right, Horse? Rest up a moment. Let me think. We need rope. At least forty metres.'

One nod from Pharaoh and a shawl-clad woman in the circle of arms broke free and ran off.

'It's that deep?' asked Horse.

'Yes.'

'You sure?'

'Yes. There's ledges though. She must be caught on a ledge. Else she'd be drowned for sure.'

The shawl woman returned with a huge tangle of blue car-tow rope, coiled in her arm. She dropped it at Pharaoh's feet.

Pharaoh slid the rope through his hands, examining, untangling. It was damaged in parts, thinning in a splay of broken nylon strands.

'It's fine,' Pharaoh said. 'Anybody know knots?'

A girl stepped forward. 'I did the rowboats at the lake. You need a loop knot.'

'Rowboats. Great. Start tying. Tie it to my ankles.'

A Peace Committee flunky had broken through now and stood by Pharaoh, shaking her head. She had a tablet and was looking at it. Her voice was in full clipboard mode.

'Peace Committee rules violation.'

'Meaning?' Pharaoh replied from the ground, as the kid continued looping the rope around his legs.

'Going below surface is banned. You have to file a request, a location map and obtain a safety certificate signed off by the Bloods.'

'There's a baby down there.'

'Be warned. We will mark against your name.'

'You do that. Now step away, I'm going down.'

The crowd was bristling round her. The flunky swept up the hems of her robe and stepped back but not away.

The kid had finished the knot. It looked like a hangman's noose.

Horse picked up the rope and two others from the ring of stretched arms joined him. Pharaoh nodded and Horse beckoned me and Dune. It made five of us in all. Horse was at the end of the rope, closest to Pharaoh's feet.

'I'm going head first,' Pharaoh said. 'Don't let the rope have too much play. I'll tap or shout if I hit problems.'

He gripped the square concrete rim of the shaft, then placed his hands inside and pressed them into the shaft's side, bracing himself.

'You got me?'

'Sure,' Horse called out to him.

'No slack?'

'We got you,' Horse said.

Pharaoh slid into the shaft, head first, veins bulging in his face. His hair brushed the sides and the cross-shaped welt of his chip implant was suddenly visible through his mussed Afro. Then his head was gone. His shirt flapped. Chest, midriff, waist, thighs followed.

We kept the rope tensed, letting it shift slowly, hand over hand. His ankles were at the rim, followed by his boots with their worn-smooth soles and the rope knot which bumped on the sides as it slipped down. The shaft swallowed him the way a snake swallows prey. And all we saw was the blue of the nylon rope rubbing across the lip of the shaft. Length after length of it disappeared. Grunts came from the shaft, but no shout to stop. We kept playing out the rope steadily. The grunts deepened, picked up an echo.

'Hold-hold-hold!'

We stiffened, took the weight.

'OK. But slowly!'

Horse was indefatigable and struck out a rhythm for us to shift weight, replace hands, play out the rope. 'And now! And now and now! And now! That's it.'

We had only a three-metre coil left at our feet when we heard the cry.

'Halt!'

We held. The faint echo of water splashing. Grunts.

It was a long hold. Beta was counting the seconds under her breath. She reached thirty.

Then finally the rope waggled; Horse called it, and we began hauling the rope up.

Pharaoh's boots emerged. The rope knot bumped out of the shaft lip, tight at his ankles. Blood poured from his shins. Horse signalled he was coming off the rope and we had to take his load. We braced. Horse rushed to the shaft edge and he hauled at the legs then torso of Pharaoh, wrenching him out. Beneath the snagged, torn cloth of Pharaoh's shirt, a bulge. The child held fast to Pharaoh's chest. And lifeless.

Screams. Cries. The aunty wailing. Shouts.

'Not breathing,' Pharaoh said, exhausted. He eased the child to the ground.

I knew CPR from the Resistance. I dropped to the kid and something in how I moved made people back off. No breath. Chest not moving. No signs of life. I did the procedure as best as I could recall it. Heel of hand. Other hand over it. Push down two inches. Count the compressions . . . Thirty. Stop. Tilt head back. Seal. Two breaths. Repeat. Chest. Breaths. Nothing. I held the kid up by the ankles, tapped her back, then placed her down again and did the procedure again. Nothing. *Keep going.* The noise faded from above me. Beta was shaking her head. I looked up. Pharaoh pushed me off and began himself. He kept at it for so long the blood from his leg cuts coloured the concrete where the kid lay. Finally, Horse called it to Pharaoh.

'There's no point any more.'

'There's always a point,' Pharaoh cried.

'She's dead,' Horse said, turning his head up to catch his tears before they fell from his face.

Pharaoh let out a cry that sent shivers through us all. Still on his knees, he gathered the child up and passed her into the mumbling aunty's arms with apologies. The aunty began kissing the child all over.

A flunky pushed through the ring of people. 'Move off now, nothing to see!' he shouted to the crowd.

Pharaoh turned to the flunky. Another one stood next to the first. This new flunky was well-muscled.

'We have to take the body,' this second flunky said.

'If you try, your dead body will join hers,' said Pharaoh, trembling.

The crowd seethed:

'Where's your humanity, give her some time!'

'Stuff your forms. A kid just died!'

'Away with you and your flunky robes!'

But others didn't call out at all. They stayed silent and watched the flunkies attentively for cues. A crowd divided.

The flunkies were unmoved. 'We have to complete forms. The death certificate, cause of death. The chip recovery ticket.'

'Let her bury her child.'

'No burials or ceremonial burnings are allowed in the camp.

We have to take the body for the Bloods to examine. We can radio for Scavengers. We don't want to, but we can.'

'You want cause of death?' Pharaoh asked. 'Then write that the *Bloods* killed her. Tap that into your forms. And mark me down for death by Scavenger for saying it if you want to.'

Pharaoh spat at their feet and walked away.

'Not good, not good,' one of the flunkies muttered as Pharaoh strode off. The crowd split. Some stayed with the flunkies, others drifted away with Pharaoh. When I looked back, the flunkies were easing the infant from the wailing aunty's arms.

We walked with Pharaoh in a silent crowd up to the tent zone. In twos and threes, with hugs, headshakes and embraces, people dropped off.

Litter billowed. Yellow noodle wrappers. Silver foil. A brown-stained bandage. A broken-up plastic chandelier. Some kid picked the chandelier up and began running around with it on her head.

Beta was walking next to Pharaoh, looking him over.

'What's happened to your eye?' she said.

'Wire down the side of the shaft. I'll be OK.'

'Get some antiseptic on.'

Pharaoh nodded.

We came to a mound of stones. Pharaoh sat on it and beckoned to us to sit with him. There was just me, Dune, Beta and Horse and the two other rope holders. We waited for him to speak. It was a long wait. Finally, he picked up a stone and flung it.

'Every time this shit happens, it wounds me. By tomorrow, that shaft will be sealed, I'll arrange it. Go now to your tents. They may send Scavengers for me. You don't want to be around me if that happens.'

'Is there anything we can do?' asked Dune.

'Pick your heads up. Watch the skies for a couple of hours, anything airborne. We need to identify patterns.'

'We've done that before,' I said. 'In the Resistance. Skywatch.'

'Good. Maybe one day we'll spot the Bloods' Second Christ ascending,' Pharaoh said bitterly.

He got up and left with Horse and the two others. Dune glanced to Beta. She shrugged. The shock of the kid's death sat heavy on us all.

We took it in turns to watch the sky. Then me and Dune went to join the queue at the food tent. We came back with lentils and some greeny, mashed potatoes, fresh cabbage leaves, and hard bread. We did our best to cook it all up on the stove into a stew.

Beta had stayed flat on her back by the tent, on skywatch.

'Seen anything interesting?' I called to her as me and Dune cooked.

'There's been a Piper M-Six Hundred vectoring east to west. Two jets at six hundred metres' altitude on reconnaissance, due south. One Sikorsky S-Seventy-six-D helicopter with a badly serviced engine limping at no more than eighty, also heading south. A Blood comms drone circling at high altitude, and a hobby toy plane not half a mile and to the west. I think it hit trees.'

'You saw all that? How?'

'I may have missed some. And I've excluded birds. They fit the category, but I excluded them.'

Dune looked at Beta for a long moment, then at me, and we laughed.

We ate together, then Beta left and the light began to dim.

'Do you ever look at paintings of the sky?' I asked Dune, as we sat at the tent opening, looking out.

'Why would I do that? I'd look at a painting of donuts, yes. But sky? No.'

'Serious. You know the blue that we call sky isn't there, like, more than any other colour. The blue's an illusion.'

'Ain't no blue up there at all,' said Dune, pointing, 'that sky's purple. With a touch of pink.'

'*Shh.* I hear something.'

We listened. The sound was gone.

'What you think of Horse?' Dune asked me.

'He seemed more interested in what kind of shaft it was than getting to the kid. But he really pulled on the rope.'

Dune chewed the food and my words.

'What about Beta?'

'What about her?'

'I'm not sure. She's a geek. And she's fangirling you.'

'Naw. Why? You jealous?'

'Yes. She's too nice. I won't be able to compete. Beta was *sucking your shoulder blade*. I looked out and saw her, don't deny it. I tell you, she's crushing on you.'

'Her mum died. They shot her mum in the *bath*.'

'And that's why she's sucking your shoulder?'

'No, she was sucking poison out.'

Dune sucked their teeth.

'Come here and shut up,' I said.

Dune snuck between my knees, facing me, and I dabbed an iodine-soaked square of cloth on their scalp wound. Like mine, the hair there had been shorn off with clippers. The bare oblong

34

was a slash of skin and sutures bordered by Afro. Little black dots showed where hair was starting to grow back. I smiled my sadist's smile as the sting hit Dune and they swore at me.

Then they turned obediently and rested their back against my chest and I set about their Afro, gently running my fingers through it to ease out knots and bits. Dune's hair was type 4C, mine was more 4B. You had to rub Dune's hair between your fingers to loosen the knots sometimes. Dune turned once and stole a kiss. I didn't tug the hair closest around their wound because the wound had been an angry red, though now, with the iodine, it was orangey-blue.

'Done.'

We'd shaped a bit of tin cut out from a cooking oil can as a mirror. Dune leaned for it, looked and nodded.

Then it was my turn and Dune showed how tender they could be. I hardly felt the sting of the iodine, their dabs were butterfly-light as they worked my hair with their fingers.

'You ready for the drones again?' they asked me.

'Sure. Bring them.'

When they were fully done, I took a look in the tin mirror and pronounced myself pleased.

We watched the spots of colour from the tents as the light faded; it reminded me of Vibrate Music Fest on the Suffolk coast. Those Vibe tents and their disco balls, laughter, Mum and Dad doing their bad Soulja Boy cranks and reggae shuffles and soul grooves, Dune lying on me, necking vodka from a Coke can, the sizzle of the burger stalls, the gloops of steaming daal and scoops of cold white rice on cardboard trays, wafts of barbecue smoke. There was a satsuma-juggling Buddha and the air had been full of patchouli and attar, sandalwood, horniness and glitter. Mum and Dad were both drunk and dreamy, as me and Dune danced together, doing half-flips, windmills and flares. We got a circle of admirers. 'You two!' Mum had muttered after the applause. Her eyes had misted as she said it though, and I could tell she was happy for us both.

Now, here we were. The Bloods' ERAC. I never thought I'd miss that Suffolk field, or wish to be on its carpet of sludge, in the smog of diesel fumes and rash of boho tents, all glowing in the dark as damp spliffs fizzled and mongrels yapped. *Mum.* Ah, shit. How she and Dad died came thudding into my mind again. I saw every detail. And I wanted to see nothing.

Dune nudged me.

'You're crying, Ax. You OK?'

I sniffled. 'I'm good.'

'See the sunset? It isn't even ugly. You'd think, the mess we're in, God would paint a sky to fit. But no, that's a pretty sunset. All pink and orange. We could be in a slushy film.'

'Right,' I said. 'If you remove the crying baby soundtrack. And the zombie folk mumbling to themselves in the tents. And the thud of distant bombs. And the smell of shit and piss. And the broken-up concrete. And the red ants crawling up our legs. And the piece of mad metal stuck in our heads.'

'Yeah. Apart from all that,' said Dune.

I looked around. 'There's also the—'

'OK. I get it.'

'Still, your point is good. The sun is doing a nice number.'

Then the drones came over and we were out.

4

The Parade

On the morning of day three, as we were both still shaking off the effects of the drones, flunkies herded us from the tent zone to an area west of the camp to attend the parade. Attendance was compulsory. As we moved, I started mapping this area of the camp in my mind. It was a routine the Resistance had taught us. Like Beta had said, the long, broad concrete lines with the gentle forty-five-degree turns at their hazy ends shouted 'military landing strip'. I looked about. The land around was flat for miles. In the distant west, the remains of some squat buildings, and, almost out of sight to the north west, a crumpled, bombed-out communications tower.

Paraders. Snare drumming. Whistles. Marchers were coming from the north west of the base. Peace Committee orderlies waved red pennants that streamed in the wind against the cold blue sky. There was a boom as a grey fighter jet with the Bloods' insignia on its tail went past. Trumpets.

Flunkies signalled we should cheer. A thrash of marching boots. Then they arrived: a snaking column of uniformed bodies, whose joyous brown, black and white faces tilted to the sky. Batons twirling into the blue. *Woop boom*. Whistling. Brass. The rustle of pressed grey linen. Mouths flexed in song.

'Mary, Mara, coming again!
Mary, Mara, sun or rain!
Second Coming for me and you!
People get ready, join the queue!'

The drummers wore red jackets and black trousers. They looked left and right in sync. A *whoosh*: little silver stars showered down on the marching band. Orderlies urged and the crowd around us screamed with pleasure. A girl in Afro pigtails swooned. By my side, Dune was muttering, 'What the fuck?', their lips curled in disgust. They'd been muttering various things ever since they'd woken, sore-headed. Beta had a fixed look on her face.

In the middle of the parade was a car. It had smoked windows. Blood soldiers walked alongside it, their left hands held high in the Blood 'O' salute. The car's roof was down. It drew near. The windows lowered. On the backseat, two familiar white faces: a woman and a man. She was wearing a green khaki jacket and had her blonde hair coiled in a bun at the back, her lips in a sneer. He was in green too. Both mid-thirties. He had crew-cut black hair and a pistol. They looked the same as in the Bloods' publicity video they'd launched for their Immigrant Lofts campaign. Finally, we were seeing them in the flesh. He fired his gun into the air and the soldier escorts ducked. He laughed at that, then waved to the crowd.

Cheers from the crowd.

'Who are they? asked Beta.

'Blood commanders,' Dune replied. 'We've seen them before.'

We'd both seen them many times on target sheets. They'd been at the top of the Resistance's kill list.

38

Dune cursed them. I kissed my teeth. We were an island of contempt in the crowd's euphoria.

'And who's this Mara they're singing about?' Beta quizzed.

'Another Blood thing,' I explained. 'Mara's their new Mary Mother of God who's going to give birth to the Second Christ and set off the end of days for all but the white believers.'

Dune spat on the ground. Beta shook her head, unbelieving. 'Fruitcakes, then,' she said.

'Yeh,' I agreed. 'Hundred per cent raisins.'

Pharaoh came nudging by. He showed the same waist-height clenched fist. I nodded to him.

The flunkies kept us there till the marching band had wound its way north up the runway and out of sight. Then they signalled we could collect a bundle from the clothes tent as a reward for attendance. Beta was hovering and I waved her over and she fell in step with me, her fingers sliding into mine. Dune was walking ahead.

'Thanks,' said Beta.

'What for?'

'For letting me walk with you. You're always kind to me.' She stretched up on her toes and kissed my cheek. I squeezed her hand, thinking nothing of it.

'*I* should be sharing a tent with you, not Dune.'

Beta had stopped, holding me back. 'What are you talking about?' I said.

'I'd be better for you. I know you. I know your shoe size. I know how many fillings you have in your teeth.'

I squeezed her hand. 'That's full-on stalking, Beets.'

Her head dropped. 'I don't care.'

'You know I'm with Dune.'

I looked at her. Was it my fault she was crushing on me? And *what the fuck*, why now, when we were in the middle of all this shit? How anybody crushed on someone with six days of sweat, and crud in every crevice, was something else. I didn't have a reply for her. I just shook my head.

She looked away and down and when she spoke next, her voice was flat, factual.

'A forty-nine step drawbridge. A moat four metres wide and roughly six metres deep. Two electrified fences either side. A thirty-six metre crane. Twelve dogs. A hundred and twenty-eight paraders.'

'You've been counting?'

As well as the head-drop, I'd picked up that Beta counted when she was anxious.

'Twenty-three guards, including the sniper in the crane.'

Dune had slowed, and turned and joined us now. Beta went quiet, unlaced our hands.

We all three walked a few steps together, then Beta slipped away.

Only when we two were in the tent and had finished arranging the piles of old clothing we'd grabbed after the parade, did Dune say anything.

'I don't like Beta's vibe. Did you feel it?'

'Why?'

'She looks at me cold.'

'She's just shook-up. Bloods killed her mum. She's lonely and lost.'

At that word, *mum,* something hammered in my chest. I found myself trembling. Then Dune came into my arms. We were silent for a moment, both of us remembering something.

'She looks at you too much,' they said.

'Hush.'

My lips brushed Dune's.

A shadow crossed our tent, then a face thrust itself through the flaps. Pharaoh. Close up, I saw the milky-brown eyes, bloodshot around the edges, the flat nose, and the thousand creases in his forehead. 'You two hungry?' he said, beckoning.

We needed no second invitation.

Pharaoh took us on a mazy route through the tent zone, circling west. We slipped across concrete access roads, then pushed through heavy-headed wild grass.

In a clearing among saplings and shrubs, someone was sitting by a small fire. Olive-skinned. Short, wavy black hair. Level green eyes. A square chin. A purpling bruise on her left cheek. Rips in her clothes. She nodded a greeting and beckoned for us to sit. There was a skinned rabbit on a skewer in the fire, sizzling.

'The skies are busy. Will they spot us?' the woman said.

'They're too busy following the commanders' limo to notice a wisp of smoke here,' Pharaoh replied.

This settled the woman, and she gave us her name, Elizabeth X, and asked ours.

I told her. Dune stared at the cooking rabbit.

'There's heavy Blood truck traffic on B-roads all around,' Pharaoh said to her. Then to us: 'The trouble-causers in camp that Dolphus warned about? That's us. We're the Underground.'

'We knew you were,' I said. 'It's an open secret in camp.'

'Does anyone ever get out?' Dune asked. 'They're going to wipe our minds. We've got to get out.'

Elizabeth X plucked the cooked rabbit carcass out of the fire, took up a knife, cut it into four pieces and handed us one each. 'We'll get out,' she said. 'But it will take time and commitment and some outside help. The Bloods have got most of the country under their hammer.'

'Yeah,' said Dune. 'How in hell did that happen?'

'My dad thought they'd be gone in three months,' I said.

Pharaoh bit into his rabbit. 'Many people did. Before the Americans blasted them into power.'

'You know all this, right?' said Elizabeth.

I nodded. 'On TV, we saw bodies floating down the River Thames, birds sitting on top of them, pecking. Madness.'

'I saw the tanks on TV,' said Dune. 'Outside Parliament. American tanks. "England is saved." Some shit like that.'

'Which for Blacks and Muslims and misfits meant people getting hanged and shot,' nodded Pharaoh. 'Commies. Queers. The wrong kind of Christians. They kept extending the list.'

'Right,' said Elizabeth X. 'They have the Americans with them. Mercenaries being paid by the Bloods too. And plenty of British Army regiments have gone over to them. Some regiments renamed themselves the Pure English Army. They're all pushing north. They've bombed Liverpool. Blown up bits of Manchester. The Rubble Revolution, they're calling it. *Pulverise, pacify.* Countryside's no better. Grain in silos, rotting. Unmilked herds dying in sheds.'

'So we're stuffed?' said Dune.

'We're never stuffed,' said Elizabeth X.

'How do you know all that,' I asked, 'from inside here?'

'The Resistance gets messages to us,' said Elizabeth X, 'and we'll break out of here. We've done the checks on you,' she added. 'You were both in the Resistance Youth Corps. You led a platoon, right, Dune?'

Dune nodded. 'A squad. Eight of us. We had crossbows, longbows, guns. Though hardly any live rounds by the end. Supply problems.'

'And you topped out? You were the best?'

Dune swelled. 'Shooting's my thing.'

'Respect.'

'I learned from my gramps. We hunted rabbits. Ducks. With crossbows. Catapults. Longbows.'

As Dune spoke, a memory came to me of Dune's shooting skills. It was during a boring summer day. We were in the back garden and Dune began showing off. They took their catapult out and hit all five cans off the fence, dead centre each time. My turn, I hit one. Then it got stupid.

'Do you love me, Ax?' Dune had asked.

'Course.'

'Really, really love me?'

'Course.'

They had me put an apple on my head.

'Stay dead still,' Dune said. 'And trust me.'

I closed my eyes. My skin prickled. I heard the *whoop*, felt the tiny shockwave that shifted the hair on my forehead. Heard the apple hit the ground. I opened my eyes.

'Put another one up,' Dune said, proud and grinning. They'd reloaded the catapult.

I placed the second apple on my head when Mum came screaming out. 'Don't you dare, don't you dare! You stupid stupid shits. I can't believe it!'

'But I never missed yet!' Dune protested. 'It's life skills! How to stand rock-steady. That's good life skills!'

Mum chased Dune. They fled into the house, up to the bathroom and locked the door.

'Hey, Ax, you there?'

'Yeah. Sorry. Just remembering something.'

'That's good,' said Pharaoh. 'I was saying, we know you can write code, that you understand programming languages?'

I nodded. It was my hobby.

'This chip hurts my head so hard. Is that normal?' asked Dune.

'Hang in there,' Pharaoh soothed. 'It's different for everyone. The head wound should settle. They heal with red welts across your skull in the shape of a Bloods' cross. Four staples in there hold the flaps of skin together till they seal. The bones knit back.'

'They cut bone up there?' asked Dune.

'Yes. They slice the scalp, then a circular saw takes out a disk of skull. After the chip is inserted, they punch the bone back in, stitch it up. Any who get infected and die, the Peace Committee comes and scoops them up into the death lorry and they're transported offsite.'

'Must you supply so much detail?' said Elizabeth X to Pharaoh.

The sudden needle between the two had Dune raise an eyebrow at me, but they kept on chewing. This rabbit was the first properly edible thing that had passed our lips in a long time.

Elizabeth X suddenly stared up. '*Hush* . . . Go low.'

We flattened our chests into the grass and listened. The grass was swishing about to our left. There came a *pssst*. Another two in quick succession.

Pharaoh answered with a *psst* of his own. 'It's OK,' he said. 'It's Horse.'

'How did he find us?' asked Elizabeth X.

'I must have told him,' said Pharaoh.

Elizabeth X frowned.

Horse came into view. He had neat jeans and a dark green bomber jacket, fresh supplies from his clothes tent bundle, I guessed. He had a good eye for clothes, wore them well.

'Take a seat, Horse,' said Pharaoh. 'What you got?'

'I found this at a drop,' Horse said, sitting. 'It's coded.'

Horse passed a long thin slip of curled paper to Pharaoh. Pharaoh passed the message to Elizabeth X. I saw only dots. She studied it and began nodding.

'What does it say?' asked Horse.

'You can go now, Horse,' said Elizabeth X, without looking up.

'Are these two in now?'

'You can go.'

Elizabeth X turned her gaze on Horse until he got unsettled and rose. She waited until he'd disappeared into the long grass. Then she spoke. 'Discipline is vital in any battle. Let's not get careless.'

She was talking to Pharaoh. The needle between them again. It was something about the message, or the way it had been delivered, or Horse and his questions.

Pharaoh waited for more, but all Elizabeth X said was, 'Plans are speeding up. We will break out soon.'

'Are we in the Underground now?' Dune asked, echoing Horse.

Pharaoh looked to Elizabeth X.

'Not yet,' said Elizabeth X. 'We've got to see how you deal with the drones' rewriting.'

'This rewriting,' I said. 'How do we fight that. Is there a way?'

The light was fading. A wave of fatigue hit me and my body was cramping again.

'It's why we called you here. To tell you. You fight off the day drones from getting to the SIM in your heads with hair gunk, which we will give you. You see me and Pharaoh, how our hair is all frizzed out and shining? That's not fashion, it's protection. It works against day drones, not the night ones. The aluminium particles in the gunk fool their radars, stop the drones connecting with our chips. The night drones are more powerful. When the night drones come, it can feel like a firework going off in your head unless you take steps. What works against them is to storify.'

'What's that?' said Dune, scowling.

'They're trying to erase your memory of yourselves. Your job is to hold onto those memories by telling them to each other. The more you share the memories, the more you're able to strengthen them in your mind so they can't be erased. If you start forgetting or fragmenting, you tell your stories back to each other. We *are* our memories, right?'

'I don't get it,' said Dune. 'What kind of memories?'

'Anything with emotion. Where you remember pain or joy. Those are the memories we hang onto best. The ones that can fight the drone rewrites. You get it?'

'Nope. I still don't get it,' said Dune.

Elizabeth X squeezed Dune's hand. 'I'll show you. This is my story,' she said to us both. 'You're both seventeen, you're old enough to hear it.'

5

Brown Paper Bag

Elizabeth X stared into the embers of the fire as she told her story.

'When I was twelve, I became a survivor. A white man raped me. I'd been walking in some wooded area when it happened. I've hated white men and fir trees ever since. It's not the damage he did to my body that mattered, it's that I never saw the world the same way again.'

'Hey,' I said to Dune. They were shuddering. I placed my arm around their shoulders.

Elizabeth stopped. 'You two OK?'

'Yes,' I said, wiping my own eyes. We were both triggered back into our own trauma. I saw the stink and green of a wood. The crunch of pine needles. Cuffs. A gunshot.

The memory receded. Dune's quiet whimpering too. They squeezed my hand to show that they were OK.

'Go on,' I said to Elizabeth X.

Elizabeth waited. When Dune's breathing settled, she continued.

'I used to sing. In a choir. The strongest feeling of togetherness I ever had was on choir nights. But since that day I've never sung. I went and read heaps of books, trying to work out how men and how whites got to thinking they had the right to do that, or whether some people are simply born bad. The books gave me some answers but not all.'

'What books?' I said softly.

'Audre Lorde was one. You should read her if you get the chance. Malaika wa Azania was another. I learned meditation, to try and cleanse my mind. But my hate was too strong for it, and I decided righteous anger was better than fake calm. I decided I would only ever have relationships with women. I decided a lot of things that day.'

Elizabeth looked up at us, briefly.

'This is who I am. You looking for an earth mother? Not me. You looking for a pacifist? Not me. You looking for we-can-work-with-these-Bloods shit? Not me. Go to the Peace Committee for that.'

Her eyes fixed on the fire embers again.

'I looked after myself. I continued to do my stretches, listen to my body's cycles. I joined night school, code club, book club, I liked online learning. Nobody can grope you when you're online. That's what happened to me. And I'm done apologising for white men, and I'm going to kill all the Bloods' white men I can find, one at a time, working my way back to my rapist. I so hope he's still alive when I get out of here, because I want to kill him myself. I envy those that can party. Pharaoh can party. I live with what happened to me every day. It's a memory that powers me. That's my story.'

'I hear you, sister,' said Dune. They were breathing hard again.

'Wow,' I said, 'that was powerful.' I wiped tears from my face.

'It connects with you, Dune, Ax, right?' said Elizabeth X. 'Something bad happened to both of you that connects you with this?'

I nodded. 'We feel you,' I said. 'I'm so sorry that happened to you.'

'Now that you have my story, you hold a part of me,' Elizabeth X said to us.

Pharaoh squeezed Elizabeth X's shoulder. 'I'll storify for them too.'

The creases of his face softened. His voice hit the same quiet tone as Elizabeth X's.

'I'm nobody special. I ran a car repair shop in Ely. Window tinting. Spoilers. Fancy exhausts. I pimped the youths' rides. I was involved in shadier things too. I did wrong. But I did my time and I cleaned up. You see this, on the palms of my hands here? These are the names of my children. Tattooed into my hands. I wake up, I got them. Every morning, I bring them together and pray to Black Jesus for them. I lost my children. I abandoned them. We were driving away from an anti-Bloods rally and Bloods militia shot up our car at a checkpoint. I got out, rolled. But my babies didn't. They were dead when I went back to the car. Propped up there. And the car, booby-trapped. I had to leave them.'

Elizabeth touched his knee. 'I got you,' she murmured to him, 'I got you.'

'Everyone I see their age, I say to myself, that's somebody's daughter, just like mine, somebody's son, just like mine. A piece of my own children in each one of you. And I care for you the same way. You got my son's eyes. You got my daughter's ways, with how you hold your hands. Sometimes I think of joining them – my children – only, I'm not sure that's not the chip inside my head talking.'

'Pharaoh, that's the chip,' said Elizabeth X. 'We been through that. Don't be saying any different.'

She turned to us. 'You tell each other your stories, you understand? That's how you resist, that's how you hold onto yourselves.'

Hearing their stories, I knew I belonged with the Underground. I never felt more strongly that I belonged to something than in this moment.

'So, when can we join?' I asked.

Elizabeth smiled, non-committal again. 'Work on surviving the drones for now. Not everybody does. People get gummed: their minds wiped, memories deleted when the drones sweep over and reprogramme them. Some wake with gaps in their memory everywhere. They become the Blanked. Then Whited. Some of them get completely hollowed out and Bloods convert them to Scavengers.'

'The zombie soldiers?' I asked. 'I've never seen them.'

'You will.'

'Take this.' Pharaoh held out a bundle. 'It's maidenhair, for you to make drinks with. Boiling it and drinking is best, but you can chew it raw too. Maidenhair's a fern that can be used as a medicinal herb to help memory retention and retrieval.'

He offered a plastic tub too.

'And here's the gunk with the deflecting particles in it. Get your hair glistening. Now go back to your tent, drink, gunk and storify. Prepare yourselves for the drones. We need to know you can survive them. Go now.'

Inside our tent, we applied the gunk to each other's hair. The soft, slow whirl of Dune's fingers on my scalp felt good. 'Am I glistening now?' I asked.

'Brighter than a lighthouse.'

The maidenhair looked like clumps of clover and smelled of

seaweed. We were tired. We each chewed a few leaves, raw. It wasn't great. Then we flopped on the foam mats. I was goose-pimple cold. Darkness had closed in. The canvas was slack and it rustled and thumped with the push and pull of the wind. The blankets smelled of horse, but I got under them. Dune followed me.

'Stinks, right?'

I nodded.

'Hold your nose. Breathe through your mouth,' Dune said. 'Good life skills.'

I smiled at that. *Good life skills.* It was one of Dune's phrases. I rested my head on their shoulder.

'Let's do it,' said Dune.

'What?'

'Storify. The stronger the story, the better, is what she was saying. Something we can remember together is best. Joy or pain.'

I pulled the blankets tighter. 'I don't know, Dune. Choose joy. I don't want to dive back into all the bad things.'

Dune had their hands behind their head now, eyes wide open. They lay there, thinking through things, sifting. 'You remember the first time we saw the Bloods?' they said eventually.

'That wagon thing in the fields?'

'No. Before that. At school. The recruitment stall. We thought it was a joke, right?'

The vision trickled into my mind's eye. 'They had the stall at school on that day celebrating all the old greybeards with portraits in the hall.'

'School Founders' Day?'

'That's it. Bloods turned up with leaflets and QR codes and high-fiving. That was off-the-scale weird, looking back.'

51

'But funny too, right?'

'Tell it me then, Dune. How old were we then? You had mohawk cornrows, nuh? And we had one of those rings that paired, we each wore a part.'

'Year ten, we were fourteen,' said Dune. 'It was summer, everybody sweating and sliding and the exams finished and general feel-good vibes like always after exams, and they made Founders' Day into a recruitment bazaar. Anybody and everybody was invited to come recruit us up. Army. Jehovah's. YouTube influencers. Police cadets. Food franchises. Census. And we went because free stuff, knowhatI'msayin'? And we heard about the Bloods stall and you ask me what I think about the Bloods. And I said it's wall-to-wall fanatics. There's not one thing I like about them. Their music? Shit. Slogans? Nazi. Wigs? Lice. Preaching shows? Yuck. You can't go fishing anywhere in London, for all the dead bodies the Bloods are throwing in the rivers. Enough burning crosses to replace the streetlights up there. And none of their Tablets of Truth make sense. If the original Mary, Mother of God was born in the Middle East then for the Second Coming, if history repeats, the Bloods would be looking out for some Middle Eastern or Asian woman, nuh? Yet those are the people they're stringing up on trees and bombing and shit. So yeah, Bloods are bullshit. But free stuff is free stuff.'

Dune had hit their rhythm. I lay back and listened.

'We filled our bags that day. Gum. Pens. Magnets. Dinky drinks cans. Condoms. Discount codes. Clickers. Everything we could lay our hands on.'

'Right.'

'Then we got to the Bloods stall.'

'Uh huh.'

'We wanted their penknives. But you had to join for them. No problem. We was already in the Police cadets, Army cadets, St John Ambulance cadets, Dolphin Divers, Frisbee Freestylers and the Society for the Appreciation of Norfolk Cheese, and we were gonna go right ahead and join them too.'

'Sure was.'

'And they gave us their pitch. Something like "God is the Father. Jesus Christ is his only born son. Mary, his mother, will come again."'

'Something like that.'

'"Right. No problem," I told them, "pray continue."

'What was the next bit?'

'I remember "Heresy and destruction and prophecy can be averted if the earth is purified by the Second Coming." Something like that.'

'Keep on,' I said to Dune.

'So I said, "Also no problem. Sign us up. Where's your free stuff?"

'Then came their clincher. Remember? "The last days of earth are upon us. Soon the Righteous Cleansing will begin."

'"Amen," I said. "I swear down, no problem," I said. "Those penknives look neat."

'"All shall bless Mara," they said.

'"Sure thing. Can we have the free gift, times two, please?"'

'You said that?' I asked Dune. I was there, but didn't remember that line. Maybe I'd been distracted.

'I said that. And they said no. Said we failed their brown paper bag test. "What the fuck is a brown paper bag test?" I said. And they pull out this paper bag, I swear down, an actual brown paper

53

bag. And put it to my face and say, "You are darker than this bag and so you can't join. Them's the rules."'

'Yeah. Sick. Tell it, Dune, keep going.'

'And I went, "Fuck the rules."

'And they came back, "And this group is also not open to LGBT."

'And I'm like, "What?"

'And they go, "We saw you two holding hands?"

'"And?"

'"Are you two of the LGBT persuasion?"'

'You were in full girly-girl mode, then,' I said, 'in your mohawk days, Dune. And I must have pulled on a frock for the day for some reason. And what did you say back, Dune?'

'I said straightfaced, "I am totally cis hetero queer."'

I smiled under the blanket, remembering it.

'And they went, "Don't play with us. Move along."

'I said, "Look at these threads. These are Pretty Urban Dreams threads. You can't get straighter than them."'

'True talk. And while they were having it out with you, I swiped two penknives from under their noses.'

'You did, true, you did. And we gave them the finger, right? Both hands, and the school suspended us for the rest of the week because they caught us on CCTV flicking the finger which was "A flagrant breach of Rule hundred and fifty-six.". That so, Ax?'

'Yes, indeedy, yeah. That was a good day. Haha.'

Dune had rolled onto me as I laughed and they were now pressed right into me, the blanket between us. And with the blanket being over my head, I couldn't see them either, but I could feel them.

'Are you trying to sex me?' I asked, my voice muffled in the blanket.

'Yeah?'

'Yeah.'

We laughed and we did it.

And fell asleep fast afterwards.

I woke in a startle. Some banging outside. Wisps of the story we told last night came to me. The recruitment stall. The brown paper bag test. Giving them the finger. Pushing over their stall. We stole the penknives. *That was a good day.* I oriented myself. I was in ERAC. I opened the flaps of the tent. It was quiet outside.

I shook Dune, lying there inert, to try to dislodge the snarl from their face.

Dune came round slowly, looked at me like I was a complete stranger, then pulled the blanket back over their head.

'Hey, get out from under there. It's me, Ax.'

Muttering from under the blanket.

'What you say?'

'My head hurts, *you no-good negro.*'

'What the fuck?'

'Did I say something?'

'Dune, wake up. How are you feeling?'

'You stole the penknives. *You no-good negro.*'

'Hah. You remember? You were with me, dude.'

'Say your name again.'

My heart lurched. Had they wiped Dune? The motherfuckers.

'Ax. Axel. Your partner in crime. The penknives?'

Dune's face cleared.

'Yeah. Ax. We did shit together.'

'The Bloods' penknives. At school. It was Founders' Day, remember?'

'Sure. Where are we, Ax? What's this tent shit? I hate camping.'

I told them. Dune took it in slowly and pieced it all together. The puzzled look cleared from their face. They replaced it with a frown that matched mine.

6

The London Wind

Pharaoh came round that morning and checked on us. I said nothing about Dune's wobble and Dune was oblivious to it. Pharaoh demonstrated how to brew the maidenhair and said the effects from the drones were strongest in the morning but wore off after a few hours, and daytime delete drones were a very rare sight, but to watch the skies. He talked a bit more, then he left.

The sun had hardly warmed our canvas when there was a squawk. I peeked out. Flunkies on the paths with loudhailers. They began barking out orders for a work detail tour. There were crop fields to be weeded. Cooking duties. Rubbish collections. Clothes needed sorting. Me and Dune hung together on the tour as flunkies and orderlies explained this task and that.

Some of the people around us were glitching. I heard them say 'White is nice'. One kid couldn't stop saying, 'I'm a mule, load me up', which had Dune giggling. Throughout the tour, despite all this, nothing left Dune's mouth that gave me any cause to worry further. I stuck close by them anyway. The air in the clothes tent jittered with fleas. The soil in the fields was hard-baked and heavy. The kitchen tents smelled foul, especially when the blue food drums were opened up. All kinds of rancid veg and stale grains spilled out. I understood why Pharaoh did litter-picking. At least the air was fresh. We did a litter-pick circuit with him. When it was finished and the rubbish was in the dump, we sat on a pile of stones with Pharaoh. An escaped scrap of paper blew up in the air. Dune snatched up a stone and threw it, smacking the paper dead centre.

'Do that again,' said Pharaoh, amused.

'Fine. Throw something.'

Pharaoh plucked up a piece of plastic and threw it. The wind made it swerve sharply up and left. Still Dune nailed it, their stone hitting with a smack and sending the plastic falling.

'Dude's showing off,' I said to Pharaoh.

'Now I believe you got skills.'

'I always been good like that,' said Dune, who didn't do humility. 'Archery at school. Javelin. Then cricket, baseball, you name it. Resistance had me training people how to shoot. Not Hollywood shooting. Proper shooting. Stance. Recoil. Target assessment. Breathing.'

'That so?' Pharaoh went quiet as a flunky passed by in flowing robes, cradling a tablet in one arm.

'What power do those Peace Committee flunkies actually have?' I asked when he'd gone.

'They're only powerful if the Bloods take notice of the reports they file. Ready?' he said to Dune.

Dune nodded.

Pharaoh threw something up. Dune grabbed a stone and hit it in one action. It jerked to a stop midair then spiralled down. Pharaoh's shoe. A laughing Pharaoh waved bye and hobbled off to retrieve it.

Not long after, the dark crept in. We were tired but we were good, and we storified.

*

I woke the next morning and placed a fifth stone in the plastic bottle. Five days.

Dune was on their back, half asleep, mumbling into the blanket. 'I love camp, it's so much fun here. We grow whiter every day.'

Then, when I started to brew the maidenhair, they said to my back: 'Step to it, you no-good negro.'

Imagine waking up with someone saying that instead of 'Good morning'? Your best friend and partner calling you a 'no-good negro'?

I put the brew to their lips, and got them to drink it.

'Who are you anyway?'

'Just drink.'

Soon Dune was quiet by my side. Their eyes softened, unglared themselves. They stared at me as I retold last night's story. Slowly, recognition crept in. They said they missed me. I wiped away a tear.

'What's happening to me, Ax?'

'They drilled the chip so much deeper into your head than mine, Dune. I think that's why you got it worse.'

'Or maybe the drones are always coming for me, like for *me* specially.'

'Could be. But you're back now. Rest up. Deep breaths.'

We did a sorting shift in the clothes tent and scratched at the fleas we picked up from it.

By late afternoon we were sitting on some mangled steel beams outside a busted bunker in the south of the camp. Sometimes it helped to sit away from everything and try to remember. It wasn't just Dune who was affected. I was forgetting the faces of my mum and dad. When I concentrated, I could see the shape of their heads and some features of their faces like the nose and the ears, but the details were blurring, and their eyes were gone, etched out completely. Something had happened to them, something bad, that the chip was deleting, but I couldn't recall what.

The London wind had got up and was blowing bomb smoke from the south, from far beyond the fences that held us in. The smoke was a wall, maybe half a mile high and wide enough to blow across the entire prison camp, which it did. Soon we were choking in it. I wanted to duck down, but Dune said 'No, let's stay out.'

So we gauzed up our mouths and noses and sat there, squinting, letting it blow over us. It surged on, tugging in its wake everything that had been trapped within it, and lifting up new stuff. Cinder from the cooking fires, rust from burned-out cars, bits of plastic, rags, a fugitive wanted poster. The smoke storm hurtled along, carrying alarmed cries from the tent zone and the screeches of birds that were pulling away before the rolling wall of smoke.

We held onto each other, me and Dune. It blew over fast. No longer than twenty seconds. When I slipped off my gauze, I saw Dune was twitching, the pupils of their eyes flexing, and their limbs stiffening.

They nudged me. 'I think I'm fading, the drones are at me again.'

'You're not. You're right here.'

'No, I can feel it, Axel. They got something on me. They always coming for me.'

'C'mon, Dune. We lickle but we talawa, right?'

'Don't joke. I know they're gumming me. Remember me, Ax. If I'm totally gummed.'

'OK.'

'Remember me, Ax.'

It was one effect of the gumming. The repetition.

'You're OK. It's passed.'

I could see it had passed. They were OK. Shaken, but OK.

'Am I?'

'Watch.'

I put Dune in a headlock the way they loved, and they laughed and pretended to struggle, squirming and bucking and laughing into my halter top all at the same time.

I didn't know it then but soon Dune would be gone and that would be the last time I headlocked them. Right now, their legs were kicking, their hips jerking, their lips rubbing the cotton straps at my collar bone, their Afro tickling my chin.

'No way can you wriggle free, I got moves on moves!'

Dune yelled back that they were gonna kill me when they got loose. They could easily heave me off if they wanted. That was the joke. They liked being wrapped in my arms.

Then the sound.

'Shhshh,' I told them. 'You hear that?'

We went still.

'It's nearing . . . I told you. They coming for me again.'

I watched. This time they'd sent the drone low.

'Duck your head,' I told them. 'Not like that. Chin up. Spread your hair.'

'Listen. It's got something wrong with it,' Dune whispered. 'The dirt in the wind's clogged a motor maybe . . . I can hear . . .'

'Shh. Your hair.'

Dune flicked their Afro and the silicone gunk glittered there with the aluminium particles. In mine too, I hoped. Doing its work, deflecting.

The drone came closer now, hovering somewhere overhead. It was a near-field, high-frequency raid drone, flying solo. They usually came in fleets of five, and at night, Pharaoh had told us. I heard it splutter. Twice. Then it smoothed itself out. Five seconds, and its front motors fired to turn it. It rotated close above us, powering down from a thrashing whine to a regular hum. The sky was cloudless, and only thin trails of the bomb smoke were left.

Maybe the drone had been part of the bombing mission and got lost. It was holding position.

I wondered what the drone saw from up there. The Bloods' Huntingdon prison city in all its four-mile-wide, fenced misery. The two bombed runways that slashed across from west to south. The smoked, broken bunkers and buildings in the zone where we were holed up. The bog at the south western edge where the saplings grew. The tents dotting the inner field where we had to sleep. The buckled tarmac roads that crisscrossed everything and looped round the tent field. The smouldering fires at the edges of the corn and marrow fields to the east, where all the books had been piled up and burned by the Peace Committee, according to Beta. Beyond those fields and further south, the forbidden zone.

The drone dropped lower. Dune began shaking. Little trembles in their feet. The drones could tune in even to sobs, so I kissed their cheek and whispered, 'Shh, we talawa, right?' It was our joke: *We small, but powerful.* Something my mum used to tell us both, back in the free days.

Mum. A memory. Almost her face. Yet seared with pain. And smeared with blood. *Why?* Something had happened to her. I couldn't recall what. It was something bad, though . . . I shuddered. There were some memories I was glad were being eroded.

Dune's legs, trembling. They smiled but their eyes were gone, the chestnut browns misting, like a thousand pins were stabbing away inside them.

'C'mon, Dune, hold on.'

A tear fell from my eye and I hugged them, and when that didn't work, I bit their arm.

That did it.

They were spluttering expletives. But back.

The drone dropped lower still. Maybe hearing something and trying to find a near-field SIM signal off us. It allowed faster rewrites. If it managed it, there'd be little hope because Dune was already barely hanging on, their memories fractured, thoughts unwired.

The drone jittered, rotating, dropping, zigging. The silicone gunk in our hair was baffling it. Lower again. Soon the gunk wouldn't work because the drone would switch recognition systems. It would have us in a moment.

'*Fuck!*' Dune stood up.

'Get down. It's still there!'

'Fuck them. Fuck it. Remember me, Axel.'

'Don't!'

Too late, Dune was up and off. Leaping over a stack of stripped-out fridges, round a crushed car. Onto the buckled road. What were they doing? Suddenly, we weren't alone out here in the bunker zone. Someone shouted, 'Get down! Get down!' at Dune from some bolthole in the rubble.

The drone picked up Dune's movement and twisted.

I scrambled after them. I didn't care, they could take me too, I wasn't leaving Dune, we'd done everything together. If we had to go, we'd go together.

Screaming, 'Wait, wait!' I raced, trying to close the gap. Dune was leagues ahead of me, the space between us felt huge and I burst my lungs trying to catch up. As they ran, they dipped a hand into the back of their pants and tugged something out. The catapult. Early that afternoon, we'd found some twisted metal in just the right yoke shape and joked about making it. Or I'd joked. The crazy fucker had been serious. They'd sneaked off and done it.

I'd made it to the road when they stopped, spread their feet and loaded the catapult in one smooth move. It was a steel and rubber beauty, with an aluminium cap for the ball-bearings shot. They pulled back on the cap.

Whoop.

I saw the ball-bearings sting into the sky. This silver array.

I clattered into Dune, my shoulders whacking the back of their knees, tumbling them down.

Small bursts of fire leaped up either side of us, making concrete dust dance.

Then the drone went skewwhiff. The ball bearings had hit it good.

We watched from where we'd fallen. It gyroscoped up, banking crazily, trying to haul itself away, made it past the first fence, small as a fly to us now, sputtering just beyond the moat and then the second fence. We heard it crash, saw the leap of little flames. The dogs barking beyond.

Dune lay there in the muck, giggling.

'You crazy fuck,' I said.

'We talawa, nuh?' Dune choked. 'Now kiss me again.'

Word got round fast about the drone strike and by the time we got back to the tent city, incense was burning on pathways in celebration, and choirs were singing high in the big tent foyers. *Someone has downed a drone.* Not the whole camp celebrated. There were still stares. Mutterings of *Which fools did that*? And shadowy figures flickering out of sight as we passed. But the balance of power between the Peace Committee and Underground had been shifted and some new energy was released that was leaping across the camp, tent to tent.

We knew from Resistance training that after any big event, it was best to lie low and say nothing. So we stayed in our tent and waited for Pharaoh. Or Scavengers, because if the downed drone had ID'd us before crashing, the Scavengers would be let loose on us for sure.

Beta ducked in. 'Was that you?' she asked.

Neither of us replied.

'OK.' She nodded. From her smile, she knew what our silence meant.

Horse came by. 'You won't *believe*. Some fuckers just downed a raid drone.'

'That so, Horse?' smiled Dune, biting their lip.

'Was one of you, wasn't it? Come on, tell me.'

We said nothing.

'OK, my lips are sealed.' Horse left, tapping his nose.

Soon after, the Peace Committee broadcast a warning on the

camp P.A., announcing that downing a drone was very high-risk
activity. Attacks on drones needed deep thought and risk assessment.
They knew it was some young people who must be new arrivals
and very naive. Any such action should only be taken by authorised
and trained persons after proper consultation with the Peace
Committee. Yes, they conceded, for newcomers to down a drone
was a startling development, and due credit had to be given for
that, it had never been achieved before. But the drones never flew
so low usually, so in the Peace Committee's judgement, it was a
probably a rogue drone or a drone operator's mistake. Downing it
was therefore a lucky hit. However, only a fool would fail to realise
that the fallen drone could be replaced a hundred times over, and
its data might have survived, meaning the Bloods would learn about
it and take action. Everyone in the camp might be punished, not
just those who were responsible. Better to wait for things to change.
The wars would soon be over. The Bloods would be magnanimous
in victory and allow us to keep what remained of our original selves.

A little later, the Peace Committee food gong bashed. A rare
evening serving. I winced and my stomach tightened. Me and Dune
joined a food queue. How did rumours work? Some people in the
queue were convinced it was us and wanted to know how we'd
done it. We were seventeen, we'd been here under a week and we'd
stood out there under a low-flying attack drone. They'd have
expected us to be burned or Blanked or both and yet here we
were, still breathing, still us. We denied involvement. The Peace
Committee speaker up on the pole by the food queue piped
more warnings as we shuffled forwards in the queue. I blocked it
all out, both praise and condemnation.

When we got to the front of the queue the server held a ladle almost longer than herself. She winked at me, and as she poured, her other hand made a fist, for long enough for me to notice. I nodded to her. The serving was a pink gruel this time, with grey bits bobbing up that were either mushroom or old ham or chicken or soya mince. It was edible. Dune snatched two bowls. I gulped mine down in five mouthfuls then drank standpipe water till none of the taste was left in my mouth. Dune didn't drink any water. They simply smacked their upper teeth with their tongue after they finished.

The Peace Committee were still broadcasting warnings as we made it back to our tent.

Of course, nobody woke listened to the Peace Committee. They were nobodies, almost completely overwritten, soon to be shipped out to become Scavengers or set to work in the Bloods' factories, or as Blood mercenaries in the battles across England.

Pharaoh showed up. He told Horse to wait outside then ducked into our tent and bumped fists. He told us in a low voice that he knew it was us and the deed was already legendary among Underground youth, the first time anybody outside of the Underground had ever downed a drone.

'So sign us up then!' said Dune.

Pharaoh smiled. 'Let's see what happens tonight.'

He gave us a bunch more maidenhair and said we should brew it longer and drink it double strength.

Then he spoke in a whispery voice as we packed the maidenhair away: 'The good news is it looks like the Bloods haven't captured enough information from the downed drone, else the Scavengers would have come for you already.'

'That's something,' I replied.

'The less good news is they'll have data that could point in your direction, and they'll try to home in with the drones tonight to find out who did it. You'll need to storify for your lives to survive the night.'

'OK, I got it,' I said.

He said he'd meet us next day if he could escape his Peace Committee trackers and we had to remember to storify hard.

Pharaoh was gone almost as soon as he'd arrived, his black beret merging into the smoke of early evening cooking pots and the squares of drying clothes, Horse trailing behind him.

Beta dropped by, but left quickly after.

We settled for the night. If the drone system had even partial intel on us, then for sure the drones would be searching fiercely to ID us tonight.

The sky grew heavy, and we lay there, scared. This might be our last night.

We drank the maidenhair, then steeled ourselves to talk. The only memories I could dredge up were hard ones. Or weird ones. Like the Holy Cowboy.

'You remember the church visit?' I asked Dune.

'No.'

Dune was motionless and frowning with effort to recall something, anything.

Something trickled into my mind about the church. I saw my mum there. *My mum.* The image of her leaped up. An outline of her. The way she walked through the church door. For the first time in days. I kept going.

'Sure you do,' I said to Dune. 'Let me tell you.' And I remembered it for us both.

It was in the early days, when the Bloods had just taken over. My mum needed to rig an antenna onto a church spire, and she took us along as cover: we were a family suddenly feeling religious and looking for a place to worship. 'Look religious,' Mum told us as she was driving. 'In case there's anyone there,' she continued, 'though the word is, it's abandoned.'

'Are you remembering, Dune?' I said now. 'Dune, you actually looked *pious* for once. You found a pure choirboy face like I'd never seen on you before. Mum loved it, patted you on the cheek, even as she drove.'

I carried on with the story.

'Now, attention, dear Axel,' Mum said. 'What is the phrase the Bloods ask you to use when you are a Black person and want to join the Bloods' militia?'

'Dunno,' I'd said to Mum. 'Why would I ever want to know that?'

'I will tell you: "I have one drop of white blood in my veins and that is the drop I worship."'

'What?'

'It's for Black people who want to declare allegiance to the Bloods.'

'Like we forming a queue for that?' Dune said.

'There've been a few converts. "I have one drop of white blood in my veins and that is the drop I worship." That's what you have to say to prove you're on their side. Now say it.'

'No,' Dune replied flatly.

I wasn't having it either. Mum pulled the car over and turned, taking us both in with her gaze.

'Say it,' she insisted.

There was another lightning flash that lit the clouds in the sky behind her. It made her face switch from beach brown to blue for a second.

Dune glanced across at me. Their eyes said, *Has your mum flipped?*

'OK, Mum, I'll say it. But I don't believe it.'

I wanted to get the temperature in the car down.

Mum's voice was brittle. 'I didn't *ask* you to believe it, I'm asking you to say it, so I know you know it. One day it might save your life.'

'Whatever.'

I said it in a monotone, word-perfect first time, so we could all move on: 'I have one drop of white blood in my veins and that is the drop I worship.'

'Great. And you, Dune.'

'Fuck that.'

They looked at each other. Dune's hand crept to the car door handle. Mum's eyes narrowed.

Mum blinked first. 'OK, we'll try again later with you, Dune, lovey.'

The church was Methodist. It was tall outside but wasn't much to look at inside. A couple dozen rows of chairs. A pulpit. A steel trough for baptising people. The cross was an electric one, glowing luminous red, which was pretty cool. Underneath the cross were fresh flowers. It had three slit-like, ornate stained-glass windows at the back, and two giant TV screens to the left and right of the cross. There were two flags on poles on either side of the small stage, one American, the other the St George flag. Mum said the

States flag was there because of the local American airbase, before they all upped and went back to the States or trundled with their tanks north with the Bloods.

A door opened at the rear behind the cross and a white man emerged. He was straightening out his blousy white cassock. A flat red, heavyweight scarf thing hung over it.

He had jeans on. The cuffs of a lumberjack shirt showed at his wrists.

'The heavens have opened in more ways than one,' he said, all jovial. His voice had a twang like in the old cowboy movies.

'It's chucking down, is one. What's the other one?' said Mum, disappointed to find anyone there. She shifted her wire cutters discreetly into her tracksuit top.

'This church has visitors!'

He'd closed the gap and was shaking hands with Mum.

'Would you like to make an offering? We take all the cryptocurrencies as well as PayPal. Church roof to maintain and all of that.'

'No, I'm good. I mean, we didn't think that this place . . . was, you know, occupied,' Mum said.

'Then come, let us pray.'

'I'd rather not.'

'That's OK, I'll do the praying for all of us. How about that? You just take a pew.'

I could see Mum was trying to back out but couldn't find the words, and by the time she went to open her mouth it was too late, the man had got us sitting in the front pew right where he wanted us. Worse still, you could tell by the gleam coming from his face that this wasn't going to be the standard English vicar

71

sermon. No, he was going to give the roof a good testing, all his pent-up sermonising let loose.

'Visuals!' he said.

And Lo! The two TVs blinked on and two fancy candles flickered, one on each screen.

I was impressed by the tech. Mum was real mean if she wasn't going to pay this guy something after this, I decided.

He raised his hands and did that Beseeching in a Cassock pose.

'Lord, we are here on this earth right now, as Noah before the flood. Yet we will row out to you, Lord, we fear not the storm. Lord, change is coming. It's in the air, it's in our blood. Who plants their seed shall reap their wheat. Hear us now in the name of the Father, the Son, the Holy Ghost and Blessed Mary, Mother of God.'

Shit. That was a Bloods line. I looked across to Mum. Her body language was saying, *I know, I know, but cool it, act like we don't notice.*

Dune had an open *whatthefuckisthisshit* look. I shook my head, to tell them to wipe it from their face.

The man's big red scarf thing flapped as he moved up and down. Suddenly he dropped to his knees, raised his hands, begging, fingers splayed. It was pure theatre.

'To be near you, Lord, we cast off from the coast. I pray they join us now before they get left behind. The blacks. The crossdressers. The gender-benders. The lost. Beware the coming Tribulations. Kneel now before the Great White Throne. The coming of God at the Appointed Hour.'

Ah, I thought, *the usual Bloods' God and White Supremacy spiel.*

The priest had the smell of mothballs and ancient sweat mingling with a woody cologne. He settled his chin on his chest, eyes closed in peace.

The TV images switched. A snowy scene played.

The images were neat. He had to have a clicker hidden in the cassock somewhere.

The standard Jesus, white as a white mouse in a flour factory, came up, all flowing locks, billowing white robes and gleaming blue eyes.

He did a few more hallelujahs and a couple Praise the Lords and Blessed Mary Mother of Gods then he was done.

'As a matter of doctrine,' Mum said, getting up and straightening out, 'I thought Methodists didn't believe in the rapture and speaking in tongues? This is a Methodist church building, right?'

That was Mum all over. The man just did a sermon as racist as the Ku Klux Klan and Mum wants to pull him up on his grammar or something.

I was looking for an out. These Bloods evangels could go nuts on you at any moment.

The sweat had gone from the priest's brow and he found his human-to-human voice again. 'Fair point. I enjoy a theological debate, I'm in the wrong trade if I don't! The signs are all out there though. I'm sure even John Wesley, living today, would see the signs.'

He turned to me and Dune, and his face went all swarmy. Dune dodged as he tried to lay his hands on our heads. He made do with the double open palm gesture. 'Jesus is my quarterback, kids. I'm merely the receiver of His messages, catching the ball and trying to get everyone across the line with it to the shore of Salvation.'

His gaze switched to Mum: 'Clearly, we are in the End Times.

Would you not agree? A great cleansing is about to happen. You and your kids need to prepare, to get on the right side of God, because His army will soon be on the move. His air force will soon be in the sky. His avenging angels will smote the wicked down and—'

'Smite,' Mum interrupted.

'Huh?'

'It's smite. Not smote. "Will smite the wicked down." Future tense. But carry on.'

The man had bad breath but I gave him nine out of ten for his neatly plucked eyebrows. His scarf had Blood crosses showing at the chest on either side.

I'd had enough. I nodded to Dune and we backed away as the priest kept on with his *yada yada*.

He noticed and called out: 'Don't be afraid of the gun.'

What? The fucker has a gun, too?

'It's not for you. It's for thieves. I have a permit. It's a good ol' Smith and Wesson. Want to see it?'

Only now did Mum say the obvious aloud. 'Oh my. So you're with the Bloods?' she said.

'Yes, and we welcome all, even the dark-skinned. Even Muslims, if they have the one drop of white blood. We are all God's creation. High or low, we are all God's creatures.'

'No. No high and low. We are all equal.'

'Well, my friend, I didn't take you for a radical Marxist, but trust me on this one, Malcolm X won't save you. That no-good negro. Only Jesus can save you in this moment.'

Mum turned and left. Like she should have aeons ago.

*

74

'Dune, you still listening? . . . Dune?'

Wind pulled at the tent's canvas. Dune's face was calm, their eyes open but clouded. I tried to cling onto the vision of Mum's face that had come back to me. But it slipped away. Instead, *blood. Tarmac. A Blood checkpoint.*

Tears streamed down my face and I didn't know why.

Dune's arm was on my shoulder, their fingers fretting my halter top's straps. Rain drummed. The night sky beyond the flaps shimmered like black sequins. I told Dune how much I loved them and how I couldn't imagine being in this world without them, there would be no point.

Dune said they'd run for the drone because I'd kissed them and they'd forgotten what it was like to be kissed and suddenly in that moment they couldn't take being fenced in, and their mind constantly swarmed and fragmented, they wanted to be free with me, like before, free in their imagination and to own everything they thought and felt, and for us to do whatever we wanted.

'And everything I ever wanted, is you, Ax.'

Dune wiped my left cheek. Another tear followed and they wiped that too. There and then, Dune wrote me this poem with their fingertip on my thigh using my teardrops. Their own eyes glittered as they wrote it:

> *We are our own sky, we are our own ocean.*
> *We want nothing more, nothing less.*

They rested their head on me, and we lay there, breathing the air, watching the thickening sky. Unease began eating my insides, spreading up from my stomach, tightening my lungs. What would the Bloods' night drones do to us tonight? I couldn't settle. I got up and dug out the maidenhair fern. The Peace Committee had banned it as unreliable, unapproved and counterproductive. As Dune looked on, I dropped three small ferns into a tin bowl, added water, mixed in what remained of the skank cider, because the alcohol in the cider would draw the maidenhair out better, then let it infuse. I nodded to Dune.

We drank. Dune first: I made sure they drank most of it. I gulped the rest, including the dregs, in one go.

Dune rested their head on my lap again and I felt their sleep pattern starting. If we were going to be gummed, it was tonight. I'd figured out that the night drones sucked up the memory and thought data collected on our implants, and tried to download new stuff, rewriting our memories if they found a way, reworking our thoughts. That was the experiment. Why we were being held here. So they could perfect the technology.

Pharaoh had said that over the six months he'd been here, the Underground had figured out new ways to resist, to block and slow the rewrites.

It seemed Dune had been targeted more than myself or else was more vulnerable, their chip more deeply embedded or more fully wired. Whatever it was, the drone rewrites had started to get through to them. I knew Dune was fragmenting. Not badly. But it was happening. We had to hold onto each other, by our stories, in our dreams, in our lives, it was the best way of resisting the rewrites.

The dark had the sky fully now.

At the gates, the slow caterwaul of the Bloods' curfew alarm started: that meant the night drones were nearing. There was no movement on the pathways. Everyone was under canvas. The penalty for not being present in your assigned tent when the night drones flew over was to risk being Blanked, Whited, Scavenged or Exploded. We were all lying still. It was quiet, apart from one baby, crying.

I heard the high hum of wind against glass somewhere. Then the faint tinkling of the night drones' high-altitude engines in hover mode. Dune was already half gone, whimpering in their semi-sleep. I found Dune's hand and held it. We locked fingers. The sky beyond the flaps was a deep black. I thought only of Dune and our stories. Would the drones pick us up?

A memory surged. *The wagon.*

I whispered it to Dune. 'Should I tell it you now?'

'Yes. Tell it,' they said to me, 'tell it now, as much as you can, I need it.'

7

The Wagon

Mum had an urgent drop and her cover story was a family picnic, so we had to go along, and Dune rode with us. Dad's tongue was quick when I asked what Mum was dropping. 'How many times do I tell you? You don't ask where your mum's going. You don't notice things. We don't ask about your work with the Resistance Youth Corps, do we? You don't ask about our work with the Resistance. Deal?'

'Fine,' I said. Dad was too worked up to hear any other answer. Dad's *keep shtum* rule was OK in theory. But Mum was the Resistance's Huntingdon Quartermaster, responsible for getting stuff to people, from guns to spark plugs to soap powder. She knew what me and Dune were doing because she supplied the pit props for our tunnel builds, and she provided the locks for the safe huts that we were burying three metres deep into the floor of the forest for when the Resistance had to hide people in them.

And Dad was always leaking code stuff he was doing when he got stuck. Which was often. One time he came huffing his way down the stairs, muttering about bugs. He flung an error sheet at me. I shinned up into the loft and glanced at the middle-left of Dad's four screens. It was a live feed. Someone was hacking a Bloods' government database called Porton Down and Dad was hacking them to monitor it all. Only Dad had messed up. There was a bug in his hack code. I swapped his code soup for something that actually ran smoothly, then went down and told him it was fixed and that maybe next time he'd be better using Logic Focus instead of Object Orientation.

'Right,' Dad said, brushing my code wisdom off. 'Thought so.' Then, 'You picked all that up in thirty seconds?'

'You're getting slow, Dad, old age. What's Porton Down then, and why are you hacking it?'

Dad tapped his nose. 'Porton Down's the big government science and defence lab. All kinds of secrets sit on that mainframe. The Bloods in government think they've taken it over but they're actually looking at a mirror site that we control, and we're feeding them bad info. Porton Down deals with virus attacks. Not code viruses but actual biological viruses. So it is somewhat important we keep control.'

'Fuck,' I said to myself. If the Bloods got hold of biological weapons, then a whole heap of new shit would get real.

Mum snapped me back into the real world by a sudden shout at Dad.

'No, no, take the B road, avoid the roadblock!'

Dispensing driving advice to Dad was the fastest way to annoy him and he deliberately drove over all the B road's potholes. The car was rattling with the things you associate with picnics: sick bags, plastic bags to wrap your feet in when tramping through mud, heavy coats in case of rain, the cool box, fold-up chairs, a plastic tabletop and its four legs that clicked and clacked in the footwells, a football, badminton racquets. And wind chimes. God knows what they were for.

Dune's face was pressed up against the glass of the rear, driver's side. Dad was talking about how they lynched Black people in America in the olden days and that was what might be coming

79

soon and, what with the political situation and all, Huntingdon was in the eye of a storm. Birmingham was almost gone, London been gone a year already. The Bloods were looking unstoppable.

Dune leaned forward, tuned the car radio to a Resistance station and when the line 'Change is a-coming' wailed out, we all joined in, and that improved the mood.

We left the car in the mud patch of a tractor turning point. Mum took out a large canvas bag and veered west into a field of baled straw that had a slight incline and became a conifer forest. Dad took us due east across the same field and kept us going, telling us not to turn round. Soon we were among tree trunks and dragonflies. There was a stream running through the trees where dark pools held shoals of finger-length silver fish. Small, black, biting flies hovered above the stream water. We kept on and as the trail got rockier, Dad started huffing with the cool box, but not letting us help. We made it past the last treeline of the woods and into a clearing that was almost lawn.

Dad got the cool box opened. It was maybe a fake picnic but there was no reason not to enjoy it. 'A fish does not know the meaning of water,' Dad began, in his 'sage on the mountain' tone as the lid of the cool box hinged back.

The air was dry, with flecks of hay occasionally flicking across.

'Is that right?' Dune said, grabbing a chicken drumstick.

'Yes, think about it. Being a fish, being always in water, a fish has no awareness of not-water to compare with the state of being in-water.'

'Carry on,' said Dune. They took another piece of chicken. Dune was an Olympic eater and you had to be fast around them.

Dad hesitated but found his mojo. 'My point is, we are

sometimes immersed in things and have no awareness we are immersed in them. Like now. With the rise of fascism.'

'I got attacked last week,' said Dune.

'What happened?' said Mum. She'd rejoined us, minus the canvas bag.

'Nothing. The usual. Some randoms threw a punch at me. I hit them back and ran.'

'Was it Bloods?' Mum pressed.

'Yeah. Bloods Cadets.'

'You know you're fam to us, Dune?' said Dad.

'Are you adopting me?'

'Might as well,' I joked. 'Seeing as you spend most of the time round ours.'

'And Dune is welcome,' said Dad. 'I'd trust them with my life.'

Dune nodded. Their eyes flicked at the chicken Dad was holding.

'Makes you fam, right?' said Dad, biting on the last spicy chicken wing. 'Now, I'm a-just lie back, close my eyes and bathe in this sunlight like a fish in water.'

Dad rested his head on Mum's stomach.

'You two, don't wander off,' said Mum. 'Appreciate nature. Look at those beautiful fields yonder.'

'Yonder?' I quizzed.

'Yes, yonder,' confirmed Mum. She was a trained librarian. She knew these kinds of words. She wagged a finger vaguely at the greenery around us.

Dad had this amazing ability to go to sleep at the drop of a chewed chicken bone, and he was soon snoring. Mum's eyelids fell too.

Dune edged closer. Me and Dune watched the countryside

around us for about three seconds. Then it was clear that the open air and sun and stuff had got Dune frisky. They began rubbing me. *This was nuts.* I trapped their hand.

Dune turned onto their chest. 'Your dad's getting old,' they said. 'See how he struggled with the cool box?'

'He's not old, he's unfit. All the days he spends staring at screens.'

'What about me, am I fit?' Dune said.

I grinned into the grass. This was Dune all over. Fishing for compliments. 'Good try,' I said, 'but this conversation has now ended.'

The sky was sheer silk blue. The fields were a patchwork of colours in pastel tones of brown and green and yellow, ruffling from the horizon towards us, all the way up to the broad grey zip fastener of the road. Then, after that, larger and larger patches of flowing green fields, right up to where my head was now resting on Dune's softly rising and falling stomach as my hands kept theirs from wandering.

I had my eyes half closed, so my eyelashes played with the sun's rays, when I heard this distant rumbling sound. I looked up. It was coming from the road. The sight confused me. I sat up to see it clearer.

I thought it was scarecrows at first, stacked vertically in the back of one of those farmer's wagons with the steel-slatted upper bodies that are towed by tractors. But as I looked more closely, I saw it was human beings, not scarecrows, every one of them dark-skinned, tall, nappy-headed, and dressed in rough clothes. They were stood up in the wagon, being jolted and jostled as it was towed along the road at some speed by a camouflage-coloured Land Rover. I called out, waving to them. I was far enough away that they might not see or hear me, but I thought at least one of them might. None waved back, or even lifted their hands as they went past.

I nudged Dune and they woke, saw what I saw.

I shouted again, more urgently at them. Dad stirred, mumbling 'What are you shouting about?'

'The wagon, there were all these people, Black people, crammed into the back like chickens in a cage,' I said to him. 'They were ghost people, Dad. They didn't shout out or move. They looked like they were tied up and they had dead eyes.'

'Where?'

'It's gone now.'

'Dead eyes? How could you see their eyes from here?'

'I dunno. Dad, they were scary.'

'You sure? Maybe you were dreaming.'

'Yes. I'm sure.'

'Dune?'

'Yup?'

'Black people in the back of a wagon. Tied up?'

'I saw it too,' Dune confirmed.

Mum stirred now. 'We need to get back. Phone this in. I've heard reports. It's the Immigrant Lofts campaign. They had vans out saying they were going to round up people hiding in the countryside that didn't have the right papers.'

By the time we were back on the estate, it was dark. Mum was on the phone for ages. Then she came down and wedged me between her knees and began oiling and cornrowing my hair without even asking. A newsflash came up on the TV. Another big bomb had gone off, this time in Leeds.

8

Blow-up

I woke, rolled over and eased up to my haunches. I looked at the skin on my arm and I saw it was brown. A voice somewhere inside my head was talking.

You no-good negro.

Axel. I was Axel.

You love camp. The sky is blue. You are white too.

A wagon flashed into my mind. The memory slithered and slipped and stuttered, but it came. A wagon in the countryside. The blank eyes of the people crammed into it. Like scarecrows. Alerting Mum, Dad.

A pain shot through me at the thought of Mum and Dad. *Blood. Tarmac. A scattering of limbs.*

You no-good—

I cut the voice off. I looked down at my skin and I knew the beauty of that brownness. I saw into the hair follicles, the black hairs pushing out, hairs as black and as beautiful as the dawn of time. I raised my hand and I felt my chin. I breathed in the air. It was acrid with breakfast smoke.

I was Axel. I was in the Bloods' experimental camp. ERAC. They'd placed a SIM chip in my head. *Had they?* I felt the bump there. *Fuck.*

The sun was burning through the canvas of the tent. I opened the

84

flaps and looked across the tent zone. It was busy with people stirring in all their cursed humanity, their black, brown and ghost-white selves stepping out once more into the hellish world we were fenced into.

I cursed the Bloods. I went out and I washed my face at the standpipe. The kid at the standpipe with me bent to drink from it and as he did, he farted and we laughed, the two of us, because that was us, that was all of us in our messy humanity: we were what we were. I felt the water flowing across my face and I remembered something. The drone. Yesterday, Dune had downed one with a catapult. When I finished washing my face, the people in the queue were mumbling that I couldn't wet my face for so long. I saw the hand on the catapult. Dune's. I'd been with Dune when they'd downed a drone yesterday. I was still here. But where was Dune?

Panic. Dune had not been in the tent. Where were they? I looked around. I noticed one or two people standing still, not sure any more who they were. A brown-faced toddler with straight, bowl-trimmed hair. A Chinese girl with a bruised face. A white youth looking at the sky and crying. All waiting for family or friends to come shepherd them, restore them. None of these stranded were Dune.

I ran across the tent zone, calling out, 'Dune! Dune!' I reached the edge of the zone.

Why hadn't Dune been by my side when I woke? Had the Scavengers seized them overnight and I didn't even wake?

I kept calling, going from tent to tent.

Mid-zone, there Dune was, alone and rocking. I called and they turned, their face blank. I hugged them. 'I was worried, so worried,' I said.

Dune stared back at me, puzzled.

I got them back to the tent. 'Who are you?' They kept saying.

85

'You no-good negro.' Sometimes they'd stop talking and look at me and hate filled their eyes. The insult grew new adjectives. 'You low-rent, stupid negro. You . . .' I held them tight and it was as if a physical, body memory, the smell and feel of me, brought Dune back, the way old people forgot faces or even what year it is, but never forgot how to ride a bike.

'Remember the wagon?' I said.

'A wagon?' Dune asked.

'That's right.'

I went through the story of the wagon, the scarecrow people.

'Your Mum and Dad were there? They loved me?' Dune asked.

'Yes.'

I realised I'd seen their faces last night in that story. And yet now I could see only their outlines. *And blood. Pools of it.* Something bad had happened to them.

'Hey, Axel,' Dune called, 'You're shaking.'

I turned and grabbed their face and kissed them. They'd called my name. That was great.

'I was loved,' Dune said. 'We went on that hill and we ate chicken, right? The sun was out?'

'That's it.'

Slowly the Bloods' memory blocks weakened in our heads, our chip-forced thoughts faded, and Dune's true memory came back. Yes, sometimes they just held my hand and squeezed it as if riding out pain. But I knew the blocks and drone-inflicted SIM rewrite attempts were fading, they always had so far. I made more maidenhair tea and thought about the drone. Dune had downed it and no newcomer had done that before and we were not even meant to survive the night. Yet here we were.

I told Dune about this. They looked at me like I had three heads. The Bloods' head chip started talking out of Dune's mouth again.

'Nah. No, that can't be, you dumb negro.'

I made more maidenhair. I kept the stories we'd told flowing, told them about the church and the cowboy preacher. I did the preacher's Yankee voice. The party at the skateboard park that ended in two ambulances and the Brit Award-winning rapper showing up for a surprise gig. Dune's Golden Shot prize at the Resistance trials when they beat the Resistance's crack shot at targets. When we made the waterslide in the back garden for Dune's birthday and they renamed it MudFest and cranked up the music.

The flickers of recognition increased. By the end of the morning, Dune started saying stuff like, 'Dude, I brought a drone down! High five!' They'd say this over and over, laughing, unaware of the repetition. But they were totally Dune, and by noon, as we finished the maidenhair dregs, they were close to fully back.

Late afternoon, some yellow-flagged Peace Committee orderly came by our tent. The Peace Committee wanted us to go for an interview. Could this be the Peace Committee onto us about the downed drone? I worried. There again, the word in the zone was that the Peace Committee simply loved their interviews. Big, perfumed adults who sat, silk-clothed and spread-legged on their cushioned, cloth chairs, flapping their fly swatters and quaffing filtered water while tapping data into their official Holy Knights DataPads, recording which tent was overaccommodated, who was late to light their breakfast fire, who ate two eggs instead of one, who failed to attend their work shift in the fields, and who missed the curfew by how many seconds. The men wore big Jesus beards and the women

87

had their hair rope-knot braided, Second Messiah style; in interview sessions, they plopped hanging judge wigs on their heads and did a lot of sucking of teeth. Pharaoh said they were appeasers whose philosophy was like that of all appeasers: if we licked the Bloods' arses enough, they were going to treat us better.

'Let's do this,' said Dune. 'It'll be routine.'

'You sure?'

'Yup. I'm good.'

Me and Dune squatted on the low bench before the Peace Committee and waited as the head honcho Dolphus read out our list of infractions: tent flaps tied incorrectly. Incorrect standpipe and breakfast routines. Exiting the tent zone without approval. Moving through tent zones needlessly. Entering bunker zone without permits. Non-approval of morning shift absence. He went through it all even though it was all nonsense because it was all overshadowed by the fact WE HAD KNOCKED OUT A DRONE.

The Committee kept up their hemming and hawing, aahing and sucking, the way they loved to. Eventually they came straight out and asked us: did we attack the drone?

'Hell no!' Dune replied. I shook my head too.

There was a moment of silence. Looks were exchanged, beards tugged, braided hair stroked.

Then they dismissed us.

We got back and Pharaoh and Elizabeth X were sitting there in our tent. Pharaoh's jet black Afro spilled from under his black beret.

He was wearing a black poloneck top. A maidenhair leaf stalk moved around his mouth. Elizabeth X's shoulders were set back in a hessian yoke top. She had crossed her arms, as well as her legs. She had on her beret too. She wore one earring in her left lobe, of a miniature, wooden Afro comb. I felt my earlobes tingling with jealousy. *I* wanted earrings.

We all four studied each other a second.

Then, 'How'd it go?' Elizabeth X asked.

'They're sure to report us to the Bloods,' Dune said.

'OK. We'll try to block that communication.'

Pharaoh nodded. 'Congratulations on surviving the night,' he said.

And Dune being Dune, they actually managed to bow, even though their ass was on the groundsheet.

'You used an improvised catapult. We've built similar but not so fast,' said Elizabeth X. 'It was impressive. How d'you get to be such a great shot?'

Dune struggled to recall anything that would provide an answer to that.

'It was their grandad,' I said for them. 'The two of them went shooting all the time. Guns, catapults, shotguns, you name it.'

'Reports are in from the Resistance. And you two check out,' Elizabeth said. Pharaoh nodded.

'You mean we finally get to join the Underground?' said Dune.

'We want you to train an army of Underground catapult shooters here,' said Elizabeth X.

'I finally get to join the Underground?'

'That's right, Dune. We want you too, Axel. We know you can code. Resistance gave you glowing reports.'

'I can code?'

'Yes. Your parents were part of the Resistance. Your dad specialised in code and you helped him.'

Dad. An image spilled onto the screen of my mind. Dad upstairs in a loft. Then the image spilled away from me again like liquid mercury balls rolling on glass.

'Your father had transmission equipment rigged in a tree in your back garden. And listening tech in your loft.'

'What else do you know about my parents?'

'Don't worry, keep storifying and your memory will come back. And your coding skills.'

So she wasn't going to tell me what happened to them? My dread built.

'We have a team working on intercepts. You used to help your father in that field. We already pull down some of the Bloods' transmissions. You could help us pull down more. Will you join us? Both of you?'

There was a lick of sweat across my back. I looked across at Dune. 'How about it, Dune?'

'I say let's do it, Ax,' Dune said. 'You know I'm way past scared. How about you?'

I'd wanted it, yet, now it was offered, I suddenly had doubts. Were these two *no-good negros* arranging our deaths?

'We'll let you think about it,' said Elizabeth X. 'It's a lot to take in. There are risks. We'll be back tomorrow for your decision.'

They got up and left. No sooner had they gone through the flaps, Dune went antsy with excitement.

'This is it. What I always wanted.' Their fingers were in the gunk tub and they were gunking their hair extra as they said it, like they were going to go out right now, even as the dark hauled in, and shoot another drone down or something.

'We can still say no,' I reminded them. 'Catapults against drones? The odds don't stack up great, Dune, don't you think?'

'What are you talking about?'

'They warned us, way back. Those two are being hunted even now. The Bloods could send in the Scavengers. Or send the drones over our tent one night, explode our heads off.'

Dune straightened and it was as if they hadn't heard anything I'd said. 'Hey, stop there. I'm all about breaking free. Break free or die trying, that's me. How about you?'

They were up close now, their chest in my face, gunking my hair as they were saying all this. They didn't see the huge smile that had broken out across my face. Now they looked down and caught it because it was still there.

'Oh, you beauty, Axel,' Dune said, tracing their fingers along the line of my eyebrows, 'you want in as much as me!'

I bit their chest and they kissed me. Then they tilted their head into the tent ceiling, made a fist and whispered, 'We are so gonna break free!'

Night fell and it was time to storify again.

Each night was a battle with the head chips.

Each morning a new part of me gone, a new fight to piece Dune back together.

The chips were as lethal inside our skulls as the Bloods' tanks were outside the camp, in England itself.

'My mum and dad. Do you have any memories of them?' I

91

asked Dune. 'Every time I think of them, I get this flash, like my brain's going to blow. There's something bad happened to them.'

'Yeah, I get that too.' Dune went quiet. Then they said, 'Let's not go there tonight, though. I don't know if I'm strong enough.'

I looked across. Dune hated to admit weakness. The words they'd just said gave me a new respect for them. Even though I was dying to see my parents again before they were totally erased from my mind.

'Remember the hanging?' said Dune. 'In the park?'

'We going to go there instead? That's your lowkey?'

Dune nodded. 'I want to remember it. It's important, I think.'

I sighed. 'Sure. Let's go there. You telling it or me?'

'You.'

A Street Justice decree was passed by the Bloods in the final week of the London takeover and all week the TV news had shown captured resistors being hanged on gallows over the River Thames and shot on the river's banks and thrown into the Thames water. By the weekend, the Huntingdon Bloods had turned copycat.

We had been playing basketball in Little Stukeley's park and after, we lay down in a hollow in the grass next to the court to cool down and loosen buttons and slide zippers. There were some birds flying around. Seagulls.

Dune let me run my hand through their short twist 'fro. They'd had side bars cut in. I traced them with my fingers. The skin by their neck was warm and shone in the sun like gold leaf. I opened my knees and Dune pushed their head into my crotch and I twisted and neatened Dune's hair as they were down there.

Then we fucked.

When we were done, Dune sang softly.

Thing was, Dune could sing. Not the rasp of the street musician, not the rolling flow of the lyricists and rhymers, not the whine and warble of the TV show contestants. No. Dune's timbre was soft and magical, and made you think of empty trains, deserted platforms, remote hotels, a lost child hiding in a forest. Dune sang this way only for me. I never heard them sing this way any place else, in front of anyone else. I rested my head on their shoulder and felt their lungs' rhythm, the vibration of the song.

Suddenly, shrill cries. We bobbed up. Two white militia had come into the park, pulling a scrawny, black-skinned man with a straggly Tut beard and no shoes on a rope behind them. He was bound, cuffed and gagged. A small crowd followed the three of them, solemnly pushing a gawky, rattling gallows that looked like a tilted Hangman game sketch gone real. The gallows' wheels squeaked.

We dropped low and peeped and listened.

They were about a hundred and fifty metres away from us, by a duck pond.

To cheers from the crowd, they put a rope over the man's head and pulled him up on the gallows by his neck. A couple of the crowd leaned their weight on the rope to get him up high. His feet kept kicking. They let him dangle and choke and kick till he became still. Then one of the militia took out their gun and shot him twice.

We flattened into the hollow at the sound of the first shot. I glanced up between that and the second bullet. The pads of Dune's fingertips were in the bones at the back of my waist, telling me to

Get down, stay down, stay still, stay low, they can't see us in this hollow so what are you doing, getting up? A streak of blood on the park path, widening.

A grey fighter jet skimmed across the sky. It did a go-around then slowed to almost a stop above us. It was a United States Air Force plane because it had the Confederate flag painted on its side. We stayed still. The plane roared off.

The rustle of leaves. The shimmer-sound from the basketball hoop's chain net. The clutching of our breathing. The pop at my throat when I swallowed. Traffic on London Road. The small crowd's jeers as the body twitched. Laughter. The scuff of shoes as the crowd melted away, leaving the body there. The creak of the weighted, makeshift gallows.

'The fuck?' said Dune, when the crowd's footsteps had faded.

'Stay low. They could be back.'

'That poor bastard. If I had a gun, I would have shot those Bloods myself.'

We were whispering all this.

We watched the wind spinning leaves in the trees, spinning the limp body. In my chest, my heart spun too.

I sat up and steadied my breathing. Remnants of the images still circled at the edges of my mind's eye, sucking at me. My head was hot where the SIM chip was lodged. I was dizzy. Dune was lying beside me, their breathing rattly. Dune. Their sweat as they lay with me in the park. The tinny ringing of the basketball hoop net. The creaking gallows. The crowd. The Bloods' soldiers. Dune's hand at my waist, tugging, *get down*. I started to unravel memory from SIM nightmare. In the park, we'd stayed low, hiding from the militia. And now, in this camp, we had to stay low too. That was Dune, breathing there. I was Axel. They'd chipped us. We were in the Bloods' prison camp.

I shook Dune.

Dune stuttered awake. They stared at me blankly.

'Leave me alone, you dumbass negro, why aren't you swinging?'

'Hey, Dune. It's me, it's Ax.'

'Have a swinging time. The sky is blue, and my eyes are too.'

Great. Just as we were about to get in with the Underground. I bit them. Yes, I said I bit them. It had worked before. Dune looked at me quizzically. I had my teeth sunk into their forearm and they just looked. The way a doberman might look at a chihuahua – tilt their head as if to say, who or what *are* you, and what are you even doing?

I stopped biting, embarrassed. Dune raised themselves right up and into my face.

'Only good negro is a swinging negro.'

'Dune. You're confused. The hanging in the park. You've got to untangle it from the SIM shit. We'd been playing basketball? The Bloods pulling the man on the rope and the gallows and the crowd dragging it behind them making that huge racket?'

'I love being here. Living here is fun. Good food, fresh water, nice guards.'

'Dune?'

'The sky is blue and I can be reborn too. Hang the resistors.'

Ah fuck. I got the maidenhair out and made a drink. I made them swallow it all and coaxed them to lie back down.

'Hey, my no-good negro?'

'Yes?'

They stared up at me, like, *inspecting* me. Something fearful crossed their brow, then rippled back across their SIM bump.

'Hey?'

'What?'

'You're just a brown paper bag.'

And Dune began this silent crying, like there was some part of them that knew who they really were, and that part of them was trapped. Their blink rate slowed.

I bent down and kissed them. Softly, with little lip movement.

'That's how we'd kissed that day in the park,' I whispered to Dune when I broke off. 'You remember now?'

'A . . . A . . .' Dune said. They were looking around, though still lying flat. They glanced at the tent ceiling. Then they closed their eyes.

As soon as Dune's breathing steadied, I ran across the tent zone to Beta. She was eating morning marrow soup with her tentmate, Footsy. 'Don't talk, eat,' Beta said, when I burst in. She handed me her bowl.

I forced myself.

'Better?' Beta asked.

'A little.'

'Now breathe.'

'Beats, it's Dune. Their mind's all over the place. Blanking.'

'Saying "you no-good negro"?'

'Yeah, but worse.'

'It's happening all over the newcomer tents. That, and "Hallelujah, Mara". Dune'll beat it. You gave them maidenhair this morning, right? Let that kick in.'

96

Beta's tentmate, Footsy, nodded to me. She finished her bowl, plucked a couple of burrs off a sweater and pulled it on. She gave Beta a brief peck on the cheek then left.

Beta licked both bowls clean, smacked her lips, belched and looked up, embarrassed. 'I don't know how much more marrow mush my body can take,' she said. 'Now tell me more, dear Axel. I'm all ears.'

I told her of the morning shitshow with Dune, how the SIM had got them bad and this time it didn't look like they could climb out of it. Beta took it in, her right hand on her chin. 'Nothing's worked?'

'Nope. Please help.'

'I've been thinking how this tech in our head works.'

'And?'

'Of course, the SIM wipes our own memories and tries to substitute its own stuff as delivered by the drones. But our bio memory network is still there, and it fights back. That's what human resilience is. But if Dune's dealing with some deep trauma then their bio memory doesn't have the resources to keep the SIM stuff out, like me and you in the normal way, even with the maidenhair. In which case, you have to outfox the SIM, to bring the bio network back.'

I didn't quite get it all but I just nodded. 'Beta, I'll do anything for you if you can get Dune back.'

'Anything?'

'Anything at all.'

Beta smiled weirdly. 'Promises,' she said. 'Now stop blubbing, I need silence to think.'

The silence grew and grew.

'OK,' Beta said finally, 'let's go see the patient. The Dune we know won't give in without a fight. We just have to outmanoeuvre the SIM. They buried it in Dune deep, right?'

When we reached them, Dune was sat up and mid-conversation with the tent's shadows.

'Listen, there is a shining city on a hill. That's where we going and it's going to be a bright white future.'

'Hey, Dune,' I called out.

They stopped gabbling and looked up.

'This is Beta. Remember her?'

'Ugly black bitch.'

Beta shrugged. 'That's the SIM. But it means something. Maybe they're feeling ugly. Let's thread their eyebrows.'

'What?'

'I'm serious. Thread their eyebrows. Dune had great eyebrows on arrival, right?'

It was true. They liked them sculpted. In only one week their eyebrows now looked wild.

'If we can wake that salon vibe, revive the "Black is Beautiful" in them, we got a chance.'

I bit my lip.

Beta snagged a thread out of her top and looped it into a rough figure-eight. She scooted behind Dune and we eased them down so Dune's head rested in her lap. She cupped Dune's face and tilted their head back by the chin into her lap, then stroked their eyebrows.

'Ready?'

I nodded. Dune was mute but compliant, staring right up at her.

Away Beta went, twisting and whirling the thread. She had me hold Dune's left eyelid down as she did the lower parts of that brow. Dune's lips began to move. We got a flicker of voice.

'Say again?' I said to them.

'Windswept, please,' Dune said, in their total salon, prima donna voice. 'And dewy, you understand? These brows should look fresh as the morning dew.'

I stuffed my hand in my mouth to stop myself from laughing. *Ha. The SIM hadn't killed the vanity in them.*

Beta held out an admonishing finger to say *We're not there yet.* She switched eyebrows and spun away with the thread. When she was happy with the alignment, she swabbed a bit of cooking grease over the final brow shapes and stroked them one last time. Two windswept, dewy eyebrows winked away on Dune's head. Beta eased that head out of her lap and sat them up. 'What do you think?' she said, holding up the tin mirror. 'They're to die for, right? Courtesy Beta's Boudoir.'

Dune stared at their reflection.

'Ugly negro.'

Shit.

'Hush,' Beta whispered. 'That windswept thing they said? Means Dune's in there. Let's just keep going, we'll find the stories to free them.'

Beta began rubbing Dune's feet for some reason known only to her, while prompting me to tell them memories. I did my best.

'Dune,' I said, 'remember when you rode your skateboard along the Holiday Inn rails and the security chased you and dropped his hat and you took the hat and skateboarded along the rail wearing it, then backflipped off. And it went viral!'

Dune blanked me.

'How about that Triple Science teacher screeching after you lit the magnesium and it blew up?' I did the voice. *'This is an unsafe environment and you are an unsafe child!'*

Not a flicker.

Beta was kneading Dune's calves now, working her way up, it seemed. I was going to grab her hands if she laid them on Dune's thighs. There were limits.

'How about the fairground?' I said. 'Me and you, Dune, crushed up on that Wheel of Death? The fairground music all wheezy and blaring? The cage slamming us together as we whirled. When we stepped off, dizzy as fuck, and we did the Waka Waka dance? "Waka Waka, clap left. Waka Waka, clap right"? And I slipped and came up in mud and we carried on and not only, like, the *whole fairground* joined in? The zombie dance. Remember that?'

Dune muttered something. It sounded like an insult. Beta was at the top of Dune's calves now.

'What about in the cinema that April weekend, getting sticky? You fed me popcorn and it got everywhere, like everywhere? And our tongues were so numb from being stuck down each other's throats.'

Dune's newly mint eyebrows flickered.

'And the moves we did in the aisle when they hit the *All Hell Breaks Loose* riff? Come on, let's do it, let's do it.'

I dragged Beta up with me. We got Dune up between us and did the dance, coaxing Dune's body into the moves like a marionette. Slowly, the steps came, and I threw in the hand roll. 'Come on, Dune, hit it, feel that beat! Let's get this party started! That's it!'

Dune was all jerky at first, then something clicked and they synced and flowed.

When we all three sat again, Dune had worked up a sweat and was beaming, their eyes connecting with me.

'Now tell last night's story, Ax,' Beta told me, 'Tell it as best you can.'

'Isn't that too big a jump? The mood shift? Isn't Dune doing fine like this?'

'No, it'll be good for them. While they're loosened up and receptive.'

So I told the story of the park hanging, as best as I could recall. And the mood dropped and Dune's face went from glowing to frown.

'Yeah, that was how it went down,' murmured Dune. 'That's when I knew we should be heading north. But we never went, Ax. We never made it. And look at us now.'

'Yeah, look at us,' I agreed.

Dune's head went into their hands and they wept.

'Dune's back,' Beta said quietly. She hauled herself up. She was drenched, and her throat hoarse.

'Thanks,' I said softly to her.

'No problem. Two hundred and twenty-five plucked hairs, four stories and three dances is all it took.'

'What happened to me?' asked Dune from behind their hands.

'Your SIM got you,' I said. 'The drones hit you hard last night and you were saying mad shit this morning and all day. Beta here came and helped out.'

'Like, what did I say?'

I told them a few examples.

'I'd rather die than be saying that shit. I'm sorry.'

'Don't feel no way about it,' said Beta. 'It wasn't you, it was the SIM. Could happen to any of us.'

'You are beautiful,' Dune said to her. And they leaned over and kissed her cheek. I kissed her other cheek.

'What is this, a kiss-fest?' said Beta, squirming between us, but loving it.

There was the noise of someone carrying a bucket of slopping water outside. Light was pushing through the canvas.

'What do you want?' I said to Beta. 'I promised you.'

She tapped my cheek. 'The one thing I can't have.'

'I promised. Anything at all,' I repeated.

'It's OK. I wish you two well. I mean, it sucks how much you're into each other, but apart from the fact it sucks, you're beautiful together.'

After she'd left, as Dune stumbled around in the tent, getting their head clear, I thought about the bittersweet of it for Beta. How she'd helped me get Dune back but to do that she'd heard stories about how tight me and Dune were. Even as I was telling them, she was learning she had no chance with me. And I loved her all the more for that too, because it was such a shit thing to have to do and yet she kept on, she helped me get Dune back.

Dune still needed oxygen, exercise. I pulled back the flaps so they saw all the other tents and I took them out and walked them around. Bit by bit, they came together. Their older memories were still patchy, but they knew who they were, who we were, and that we'd landed in this camp where the water came by standpipe and the Peace Committee ran things but the Underground existed, and were getting stronger and stronger, and we were joining it. I had them feel the SIM bump on their head and on mine. They understood about the drones, the SIM chips, the explosives, the fence, the guards, the dogs. When we came back from the walk, they summed it up pretty neatly.

'Basically, this is a shitfest?' they said.

'Sure is,' I replied.

'But I got the best eyebrows in camp, right?'

I looked across. Dune wiggled them imperiously.

9

Baby Snatch

Elizabeth X and Pharaoh came to the tent. Me and Dune had
discussed it and it didn't feel right to not let them know about
Dune's crash, even though this panicked Dune because they so
wanted in. So I told them about how we'd struggled to get Dune
back and did they still want us, because it was both of us or neither?

'We need you both,' said Elizabeth X.

Pharaoh squeezed Dune's shoulder. 'We don't abandon those
who go through troubles. That's not our way. Anything we can do
for Dune, let us know.'

'What's the plan?' I asked.

'Someone is bringing hack code that is vital for our escape
operation,' said Elizabeth X. 'They're close by. They will arrive in
the area any day with a phone that has a drive in it, an SSD drive,
that holds the code.'

Pharaoh took up the flow: 'The Resistance here in Huntingdon
will get that phone from her and load it on a drone and fly it into
the camp.'

'This is a critical phase,' said Elizabeth X. 'We need to get ready.
We need an army, and Dune to protect the airspace for the
Resistance drone. We need code skills, Axel. The phone will contain
vital code for downing the Bloods' SIM rewrite operation. The
skills you two have match exactly what we need to get that Resistance

drone landed and the hack code on the phone it carries successfully deployed. Only then can we break the grip these SIMs have on our heads.'

'Can we get more maidenhair?' Dune asked. 'We've run out.'

'We'll look into that,' said Pharaoh. He placed a hand on Dune's forehead, his head dropped, and he began praying. Yes, praying. I glanced at Elizabeth X. She had a wry smile on her face that said, *Roll with it, everybody got their quirks.* So we did. And Pharaoh gave up major Godlies to our tent ceiling:

'In the name of Black Jesus, heal this person's soul, fend off the malevolent Blood software shit attacking them, and feed their heart with all the love in the world that they deserve. Verily we call upon thee for all strength for this son of the true Lord. In the name of Black Jesus, amen.'

'Amen,' I said.

Apart from the 'son' reference, which I knew would have got Dune scratchy with irritation, the prayer seemed harmless.

'Can I have an amen?' Pharaoh called.

'Amen,' said me and Elizabeth X.

'Can I have an amen in the name of Black Jesus?' called Pharaoh.

Dune hadn't been to church as much as me, so they didn't know the preacher kept on till everyone joined in.

Finally, Dune got it. 'Amen in the name of Black Jesus!' The phrase rolled off Dune's tongue and the laying-on of hands was done. Elizabeth X and Pharaoh didn't miss a beat, like this was a normal prelude to an Underground meet-up. They set out what they wanted us to do. First came the formal bittercoated sign-up.

'We don't want to fairy tale this,' Pharaoh said. 'People have died working for the Underground.'

'But we're the living dead already,' said Dune, tapping their head. 'Anything's got to be better than this. Right, Ax? We got to fight back. Right? Together we can do this. Right?' Dune again. Making sense. But repeating.

'Yeah,' I said slowly.

A phrase from my mum suddenly flashed into my mind.

'Sometimes you have to take a stand,' I said.

'Welcome then,' said Elizabeth X. 'You've joined the revolution.'

Dune began high-fiving. I let the moment ride itself out. They got serious again.

'Listen good now,' said Elizabeth X. 'So the Resistance are going to fly a drone into this camp, carrying the phone with the code that can neutralise the SIMs in all our heads.'

'Someone's coded up a kill-switch for the head SIMs?' I asked.

'Exactly,' she replied. 'The phone that flies in will have that kill-switch code on it. Somebody's bringing it to us right now. But it's going to take preparation. A series of things have to happen first. We have to clear the skies to get our drone through. If the Bloods catch wind of this drone, they may swarm the airspace. That means we need an artillery to clear it. We want you to train and lead that artillery, Dune. Can you do that?'

Dune swallowed, but nodded.

'And we have to figure out the handshake protocol to get into the Bloods' SIM software in order to hack it and upload the kill-switch. That's where we need you and your coding skills, Axel. You follow?'

I felt my heart flip at the word *coding*. I took a breath.

'Yes, I get it.'

I knew that hacking handshake protocols was Hack Camp 101. I'd done it in the Resistance outside. And yet. I told them my fear.

'My coding mind's been blank a long time. I don't know if I have it in me any more.'

'Don't worry about that,' Elizabeth X said. 'We have faith in you.' She turned to Dune. 'Dune, you'll train to knock out the Bloods' drones. Using catapults.'

'Catapults?' repeated Dune.

'Yes,' said Elizabeth X, 'you showed it can be done. First step is making them at scale. We will gather old tin cans, aluminium, any stuff that has a low melting point. We'll melt it down and cast the catapults, a hundred or more. You will train up a platoon and lead them.'

'I could do two, maybe three squads,' said Dune. 'Train each squad separately. Then bring them together. That's how we did it in the Resistance. Also set each recruit tasks to build technique, make them better shooters. I can do this, only, like Ax said, I'm blipping.'

'Don't worry,' said Pharaoh. 'We'll find a way to increase your maidenhair supply.'

Elizabeth X paused. 'Axel, let's talk about you and coding now.'

'Yeah.'

'The sky looks clear most days but it's full of transmissions. We're plugging into them. We know more about the Bloods' movements out there than the guards running this camp. We hear the pilots of the planes. We hear the foot soldiers' shortwave radios. We know what deliveries are arriving and when. We monitor their message boards, BloodChan and SupremacyChan.'

'That's cool,' I said.

'Yes. We have the tech for that. Which reminds me. We want you also to look out for any usable electronic equipment in the camp.'

107

'That I can do,' I said.

She pulled out a device the size of a matchbox and showed it to us. Code was scrolling across its LCD screen. 'Here's an example of what we're picking up. We think this data stream is what they're scraping from the SIMs in our heads. We can't decode it yet.'

'Run it back,' I told her. She did.

'Now freeze it there.'

The screen froze on a six-line subroutine.

'You recognise anything?' Elizabeth X asked.

'Yeah. The language is Python, and it's pulling up LightSabre as backend data.' I said this before I even thought about it. 'See the line of text in there. "I have the bluest eyes".'

'OK,' said Elizabeth X, looking intently at the device's screen. 'Good spot.'

'You hacked this stream?' I asked.

'Sure did,' Pharaoh said, his voice heating up. 'And we're going to use everything we've got to break out. The plan is we destroy the Bloods' drones, brick these SIMs in our heads then storm the gates. There are many of us in the Underground and we communicate by many means. You've heard our drums. Those speak to everybody who listens. For our soldiers, we use signs. Similar to the Resistance. They're chalked or scratched onto tarmac, concrete, whatever is around. You read them, then scrub them out. There's a decrypt guide for the most sensitive signs. When you're ready you'll get the full guide but for now, we'll just teach you the direction codes.'

Pharaoh took paper out of his bag and began scribbling. He showed us what he'd written. I read it.

2 U 60. 100.

'The first number tells you which runway,' said Pharaoh. 'The line drawn under the U is the orientation line. You stand that side to know which way you've got to move next. Then sixty. That's degrees. The angle you turn. Last number one hundred. That's how many metres you've got to go to find the next stage. You got it? Four steps: Runway. Orientation. Degrees. Metres. Try another one.'

Pharaoh scribbled another.

1 U. 90. 20.

'Runway One, straight ahead, ninety degrees, twenty metres,' said Dune, straight out. 'But rain will wash chalk away out there.'

'Sometimes we might make it from bent wire. Or scratched into discs. Or on the side of some metal.'

'Stay alert,' Elizabeth X said. 'We also use morse code. And whistles. The whistle codes we keep encrypted. When you need to know them, we'll give you the decrypt.'

I'd noticed that when Elizabeth X was nervous, she flicked her eyes leftwards, and she flicked them now.

'Pharaoh and I are being hunted inside here. There's a reward for our identification and capture. The Bloods know we're organising this breakout, they just don't know how and when and who. Me and Pharaoh are on borrowed time. That's OK. The vanguard always gets shot. But you are the future. If we go down, you must keep the plans active, push on. You'll hear lies about us inside here. Generated by the Bloods and spread by the Peace Committee and other cowards and turncoats. Don't be deflected. Don't let them sow doubt. Me and Pharaoh are not on drugs. We're not confused or ill-informed. Don't let anybody sideline you with subcommittees and delays and derails and hesitation. When the time comes, we strike hard. Strike strong.'

'Amen to that,' Pharaoh intoned. 'The lives of me and X are not important. What's important is that this camp falls. We are close. So close. Let's get to work.'

He pulled out something from his drawstring bag. 'This is a sketch of the drone that will fly in to deliver the software. It's tiny, right, compared to the Bloods' drones that you've seen?'

'Yeah,' said Dune, 'small but talawa.'

'Ha,' said Pharaoh, 'damn right.'

I looked at the scale drawing. The Resistance drone had a black body, four helicopter propellers, and a small payload bay at its base. It was not much bigger than a fist.

'This is everything,' said Elizabeth. 'If we land this drone intact, get the phone out of it and make the code on it work, we are free. All of us.'

'A lot of ifs,' I said.

'It looks like a toad,' said Dune at the drawing.

'It's camouflage. The colouring of the sky. It will fly low to avoid radar,' Elizabeth X said, 'skim above the fences, and land on Runway Two. Just before it comes, a red mist will cover the sky above the camp. When you see the red mist, get ready. Dune, your army's job will be to get it landed safely.'

'OK. I'm game.'

'We're done. Anything you want to ask us? Axel? Dune?'

Dune was resting their chin in the palms of their hands, thinking about it all.

'What?' Elizabeth X pressed.

'How do you know they won't decide one day to, you know, shoot us all up? You know, come through the gate and score a record body count?' Dune said.

'We monitor their comms. If we hear such plans, we'll fast forward our own.'

'Why not fast forward them anyway?' replied Dune. 'Maybe they'll press the explode button on our SIMs, end the experiment.'

'Sure, if they activate the detonators on our head SIMs, we're all dead,' Elizabeth X intoned. 'That's why we need the code that's flying in. To get that SIM software neutralised. It's why we've got to get the drone landed and the code it's carrying up and running. The breakout depends on that SIM neutralisation.'

'Why's it taking so long?' Dune again.

Pharaoh steupsed. Annoyance ran across his brow. 'Because the only copy of the hack code has been given to some fool kid who's meant to be making her way to us from the north. Everyone's searching for her. She's out there and close. We're hopefully talking a week, maybe only days before she delivers. And when she does, we have to be ready. Now, we got you something special, both of you.'

Pharaoh delved in his bag and pulled two black circles out. Patted them. They flopped into shape. Black berets. He held them out. We took them. 'Cool,' Dune said, placing theirs immediately on their head and posing.

Pharaoh ignored Dune's vogueing. 'Feel how rigid they are. They're made with a wire mesh lining that blocks electromagnetic waves.'

'Like a Faraday cage?' I asked. I was pressing mine between my fingers. It felt like chicken wire under the felt.

'Exactly,' Elizabeth X said. 'Day to day, carry on using the gunk. We mix aluminium particles into the gunk, and it works the same way, baffling signals. The berets and the gunk are not proof against the night drones. The night drones use a different radiation. But the daytime drones can't pick us up if we wear the berets, and they get confused by the gunk.'

'The only ones picking us up in the day with these are the Peace Committee spies, using their bare blasted eyes,' said Pharaoh.

'Can anything stop the night drones?' Dune asked.

'Storifying. And the maidenhair helps,' Elizabeth X said. 'We'll get you some more. Drink it at night, before sleep. It's the last line of night-time defence. Then in the morning to clear your heads of shit. You've been drinking it, right?'

Dune started giggling.

'What's so funny?' Elizabeth X asked.

'Just something I been thinking for a while.'

'What?'

'Tea,' Dune said.

'Huh?'

'The final line of defence is . . . tea?' Dune fell into me.

And that got me. Dune bit my shoulder to try stop themselves from laughing more and I nipped them in the ribs.

Elizabeth X's voice went all warm and interested: 'What are your pronouns, you two? Are you intimate? What do you like about each other? I'm curious. You get an adrenalin rush when Dune comes into sight, Axel? You go weak at the knees when Axel's eyes twinkle, Dune? You ever switch pronouns on each other?'

Dune straightened up and kissed their teeth. 'What are you, our relationship counsellor? We good together. That's all you need to know.'

'This work will test any relationship,' she said back at Dune.

'What else do you know about me?' I said. 'What happened to

my parents? I can't picture them any more. The last few days, I can't recall them. Something bad happened to them, didn't it?'

Stupid tears were rolling down my face. Stupid, because I didn't even know what they meant except it was something bad and, fight as I did, I couldn't recall it.

'Hey.' Elizabeth X held me.

Pharaoh landed a hand on my shoulder. 'We got you, child,' said Pharaoh. Dune moved in and the group hug was complete.

'I'm sorry,' I said. 'These tears are daft. I don't even know why.'

'They're not daft. And you'll get those memories back,' said Elizabeth X as she released me. 'Keep storifying and they will come. Don't try to remember directly, that doesn't work. Try remembering something that happened that connects to them. Something that holds emotion. You manage that, and stuff will come streaming back, sometimes more than you would wish. So be careful. Gauge your strength.'

There was a noise outside: a series of low clicks.

'Time's up,' Elizabeth X said.

The two packed in a hurry. Elizabeth X turned one last time at the tent flaps. 'Look after yourselves, right? Hold on to each other. Keep human. Keep storifying. Don't let them gum you.'

They each raised a fist in salute.

We raised fists back at them.

I watched from the tent as they stepped through camp together, and I saw the outline of Horse following them at twelve paces. Then they were all three lost among washing lines and smoke.

We spent the rest of the afternoon on a work detail, digging. Crops were the main work activity of the camp. It meant shovelling.

Forking. Raking. Sieving. Watering. Hoeing. Turning. To the north of the camp were fields and fields of turnip, marrow, squash, pumpkin, corn, carrot and potato plants, and tall rows of peas and runner beans. Winter cabbage grew under thin nets. The Peace Committee assigned the teams and directed the work. The camp had expanded, so another job was breaking new ground by digging up saplings, crushing rabbit holes, and generally making fallow land good for growing. Mainly we dug. It was no simple job. If you dug too little, the Peace Committee made a note and you were meant to be fed less at mealtime. If you dug too deep, the Bloods' anti-tunnelling sensors were triggered and you'd hear guard dogs reacting to the alarm. Then specks of guards could be seen beyond the fences and a spy drone might come over to investigate and again the Peace Committee would sanction you. If you messed up big time and dug both deep and close to the fence, rumour was, they sent in the Scavengers and you were hauled into the Bloods' Reeducation Unit. Nobody who was hauled there ever came back.

Me and Dune did our dig shift together without drama and, come evening, after the marrow compote meal (the Peace Committee excelled at different names for what was basically the same food – mushed turnip, boiled peas and pulped carrots), we headed back to our tent.

There was always this sense of dread heading back, because it meant nightfall was close and with that, the night drones and all the rewriting to fend off. Beta dropped by to check on Dune, which was sweet, and she gave us some maidenhair, which was even cuter. Then the curfew alarm went and she had to scramble back to her tent.

Dune was gazing at the blisters on their hands from the digging.

114

'We've dug before,' they said. 'My hands know it. I'm too good with the spade. We both are.'

'We've got to storify,' I said.

I had this thought that reared up as me and Dune lay there, wondering if we would wake up the next day. I thought, if we died like this – or if we were Blanked, which was pretty much the same thing, I couldn't complain, it was a great way to go: to go out together.

'Axel, you're snoring,' Dune said, prodding me. 'You hear what I said?'

'What?'

'The baby snatch. Let's storify that.'

'You remember it? I don't have it.'

'I think I got it,' said Dune. 'Listen up. Stay awake.'

Dune told it.

'The guy they hanged in the park had been an official enemy of the Bloods; the Bloods had caught him in a bolt hole. The Resistance needed more hideouts, and they wanted them built by people who hadn't been involved last time because they were, their word, traitors. They gave us a motorbike, stashed in a culvert behind some gates. The site was out in the sticks. For weeks we rode up there and dug out a tunnel, prop by prop, banging in wedge after wedge. It was prep for a bunker saferoom. People on the run from the Bloods could hide there. I think they were going to place a Portaloo down there at the end of the tunnel. The day we finished off the tunnel, Ax, we celebrated by snogging, right, then we got on the bike and rode back to Stukeley. Ax, you were rocking your Twisted T-shirt that you'd got for your sixteenth, looking well cool, and you kept your arms round my waist, tight-tight. We were hurtling at about sixty when you nudged me, Ax.

' "Look down there," you said. "Lo, verily, a cloud is descending, and Moses be wetting himself. The baby snatchers."

'I followed the line of your finger. It was Bloods' Witnesses, down on the estate. They'd parked their vans on the mini-roundabout. Witnesses used to be the mildly annoying, doorstepping Jehovah's Witnesses. The Bloods converted them and had them ramp up their doom stories, so they went big on the coming apocalypse, Armageddon, Hell, damnation and all of that stuff, preaching that people needed to convert before it was too late. They'd added a cute Bloods side to it, offering to take any babies under thirty months further south to safety, especially male babies of people they weren't keen on, like resistors and Black people and anybody really who was not a red, white and blue flag-waving Blood. Most families with little kids shoved them upstairs or into their back gardens till the Blood's Witnesses passed through.

'I sped on down. Witness vans were still on the *No Ball Games* green when we made it back.

' "Let's watch a bit," I said. Your neighbour on the other side with the asthma was at the front door with his polite face on, nodding to a tag team of Witnesses. One of them had trapped him in a handshake that didn't look like ending any time soon.

'We snuck down the side path, slipped the back garden gate lock and took to the tree. Way back, your dad had whacked horseshoe-shaped steel steps into the trunk all the way to the top and hid an antenna up there. He'd be in deep shit with the Bloods if they ever found it, for sure. Or if someone snitched on him. We climbed up to the ledge where there was this electrical equipment painted green, and we squatted there, and watched the Witnesses. They were on every doorstep of the close. The *heat*. Number twenty-three's aircon was humming on full. Number twenty-five's two cats were hissing at each other under a car. Coco was barking at the back of number twenty-seven. I took him for walks sometimes. His bark had four meanings: bored. Hungry. Horny. Walkies. Right now, it was something different. Frantic. "Quiet, Coco!" I heard Charlotte, who owned him, shout. Coco howled.

'I guessed the Witnesses were at Charlotte's front door. The howl again. You were tugging at me but I shuffled round the ledge and peeked further out. Coco was going ape by the shed in his back garden. *Why was he clawing at the shed door?* I thought. I couldn't see much. Only number twenty-seven's little pool, glinting all greeny-blue in the sun. And the rubber ring, floating empty at its centre.

'Then the shed door opened, and little Reuben toddled out, snot streaming from his nose. He'd been hidden there by his mum and now he was racing for the side gate. I saw the Witnesses turn at Reuben's wailing, and they stepped towards the side gate. I said to you, "Sheesh. Shit-hits-fan time, Ax. You see?" You didn't answer. One thing I love about you, Ax, you got this big heart that is so, so stupid but so, so you.

'So, while I'm saying wait, you're already leaping to the ground. You cross the garden in three strides and plank right over the panel top, roll into my back garden, where my gramps' security lighting flicks on, even though it's broad daylight and my gramps' alarm robot barks a warning in a total Bloods' Texan accent: *'Don't move, motherfucker!'*

'You run on, hit the fence between twenty-five and twenty-seven, tumble over. I'm behind you, thinking, *You idiot*. We can hear Charlotte shouting, running down the side path. Reuben's heading into the Bloods' arms. You rush for him. Coco the dog's out now and between my legs. I crash into the pool's side, and the plastic rips and there's water gushing over me in a wave. I claw myself back up. Charlotte's screaming, *"My baby! My baby!"*

'I hear the grunt as the Witness delivers a Godly thump right in your face and you fall down.'

'Right.'

'Then one of the Witnesses is standing over me, nursing his fist. Like the fist in the face is their new baptism ritual. And I feel the blood pouring from my nose. Taste the wet and the metallic taste of it. I pass out and when I come round everything is blurred. I can make out a Witness at the gate. She has Reuben tight to her chest. Reuben's gurgling, like it's all one big game of Hide and Seek.

'Charlotte is tearing to get to Reuben, but the other Witness holds her easy as cheese pie against a wall as she kicks and wails and screams. Coco's biting the legs of the man holding Charlotte, biting his thighs. You and me are on the grass. I'm winded. You're out cold. I begin to crawl on my hands and knees towards the Witness with Reuben. Reuben's still in the Witness's arms. "Reuben," I call, "Reuben!" He holds up his little head and waves at me. Someone kicks me in the ribs. Reuben wails. The Witness pressing Charlotte against the wall says to her, "He'll be safe with us. He will be saved. *Praise the Lord, Praise Mara, Praise the Second Coming.*" Charlotte sobs and kicks. Then the Witness van engine starts up and the woman holding Reuben gets into it. The Witness on

Charlotte lets go of her and jumps back. He holds his hands up to the sky, hallelujah style. Then backs away.

'I get up. You're up too, but you don't have legs. You're pointing and I get the message, I don't *need* the message. Me and Charlotte chase them and she falls onto the road as the last Witness van speeds off. Charlotte lies in the road, crying into the tarmac. I go over and we sit in the road, holding each other. She strokes my face and calls me Reuben. I hold her, and you join us and we sit there in the road and cry. A complete snotfest.

'Then we went back into your house and your parents came back from wherever they'd been, and we told them what had happened and they went to Charlotte's and when they came back they were saying, *"This is deep water, this is deep water."*'

10

Bunker

I woke. I was Axel. But Dune. How was Dune?

I shook them and they came to, glitching, cursing me with the usual phrases. I got them sat up and drinking and by mid-morning they were doing OK.

Soon after, a message came from Pharaoh that Dune had to go off, the task they'd set Dune began today. They wanted only Dune. I was to carry on with my normal activities; when they needed me, they would let me know.

I dug soil all day. Dune came back with welts on their wrist. This pattern repeated itself for several days that became a week. In that week, the night drones didn't fly over. The Underground said it was because the drones had been deployed to a big battle going on up north. Those mornings, Dune barely glitched and was out early and came back with more welts and all scratched up, and never volunteered why. They had the same 'no talk' rules in the Resistance, so I understood. But I asked Dune how it was going, and they said OK, and from the way Dune said it, I knew the artillery was being trained.

Dune came back one morning with a set of small plastic pots, each filled with coloured liquids.

'What are those?'

'Paint.'

'Why?'

'Underground. They want us both to use it. Make it difficult for overhead drones to pick us up.'

'Anti-face recognition?'

'That's it.'

'Why now?'

'Wait and see.'

It wasn't a long wait.

'Pssst!'

Clicking outside the tent.

I pushed outside. The shadow was gone. But a piece of card held directions.

1 U. 90. 250. _3

Quickly, me and Dune gunked up our hair, slid the berets on, applied the paint and then set off.

The directions led us across the bunker zone into the rubble of a blasted air hangar. There was a half collapsed bunker underneath, unconnected to anything else, as far as we could tell. The Underground had rigged it with battery-powered lighting.

As we shuffled down, somewhere outside and above us a child burst into a nursery song. Their voice carried down to us, faint and breaking up into echoes. It was unnerving.

We kept on deeper into the maze of concrete rubble, across twists of steel, through hidden openings until we reached the third lower level. It was warm there. They'd left some water bottles. We sat on rubble, sipped the water and dusted ourselves off.

A light dangled from a steel tine in the ceiling, if you could call the tangled mess of concrete lumps and steel bars dangling down into our faces a ceiling; a bicycle lightbulb filament dimmed as if its battery was dying.

Elizabeth X emerged from somewhere into the half dark, Pharaoh beside her. I made out Beta and Footsy. There were a few others.

Elizabeth X spoke. 'Welcome. This is a base bunker. You two are the last. Let's get going. You are all members of the Underground, some of you newer than others. You may be working together. It's time to introduce you to one another. Say your name and why you joined.' There was a snap to Elizabeth X's words.

First to speak was Storm. She had a smooth face, honest eyes, a big body, and grungy clothes. 'I'm Storm and umm, freedom,' said Storm in a firm, clear voice. 'I want to see those drones burrrn!'

Beta went next. 'I got skills that you say could be useful,' she said, 'like wiring and engineering skills.'

Horse spoke. 'I'm Horse. My word is escape. We get to break out first, right?'

'The opposite,' Elizabeth X cut in. 'Let's not sugarcoat this. Chances of dying in an Underground unit are higher than if you didn't join up.'

She gestured with her chin to the next one along the wall. 'Sly. One word for why you joined?'

'Liberty,' said the one named Sly. He was tall and thin and his voice was calming. He wore a dark, baggy tracksuit, and two leather bracelets on one wrist.

'Next. Footsy.'

'Name is Footsy and my word is revenge,' said Footsy. She swallowed, crossed her arms and tugged at the sleeve of her holey, dark-blue jumper, sniffed, then spoke on. 'They raped my sister then hanged her on a wind turbine. They placed a sniper to cover it. I had to watch her body go round all night.'

Footsy's face went blank once she'd said this and I knew she wouldn't say anything more for a while. Beta hugged her.

Elizabeth X pointed again. 'Go ahead.'

'I'm Wires and my word is truth,' said Wires, loud and confident. He was wearing chino trousers and a collared shirt that he somehow made look crisp and new, even though it was grubby with dirt. 'Our true selves are out there. We have to find a way back to that.'

I thought, *Our true selves are here, inside us, just cut off from us.* 'Dune?'

'Because this isn't living. I'd rather be dead than this.'

'Ax?'

'Future. Because there *is* a future. But we have to fight for it.'

'That's good,' Elizabeth X said. 'You're all going to need that courage.'

Pharaoh demonstrated for anyone who didn't yet know how to use the silicone gunk in your hair when you moved about, and that braids were OK, but the Afro was the best style for protection.

'How the hell do I Afro *this*!' said Footsy. We laughed at her straight red strands.

'Afros aren't essential, we'll sort your hair,' Pharaoh said. 'Second requirement. Each day, after operations, tell each other your stories from before this camp, from when you were free. It prevents the memory from being erased by the SIM in here.' He tapped his head.

'We are one another,' Elizabeth X said. 'Their SIMs can never rub out who we are if we hold onto each other. Each evening before the drones come, storify. Practise now.'

Twenty minutes later, when stories of lives led outside were filling the bunker to its tangled ceiling, Pharaoh called time.

PETER KALU

'Let's get gloved up, berets on. The task today is simple. Find tin cans and aluminium to make the catapults with. Spot any silicone junk, and that's good too. We use it for catapult straps and we cook it down to help make the hair gunk. Gloves on, masks on, bags on backs. Listen out for any alerts. Let's go. Two teams.'

With Elizabeth X and Pharaoh leading, we emerged from the base bunker and journeyed further into bunker zone. Elizabeth X veered off with her team while me, Beta and Dune followed Pharaoh.

Bunker zone sat to the near south of the prison camp and was what was left of the Huntingdon airbase outbuildings after they all got bombed. Pharaoh's eyes hardly left the sky as he gave us the place's history.

'Welcome to B zone. This whole camp was called RAF Alconbury not that long ago. Twin runway strips, two miles long for blow-everything-up intercontinental bombers. When the civil war got going, the Brotherhood of the Blood of Jesus – the Bloods, to me and you – shelled the camp. That was after they'd been driven out of it by the British Army at a time when the British Army was still in opposition to the Bloods. Keeping up? Good. Next, the Bloods joined up with the Yanks. Suddenly David was Goliath. Everything here got bombed again in that second battle. Not liking the bombs, the British Army soldiers either fled or became the Pure English Army which made an alliance with the Bloods or else they simply took up with the Bloods on their crusades north with the White Army. The Bloods took over RAF Alconbury again and this time made the site their beloved Evangelical Realignment Centre, which, since it doesn't roll off the tongue very well is also known as ERAC. Purpose? As we all know, to test their new conformity SIMs. That was their original name for what

124

they've stuck inside our skulls. Brain enhancers, they sometimes called them too. We are the Bloods' lab rats. Now behold the lab.'

Pharaoh gestured. We looked back north across the camp.

'It's a good view, if you want to understand the layout. Memorise it. The bombed-out aircraft hangars. Behind the buildings, the tent zone. Could you navigate from here to there in the dark? You may have to.'

I glanced across at Beta, busy memorising. By now I'd bet she could draw it with her eyes closed.

Pharaoh kept going. 'You see the fields to the east where camp crops are grown? Never underestimate the importance of those crops. They give us a break from the blue barrel shite the Scavengers bring in and call food.'

As Pharaoh talked, bubbling into my mind was a phrase.

White is better.

I glanced around, embarrassed. Had I thought it, or had I said it?

White is better.

What is this shit? Dune was nudging me. They whispered. 'You getting what I'm getting? Ignore it. It's the SIM.'

'What you getting?'

'*No-good negro.*'

'I'm on *White is better.*'

'You think it's a drone or something?' Dune asked.

'No. The chips just quietly hacking away. Mine's gone now. You?'

'Yeah.'

Pharaoh was still pointing stuff out, like the devil's estate agent.

'Can you see far north, beyond the fencing? The cubes there? That's the Bloods' Hallelujah Camp where the Scavengers take you for final education if their drones manage to wipe you. Their idea of a finishing

125

school. The parades also begin and return there. The security fencing all around is still functioning on forty-nine-point-five hertz and instantly lethal. We're looking at finding the power supply and cutting it off. We've also got a comms line into the wrecked communication towers inside the camp that is north-north-west of here. Some of the signals we're picking up are due to that. Now turn again.'

We did.

'See the rubbish tip just beyond this zone? It runs from lower south to lower east right up to the bog zone at south west. Sewage from the camp runs in channels to the westside bog where it collects in pits that we will have the pleasure of digging out as soon as the Peace Committee assigns that particular rota.'

'I can't wait,' said Dune, all scowls.

Suddenly, Pharaoh dropped to a crouch.

We all ducked down with him.

He was looking up and east.

'Hear something?'

'Nothing,' I said. 'Dune?'

Dune shook their head.

We remained low like that. Me and Dune turned to Beta. Beta shook too.

Pharaoh gave it a few more seconds, scanning the skies, then he nodded and we got up.

'Let's search over there,' Pharaoh said, breaking from his tour-guide voice. He led us on a scramble along a strip on the outer edge of bunker zone where the last jagged line of buildings stood like broken teeth.

I was placed on lookout duty. I watched the skies as Dune, Beta and Pharaoh started pulling at the rubble.

Pharaoh was something else in that rubble. He worked up a small cloud of concrete dust around him. Dune and Beta chucked up the lumps that Pharaoh handed them. The procedure had me worried because of the noise. In a flurry of wrenching and a rumble of collapsing rubble, they dragged a window frame to the surface. It was plastic, but the rubber beading was good. Then Dune took a turn as lookout. We found two more plastic frames, small ones, like toilet room windows. We dragged them up and stripped them. We had just prised the window handles off because they were light and so probably aluminium, when an Underground alert whistle sounded.

'Scavenger alert!' called Pharaoh.

'Who are they?' asked Dune.

'The Blanked.'

'What d'you mean?'

Dune's memory glitching again. Pharaoh explained.

'They've been snatched from camp and they've had their minds fully blanked, so they've got no memory at all. They're just shells of human beings. And they operate strictly to a set of Bloods' SIM instructions. There's at least fifty Scavs based at ERAC. They have body cameras, sensors and stuff, and their controllers can send a drone over with them to inspect anything the controllers want to poke an eye at. If they get close enough to you, they can ID you because their near-field scanners catch the frequency of the head chips.'

'Despite the gunk?' I asked.

'Yes. Despite the gunk. When they find a target, they swarm, and if you resist them you get a beating or worse.'

'How do you stop them?'

Pharaoh shrugged. 'Scavs don't feel pain. Unless you physically

127

block them, like with a tank or something of the kind, they're pretty much unstoppable.'

Another whistle. Same pitch. Double length.

A second alert. The Scavengers had entered the camp.

That meant only one thing. We had to retreat.

We stuffed the window seals and handles and some rubber out of some wrecked car doors into bags, then scrambled back into the base bunker and down. The others were already settling there.

A burst of drums were indicating direction of travel. The Scavs were heading south. Towards us.

The base bunker had been rigged up with a set of twin mirrors on a telescopic arm. It worked as a crude periscope.

We rested up, held our breath and watched the mirror as a team of four Scavengers approached.

We could hear them above us in the broken-up asphalt and concrete. They toted their own scrap bags. Scouring. Picking. Recording. Listening.

But I felt sorry for them as I watched them stumble around. They walked in jerks, occasionally stopping and sweeping their batons, scanner mode on them activated. What were they looking for? We knew some of the things. Maidenhair sprouts. Bits of circuit board or electronics. Pens. Knives. Machinery. Unauthorised posters. Trail signs.

Of course, they'd have new instructions now too: to find and seize whoever had brought down the drone.

Up there, the four Scavengers locked arms and closed into a circle. Maybe sharing information. They were directly above us. I looked across to Pharaoh and Dune, sitting next to each other. Those two would be high on the Scavengers' most wanted list.

The Scavengers were staying too long above us; they had to have found something.

It was like Pharaoh had arrived at the same thought. He signalled to Dune and whispered: 'Go lower.'

Dune shifted.

'You too,' Elizabeth X whispered to Pharaoh.

Pharaoh smiled a thanks but shook his head.

The Scavenger circle broke. One of the Scavengers stuttered, circling our bunker entrance. They glitched into another stutter, then started waving the baton and beckoned to the others.

Carbon dioxide was what living bodies gave off. The Bloods used this fact to trace resistors hidden in trucks moving around the country. The Scavs probably had the same technology. Holding your breath made no difference.

What now? Would they scrabble down and fight us here? Drag us off to their centre and Blank us? Or . . . ?

We were all glued to the periscope mirror. The Scavs were clustering, digging, rooting for the entry point. They were almost on it. Should we go out in a blaze? Surely some of this rubble would dent their heads, if we chucked it? Dune had their catapult in their hand. But Scavs were a different game to drones.

Pharaoh and Elizabeth X murmured to each other. Pharaoh got up.

He whispered to us all. 'I'm going on a decoy run, have them chase me. When Elizabeth calls it, you guys get out of here and shift back to tent zone with her, fast as. Before they send a drone over. Everybody got it?'

We nodded.

What chance did Pharaoh have against the four Scavengers? At that point, I was thinking close to zero.

He started up. His feet disappeared through the rubble gap. We watched the periscope mirror.

The four Scavs were tall. They had meaty arms and charged batons. Pharaoh threw himself up and bolted.

The Scavs still hadn't found the entry hole and he blindsided them when he emerged. They swivelled round and the chase started. He actually slowed down at one point because the weight of their armour had them struggling to keep up.

Pharaoh twisted and turned and eventually there was nothing in the mirror but the dust slowly settling.

Beta rotated the periscope in a slow three-sixty. There was nothing out there.

Elizabeth X's voice was soft and troubled. 'Go now,' she ordered. 'Cross back to the tents, and do normal things.'

'You think Pharaoh survived?' Dune murmured.

'If anybody can, it's him,' Elizabeth X replied.

It sounded like a no.

'Put it out of your mind,' she insisted, 'get back to tent zone. And tonight, storify a tale of resistance, of fighting back. OK. Go. Do. Storify.' She rubbed her face and her eyes had reddened.

We clambered out in ones and twos.

Entering tent zone, it looked good. No drones came overhead to check on us. There were no signs of Scavengers. Me and Dune took twilight standpipe showers to get rid of the bunker zone grey dust that was slicked all over us.

The food gong sounded and we went and queued. They gave out scoops of cold boiled corn mash topped with a handful of fried beans. Back at our tent, we heated it up and ate. Then lay back.

The sky dimmed.

Dune came into my arms. I felt their face, ran my fingers along their cheek. Dune traced a finger along the groove of my spine.

We slid further down into canvas and I eased the tent flaps shut. A mild evening heat settled on us. Dune was slipping along my arms. Their thighs were on mine, gleaming like lodestone or that blurt of fluid when a knife first goes through fresh yam. I turned into them. I held their head in mine and smelled the body heat from their scalp, felt the slick and slide of gunk in their hair smearing my hands, and the freshness of standpipe-washed skin on my tongue.

'Let's do it,' Dune said.

So we did it. As the wind blew outside and maybe a stealth drone somewhere high above silently tried to get outputs from our SIMs.

We fell, tired with nerves and exhaustion, into the blankets. Dune nudged me.

'We have to storify now,' Dune said. 'You remember the Blood commander?'

My body trembled and my hands tensed.

'That? Oh God.' *Gauge your strength*, Elizabeth X had said.

'Do you have it?' asked Dune.

'Yes. Just.'

'Then tell it.'

'For sure?'

'Yes.'

So I told it. Our biggest Resistance mission in the Youth Corps outside. The events flooded into my mind and began screening there.

So pull out the popcorn, dear reader, and enjoy the show.

11

Molasses

Me and Dune had finished fixing up a timber hide in the woods
for a munitions store and were kicking back. We swallowed the
fish paste sandwiches Dad had made us and got rid of the taste
with Mum's walnut cake, then lay there. Times were good. I noticed
tiny buttercups nestling amongst the blades of grass and there was
one by Dune's jaw, making a bounce of yellow light gloss their
chin. I picked it and moved it around. Saw the soft play of yellow
on Dune's lips. The beautiful and sharp taste of those lips, their
warmth, how they gave back pressure when I pressed my own lips
against them. We had just got going when we got a signal and my
phone hummed, which meant Resistance. Huey wanted to see us.
I could hear in his voice that this wasn't another tunnel or message
drop. He said we were to stay strictly where we were, that was an
order, they'd come to us.

Huey's face was thunder when he arrived, trailing two others,
and they jumped out of the car. There was a bearded man I'd seen
before, crossing town in twilight, an assault rifle strung on his back.
The other one, the one with springy yellow hair and red skin, had
talked urban guerrilla tactics at a safe house, just before a Bloods'
Special Investigations Unit hit town with mobile search beams and
tracker dogs.

Dune raised an eyebrow at me. I shrugged.

We did fist knocks. Huey didn't introduce the other two. The bearded one stood guard by the roadside and Huey got to it.

'I just came from the hospital,' he said. 'And we've got a special job for you.'

His yellow-haired sidekick interrupted him. 'I understand you two are sexually intimate?'

Dune prickled. 'What's it to you?'

I looked to Huey. He nodded. Meaning it was a genuine question. I was embarrassed and Dune was bang on: what business *was* it of theirs? But I knew Huey wouldn't be messing us around, and anyway we probably smelled of sex, with what we'd been doing only ten minutes ago, so I answered flatly for us both. 'Yes. So?'

The sidekick answered. 'We had to ask. It would be unfair on you otherwise, is what we agreed. Now go ahead,' she said to Huey.

The way she called it, she wasn't the sidekick. She was the boss.

'The job carries unusual risks,' said Huey. 'If you think it's too much, just say no.'

'Spit it out,' I said. 'What?'

'We're going to trap one of the Bloods' commanders. We want you to be the bait for the trap.'

Dune turned away.

'Hear me out. We have Resistance youth working in cafes and restaurants in the town centre. A Bloods commander goes to Cerberus cafe and he likes to try to have sex with the young waiting staff, both boys and girls. He's raped two already, and put a third in hospital. He's untouchable, the Bloods own the courts. We're going to get him. He has accounts on social media and grooms young people there. Sometimes he offers them money, sometimes an adventure. Last week, we set up a fake account and got him interested in a threesome out in the forest, a boy, a girl and him. We want you two to be the bait, meet him in town, let him drive you to the forest. He'll be thinking he's going to have sex with you. Your job is to get him to the forest. Only that. Then we take over.'

Dune cut in. 'Let me see if I got this right. You want us to go on a threesome sex date with a raping, gun-carrying Bloods commander, including getting in his car and letting him drive us to a forest to fuck us. Then, so long as he doesn't detour or rape us right there in the car along the way or any other of a thousand fucking possibilities, you promise to step in before he does actually fuck us and we land in hospital or worse?'

The woman nodded. 'It's risky. Undeniably. Just get him to the forest. We'll do the rest. Trust us.'

A series of questions rushed through my head.

'Why both of us?' I said.

'To be sure he'd say yes,' she said.

'And it's safer with two,' Huey added.

'What are we supposed to say to him?'

'Whatever you want,' said Huey. 'Let him do the talking. He doesn't want to talk to you, he wants to fuck you.'

'We get in his car. How do you follow us?'

'There's a tracker planted on it. And we'll show you where in the forest we want you to take him.'

'If we do this, I'm taking a big fuck-off knife,' I said.

'He likes to fuck kids our age?' asked Dune.

'That's his thing. Young teens,' the boss replied.

'And Black?'

'Yup.'

134

Dune was shaking their head. 'A white supremacist who likes to fuck Black kids. He needs a shrink, right?'

'He needs a bullet,' said Huey.

'And we'll be supplying one,' the boss said.

There was a pause.

'Any questions?' Huey looked at us both.

'Am I the boy or the girl?' asked Dune.

'What?'

'You said we go as a boy and a girl. Which of us is which?'

Huey hummed a moment. 'Umm. Ax, be the girl. Dune be the boy.'

'This time,' said Dune.

Huey smiled. 'Yeah. This time.'

'I'll do my best,' Dune added.

'That's fine.'

The bearded man gave a low whistle.

'*If* we do it,' I added.

'Think about it,' said the boss, already in the car, driver's side, window down.

Huey held out a fist from the passenger seat. 'You have twenty-four hours. Text me your decision.' The car sped off.

When they were gone, Dune was mad and laughing at the same time. '"Are you sexually intimate?" What kind of question is that? Do we look like we've been fucking?'

'It's none of their business.'

'What do you think of the job? Let's do it. Take this bastard on.'

'I dunno,' I said. 'Sounds like a sadist. The risks . . .'

'We should do it for the waiters. The ones he's already raped. The one he's hospitalised.'

Dune had always come across to me as more self-centred than that. I was impressed.

'It might damage us,' I said, cautiously. 'I've only ever . . .' I struggled to find the words. 'I mean, whatever happens, it might make sex feel dirty after. You know what I mean? When *we* do sex, it's not just sex, is it?' I asked Dune. 'It's also love?'

'Right,' said Dune, leaning their face into me.

'I'm serious,' I told them.

'Course. I never shag. I *make love.*'

We both laughed at that.

'But why are we even considering this?' I asked. 'And why are you looking all excited?'

'You calling me a ho? *You're* the ho. I can see what you're dreaming about already.'

'What's that?'

'The dress you're going to wear for your girly flirty thing.'

'What about you? "This time", you said. Like you already thinking of making a career of it.'

We laughed again. We had to. Because inside our laughter, there was stark terror.

The Resistance told us we had to cut Mum and Dad out of the loop on this one. Understandably, since if Mum heard about it, she'd go apeshit. 'My only child and their best mate Dune are sex bait for Bloods commanders? Did I hear that right, Huey?' Followed by the application of her knee to Huey's groin.

The afternoon came and I got ready. We didn't know anything about this commander. Only a first name, David, and that by day he shot and hanged Black people, by night he liked to fuck them. People were weird like that. I was to dress as Girl. I had to keep telling myself. I pulled on a dress, shaved my legs and cocoa-buttered my skin, flicked out my hair. Dune was to come as Boy. My heart speeded up at the thought, which was weird, and I decided it was because when Dune dressed up, they dressed up properly and they were going to bring their own version of Boy, no doubt. I checked the mirror. It was a long time since I'd dressed like this. Slinky. The house was empty, Mum and Dad out at a Resistance meeting. Nevertheless, I felt like I was sneaking out, and my dad was going to be suddenly yanking me back, saying *Over my dead body are you going out like that, dressed like a whore.*

I was running late. There was a boom in the air behind me, and the downtown sky lit up like a huge bunch of electric chrysanthemums had been thrown up there. The Bloods militia had taken to letting off fireworks whenever they won a fight at a siege house or their roadblocks captured a resistor. Mainly the militias were big kids who liked shooting fireworks into the sky.

Three burned-out cars decorated the park by the basketball court. Yesterday there'd been two. The wrecked cars were reproducing. Sex was on my mind. Mum and Dad had no idea how the metal tubes of their bed rang out like the bells of Notre Dame when they screwed. It woke the whole neighbourhood, even Dune heard them. And the more bombs went off, the more they screwed, like they got the 'make love, not war' thing tangled up and thought it was 'make love when war'. The thought of Dad on top of Mum with a come face on him was *ugh!* And with Mum's knee gone, she'd wreck her leg completely if she carried on. Old people should not have sex. At least when me and Dune banged,

we were young, so we looked good doing it. I thought about us
doing it for a bit.

At the basketball court, the park floodlights were broken and
everywhere was glittering with broken glass. Someone was riding a
horse across the plains. They were hitched low on the horse's back
as it galloped, holding onto the mane with both arms. You saw
some strange things, these parts. The Roma had been on the move
recently so it could be one of them. The horse and rider disappeared
into the green and the hoof sounds sank away over the park's slopes.

'Hey, Girly!'

Great. It was going to be that kind of afternoon. I looked up.

'That's a nice dress you got on. It would look even better on
my bedroom floor! Come to Jay-Jay, he'll keep you warm all night!'

Little Stukeley's inbreds were not blessed with originality in
their chat-up lines. There were four of them, by the burned-out
cars. I cut-eyed them.

'Darling, you not stopping? Don't you like us?'

Guffaws. Footsteps approaching. I felt for my knife. I'd almost
made it to the turn by the shrubs when Loverboy blocked my path.
He was panting slightly but tried for the formal approach.

'Let me introduce myself properly. I'm Jay. People call me
Jay-Jay.'

He'd closed the gap as he'd talked and now had an arm around
my waist. His thin cotton T-shirt pushed into my chest, while his
free hand rested on my left shoulder.

Poor Loverboy. He didn't know I'd practised for hours solid,
getting the knife into my hand surreptitiously. For this commander.
Now I slipped my hand under his T-shirt and thrust the knife
upwards. Then looked right into his startled brown eyes.

'You feel something cold in the middle of your chest? Where my hand is? Between the chest bones where your heart is?'

He nodded, gulped.

'That's a bowie knife. If I press a little more it will go straight through your chest bones into your little heart. Keep hugging me though. Good, Jay-Jay. Now walk backwards a little with me. Keep your arm around me. That's right, they'll like that, your mates, you'll look cool.'

Jeers, laughter and whistles winged over from the wrecked car. We turned the corner. Now bushes obscured us from Jay-Jay's mates.

'Pay attention now. On the count of three, I'm going to jerk the handle of this knife and the only way for you to not get stuck through your sweet little heart is if you move back and run like fuck. On three. Not yet. I nearly went through you then, you see, I'm getting attached to you. There's a little blood flowing now from your chest, I can feel it trickling into the crease of my elbow. On three. Get it?'

Jay-Jay nodded.

'OK. One . . . Two . . . Thr—'

In a blink he had shot through the bushes and across the park. Like the horse.

Girly. I smoothed my dress. My hand was sticky with blood from Jay-Jay's chest. I bent down to a puddle, washed the knife and my hands, then hitched the dress and stuck the knife back in the band of my underwear and walked on.

People were always underestimating me, I thought, thinking they could read me like a book. Maybe like you're reading this book. Most people don't even know the Chapter One of me.

139

Dune was waiting at the corner of the close with their Yamaha, working their wrist on the throttle.

'Ax, babe! Afros are the sweetest, sexiest thing.'

'You look a picture yourself,' I said.

'You got the knife?'

I showed them.

My stomach was in knots. I got on the Yamaha. Dune sped us to the town centre.

The commander was tall. He had big arms, wide shoulders, and a taut midriff. He'd tucked himself into the shadows of the Cerberus cafe awning. He was in jeans and a grey North Face windcheater, smoking a cigarette. There was nobody else around. His eyes were steady and wary as we approached. His nails were short and grubby and there were scratches on his forearms. He wanted to shake hands. I stayed silent, Dune did the talking, and they did a good job, maybe overdid it. Resting their hand on the commander's when accidentally going for the same egg mayonnaise sandwich triangle. Slurping tea with their little finger cocked. And a bit of eyebrow tennis. David this. David that. Dune was a duck in water at it. *Bitch.* Their brown dungarees, white Polo top and Kickers were accessorised to the nth degree with earrings, necklace, a Caribbean auntie lace choker, and full-on strawberry lipgloss. I chuckled inside of me. Dune's idea of Boy. Huey would be choking. The commander didn't seem to mind. They'd done a better number than me with the threads, somehow it made my slinky black and white flower-print to-the-knees-and-higher-if-you-get-lucky dress look drab.

'You are both sweet like honey,' I heard the commander say.

'Like molasses,' corrected Dune. 'Who needs honey, David, when they can have dark brown molasses?'

It drew a lewd smile from the commander.

Unlike Dune, I had no repartee. I left them to it.

The chat soon turned serious.

'Two pretty brown things. It's time to taste the sugar. Are you ready for our little escapade in the forest?'

'Give us the money first.'

'What money?'

'You said.' Dune held out. 'These earrings are not cheap.'

The commander smiled, gave in, and slid some notes out of his wallet, palmed them to Dune. Then he got up and strolled to a grey four-wheel-drive car, beckoning us to follow. Grey was his thing, even though the official Bloods colours were red, white and blue. We got to the car. There were a few passers-by, but he didn't seem to mind. I thought I saw Huey in the passenger seat of a delivery van but the van took off before I could look twice.

'This one,' he said, lifting his head at me. 'Thug Rose. I want her in the passenger seat. She's too quiet. She makes me nervous. Orchid, scoot into the back.'

Those were our whore names. Rose and Orchid.

From the back, Dune leaned forward and rested their elbows on the front seat headrests. 'I'll show you the way. We know a very good spot.'

'Have you done this before?'

I didn't know for sure what the 'this' was.

Dune answered. 'No. You're our first.'

He smiled. 'I'll have to make it special then.'

I had an urge to take out the knife there and then and stab him. I'd let the dress zip fastener ride up a little and I could reach the knife fast, through a slit in the lining.

There were Bloods leaflets strewn over the passenger seat. He saw me looking and swept them into the footwell.

'Ignore those. Do you like a breeze? Roll the window down.'

The car moved off and David began tapping the music system.

'Let's get up some of your people's music. What would you like? Beyoncé? Kanye? Tupac?'

He had a decent playlist. As he chatted to Dune about music, his left hand slid across my dress to my right thigh. I tensed and my arm reached slowly towards the knife. Dune leaned right over into the gap between the front seats and started messing with the music controls and the groping stopped. I turned in the seat away from him. Dune stayed pressed into the gap between the front seats and the two of them talked music again. I checked the car wing mirror. I could see no van or car following us. The late sun was streaming down. It was a great day to get raped.

A fifteen-minute drive felt like three lifetimes. We'd sent Huey the GPS location and marked the location on an Ordnance Survey map that we'd sent as well. Yet I saw no signs of any Resistance. Trees flicked by. We hit smaller lanes, some old farmhouses, a barn; then, in a big sweep uphill, we drove up to the location. It was a layby, with beech trees overhanging. No other cars. No people. Not even any tyre tracks. Looking through the car window, something didn't feel right.

The commander was breezy. He bounced out of the car and loosened his shirt. Beechnuts crunched under his feet as he came round from the car and opened my door. He'd loosened his windcheater and a gun showed in its shoulder holster. Dune got out the rear passenger side, and when they did, the commander immediately clamped Dune's hand in his. He asked me to walk ahead of them. I listened to the crunch of their footsteps and when I looked over my shoulder, I found him staring at me with his grey, wary eyes, but no gun in his hand. I looked away.

Dune was a class act. They showed no nervousness, walking with him as if it were a leisurely stroll in the park. I could hear Dune agreeing with the commander how pretty the small flowers that looked like miniature bluebells were when you got close to them. The bowie knife was digging into the small of my back. I hoped it didn't show. *Where were the Resistance?* I heard a click and turned fast.

What the fuck?

Dune had handcuffs dangling from a wrist.

'Cuffs?'

I looked to Dune. My face said, *What the fuck?*

Dune shrugged a *He sprung it on me* expression.

The cuffs were black and had a fluffy black covering. But they were cuffs.

'Adds to the fun,' said the commander, 'Come over, let me snap one on you.'

'No thanks, you're OK.'

'They're play cuffs,' he said. 'They open easy. Let me show you.'

'Nah.'

The guy needed shooting. Now.

He made the move then. Pulled the gun out, put one shot into the ground by Dune's feet and it thudded and spurted up soil. Then he put the barrel to the side of Dune's head.

'Come on, Thug Rose. This is how we play. Don't be awkward.'

Dune's face was panicked. *Shit.*

I went over.

He snapped the cuff on my right wrist so I was cuffed to Dune's left.

'There you go, Thug Rose,' he laughed, 'suits you. On your knees, now, both of you.'

We were deep into the trees. Nothing but green and shadows all around us.

I looked across to Dune. *Say the word.* If we both hit him fast, we had a chance.

Slowly, Dune lowered till they were on their knees. *No way.* With my free hand I felt for my knife, even as I followed Dune down.

The commander dropped his trousers. Black underwear. He took out his dick. A gnarled parsnip.

'Open your mouths.'

'What the fuck?' Dune blurted.

'Open them. I'm going to piss in your mouths.'

His dick was soft. His gun hand jumpy.

'Orchid, last time I say it. Piss or bullet?'

Where the fuck were the Resistance?

He took a step closer so his dick brushed Dune's face. The commander's face was swollen, his eyes rolled back. I felt Dune shift and their free hand groping at my back. I shuffled and nudged the knife handle to it, felt Dune clasp it.

A swift arc. Dune plunged the blade up and in.

The commander screamed.

Dune must have sliced an artery because his blood spurted everywhere.

His gun hand whipped up. A shot. Red spatter. My head felt like it was splitting. Another shot. He fell on top of us and I was trapped in his stink and blood and sweat and the cloy of his windcheater.

Someone dragged him off.

Huey. Standing over us.

'You two OK?'

Other Resistance fighters emerged from the undergrowth. They stood around Huey, frozen-faced. One looked at us and sobbed.

Dune lunged for Huey then with the bowie knife: they still had it in their hand and they dragged me with them as they lunged. Huey skipped back. Other fighters threw themselves at Dune, pressed Dune's arms to their sides. Dune wasn't done though, and ducked low this time, fell on the commander and stabbed him again and again. Three of them fell on Dune and locked Dune's stabbing arm. They prised the knife from their hand.

One rolled the corpse of the commander with her foot to check he was dead. Not that there was any doubt now, after all Dune's stabbing.

'Somebody get this thing off,' I said.

I was down there with them all. Dune's lurch down to the commander had almost snapped my wrist.

They used boltcutters to snap the chain. They searched the body and found keys and freed us from the cuffs. Huey stood over us.

'A roadblock delayed us.'

Dune spat at him from where they were sitting, their lungs still heaving.

'We're done here. We got him good.'

I smeared tears from my eyes. I tried to breathe.

'You did a great job,' Huey continued.

'You bastard,' I said. 'Never again.'

They were shoving the corpse into a body bag, limb by limb. The limbs kept slipping out.

I straightened Dune's clothes, closed their mouth. Blood was stuck to their hair, making it clumpy. Red had joined the black and white of my dress. 'What about HIV and stuff?' I said.

Huey and his team were moving around the scene methodically, picking up bits of cloth, rubbing out bootprints, trying to wipe all traces.

'We'll look after you,' Huey said. Then, 'I'm sorry. Lessons will be learned.'

'Did you bring my bike?' Dune called. I had them in my arms now.

'No. We had no room.'

They loaded the body into the back of the van and had us ride with it in the back. We were told to stay alert, there might be further roadblocks.

There were six of us crammed into the back with the body. Two of them had pistols and kept them in their hands. The van bounced along lanes. I watched blood leak slowly from the body bag where they'd ripped it when hefting it over the van's tow bar. Dune was in my lap, eyes closed.

They dropped us off in town.

'Good job. Stay off the main roads till you've cleaned up,' Huey said. 'And lie low for a while.'

The van sped off.

Dune's motorbike was still leaning against the Cerberus cafe chair storage area, at the rear of the shuttered cafe. We cleaned the blood off our clothes as best we could, using the cafe's outside tap. Dune got on the bike, unlocked it and kicked the engine alive. I jumped on. They drove fast and without a word on B roads all the way to Little Stukeley.

We pulled up outside my house. Dune rested the bike on its stand. On the drive home, I'd been reliving everything, and there was something I needed to ask them.

'Dune, did he actually piss in your mouth?'

Dune looked away. 'I tasted blood, not piss. No way I'm doing that again. We go back to building tunnels and stuff. Else I quit.'

'I'm going in now.'

They held me back. 'You can't go in there like that.'

'What do you mean?'

'Shaking.'

I tried to stop them. The shakes. It was funny. Like, hysterically funny. Because I couldn't. Eventually, Dune admitted defeat and they got me to sit down and rang the house phone and rang off when Mum answered.

Mum came running out and saw us and let rip. 'What's this, *Night of the Evil Dead*? What happened? You meet the Stukeley Psycho? Ax, what's Dune done to you this time?'

Dune shook their head. 'Wasn't me.'

I said I'd fallen off the back of Dune's bike, that was all. But Mum wasn't having it, so Dune said, 'I'm sorry, it's my fault, I let Ax try riding the bike and the idiot stuck the throttle and that's why we came off bad, I should have known because Ax can't ride jackshit, not even a skateboard.'

Mum bought it. She stopped shouting and looked at our cuts,

saying we had to dab them with iodine and get the dirt out and I said, 'Iodine? What am I, radioactive?'

She smiled and cooled at that.

Inside, I stood under the shower for a long time, washing the commander's blood out of my hair.

12

Hiding in Plain Sight

I woke up to jitters. A kaleidoscope of sounds and images shuttered through my mind. Blood soaking into pine needles. The black snub of a pistol. Trees. Crunching, underfoot. Black bodies in ditches. Cackling. The sound of a gun firing. A gold earring. Somebody crying. Then it all fogged out.

I was Axel. I was in the Bloods' ERAC. I had a SIM chip in my head. I had to keep myself together.

We'd been given a fresh supply of broadleafed maidenhair. I boiled it and woke Dune. Dune opened their eyes and shut them again fast. They began cursing. 'Get out of my face, negro, you should be swinging.' I got the maidenhair down them. Yesterday morning, it had been 'Haha, this mirror lies. I'm white. Ugly bitch.'

I picked up our tin mirror. Unlike Dune, I wasn't so down on it. The little piece of tin added a gold sheen to our faces. I looked seventeen going on seventy-five. Bits of dirt in my crushed hair. My eyebrows were two earwigs, my lips all broken up with dry skin. The whites of my eyes blotched, and hairs sprouting in all kinds of places you wouldn't want. The remains of some anti-ID paint clung to my neck.

Dune snatched the mirror from me. They took one look then flung it. 'Lies, lies, lies.'

Yet a stomachful of maidenhair later, Dune was fine.

News from the drums confirmed what I'd figured: the night drones had not been over last night.

Clicking from outside the tent: Dune had been summoned again.

When they came back in the afternoons, their inner left forearm was always lined with red welts.

With Dune gone, I was alone. I watched the morning cooking fires sputter out and the washing lines go up. I had work duty in the afternoon. Digging. Beta dropped by the tent with Wires at her side. He split as Beta waved to me. I let her in. Her eyes glittered. She had a gizmo for me. A little grey cube with an LCD screen.

'What does it do?'

'Turn it on.'

She leaned across and pressed a button on it.

'Wow. OK.'

'I made it. It's a copy of Elizabeth's. Running on an M-one chip.'

'Where d'you get the parts?'

'The tip. The Underground have got pickers working right under the Peace Committee's noses. Every single circuit board they find is smuggled away. We even found a job lot of microprocessors. Looked like an office clear-out from a computer firm. They just shoved all their spare parts into rubble sacks. Raspberry Pi chips. Cooling fans. Motherboards. Heat sinks. RAM storage. The lot. I nearly fainted.'

Suddenly, Beta halted. She looked at me. She'd broken the rules. Said too much.

I reassured her: 'I wasn't listening. What am I meant to do with this thing?'

'Try it. It has an antenna in the body. It streams code. They want you to look at some streams. Watch this.'

She hit another button. A set of jumping hippos leaped onto the screen.

'Cool, right? That's your cover. Hit the blue button and the hippos come on. You tell anyone who gets curious that it's a game. The game actually works.'

'Neat.'

I tried it.

'It's got a burner too,' Beta said, as hippos jumped. 'See that red button on the side there? Never press and hold together with *Start,* except in an emergency. That combination wipes all data and turns it into toy mode only.'

'A burn key. Right. Pretty good.'

'Isn't it?'

She made to get up.

'Beta, one last thing.'

She looked at me.

'Pharaoh? Did they get him? The Scavengers?'

'No,' Beta whispered. 'Word is, he's still with us.'

I gasped relief.

Beta gave me one of her megawatt smiles, then ducked out, leaving me with the gizmo.

At first, all the Underground wanted me to do with the gizmo was watch data flows and interpret them when I could. I spent mornings squinting at the matchbox-sized LCD screen, watching local logistics movements by the Bloods. The Bloods were mainly using

151

DPD, Hermes and JustGet to deliver ammunition to Huntingdon militias. The occasional machine gun. A couple of land-based radars. A batch of laser-detection systems for airplanes and drones. The Bloods' intercepted communications systems were talking about the lasers the most. Someone had stolen them and the Bloods were going apeshit about it. I sent encrypted reports at the end of the day.

Elizabeth X came round personally to thank me when I decoded the missing lasers report. She moved me on from logistics channels to the Bloods' war comms. I took it as a promotion. No extra pay, though.

War is code and code is war, right? Here's how that worked in reality. The Bloods' code wars involved a four-step cycle:

1. Find.
2. Fix.
3. Track.
4. Target.

In the 'Find' stage, the Bloods hunted Resistance members. But, unless they were on operations, Resistance members looked pretty much like civilians. So the Bloods vacuumed up huge amounts of data off mobile phones, Bluetooth devices and anything else that hit the 5G networks they had backdoor access to. Then came 'Fix'. In Fix, they did nodal network analysis and aggregated matrices. That was all crunched and presented as a percentage likelihood of any one data cluster (or 'human being', to me and you) being Resistance. The kill per cent threshold was seventy per cent. That activated 'Track'. So, if it was seventy per cent likely according to the Bloods' pattern-of-life data that you were Resistance, they would monitor your every move by data analysis and plans would be put in place to permanently neutralise you. That was the 'Target' bit. You've guessed that already, right? Bloods-speak for *kill you*. The Bloods had a long, long kill list. Unless you were up there in the top one hundred, you'd have a big wait. I hacked the Bloods' top hundred list and sent it on.

It was likely the Bloods could run the same pattern-of-life analysis on camp occupants as they did outside the camp. That was how we ended up in shifts like the clothes tent duty. Underground members were told to keep as full cover as possible, including doing as many work rotas as we could. Me and Dune did mainly crops. But the rotas worked their way round and one afternoon we found ourselves in the clothes tent, sorting – you guessed it – clothes.

Some of the clothes there stank of piss. We fooled about with the hats pile, trying on straw hats. Floppy hats. Even an Al Capone hat. My thoughts went creepier. Whose clothes had these been, and why had they been given up? I found a piece of cardboard tucked behind the broken pocket lining of a small coat. A kid's handwriting. *Help me.* Written in red biro. I didn't let Dune see it. We finished the shift without catching too many fleas, then headed back to our tent.

How was Dune doing in this time? They were doing fine. Every morning they were off somewhere training their army. How, with what, and where, I didn't know.

I was being given a series of code puzzles. They were exercises for when the phone with the special code came in. Sometimes, to work the code puzzles out, I had to scribble stuff on paper. I had all these scribbles around me one time when Horse dropped by.

'What's this?' Horse asked, picking up a paper.

I switched the gizmo to game mode.

'It's code for a new game I made,' I said. 'It's called *Hippo Hop*. Like digital Tic-Tac-Toe, but with hippos.'

'What you doing that for?'

'No reason. Bored.'

'You can write code then?' Horse picked up a sheet and squinted at it. 'Do the flunkies know you're doing this?'

'Is it their business?'

'How will you play it?' Horse picked up the gizmo and played *Hippo Hop* for a while. Then he abruptly seemed to get bored and left.

Next day, I was walking with Horse to the standpipe for a drink when the flunkies swooped. Me and Horse fought them, but they wrestled the gizmo from me. Though not before I'd managed to hold down the burn key.

The flunkies switched it on. The *Hippo Hop* game played on the little LCD screen. Complete with sound effects. *Croak!* I saw them look amused for a microsecond. Then they went all officious.

'This will be marked. It is not authorised. You are not blessed.'

'Sorry. I'm a no-good negro,' I replied.

They confiscated the gizmo and Horse ran after them and got himself a baton beating for trying to get it back for me. Horse trudged back. I thanked him but said it's only a game, and he didn't need to even bother filling in a Peace Committee petition form to get it back.

That afternoon, I relayed the news to the Underground about the gizmo. Soon after, Beta walked up, with Sly loping alongside her, his tall frame and straight back unmistakeable. Like Wires before, he split when they reached the tent. When I asked, Beta told me to be cool, she was sure that when I triggered the burn switch all the Underground data on the gizmo would have fried.

It was another mark against my name though. I'd be moving up the Bloods' list of camp suspects.

Pharaoh came calling and I had to go with him. He wanted to see if I could spot Dune's artillery trainees or not.

I noticed Pharaoh's left eye was still not right since he damaged it down the shaft, the iris cloudy. 'Your eye,' I said. 'Has it not healed?'

'Not yet. But it's no biggie. My right's the strongest and that's intact. Now try to spot soldiers. Flag up anything you think isn't normal. Let's go.'

I walked through camp with Pharaoh and at first I was flummoxed. Because what did normal look like in ERAC? The washing lines blew in the wind. The litter swirled this way and that. The Whited went their way, shuffling and mumbling stuff. Children played in the rusted wrecks of car carcasses.

Occasionally I stopped and studied a scene.

Was the youth throwing stones at the wet blanket mad at something, or was she practising how to hit a shifting target?

Was the man on his knees with his arms raised in a SIM-affected, slow-motion Muslim act of prayer, or was he building artillery arm strength?

Which, if any, of the four people planking out by the concrete plains were in mental shutdown and which were doing core strength training? The giveaway there was Storm. I recognised her from the bunker meeting. Her smooth face hardly grimaced as she held her taut body as rigid as a barrel.

How about the boy in jeans and grubby vest holding a pebble in his outstretched fist, which he kept hold of even as the strain popped sweat all across his brow? I'd seen Dune doing that, before camp. Strength conditioning for the catapult brace position? Or just a kid with a thing for stones?

I saw two arm-wrestling contests going on. Biceps bulged. Had arm wrestling suddenly become popular?

And so it went on. Folk throwing pebbles into trees were either brain-fried or on target practice.

Two litter pickers had started spearing litter instead of using their grab tools.

Soon, I was able to call them out correctly all across the camp. It was an army, hiding in plain sight.

Pharaoh wasn't bothered by how well I started doing. 'You spot stuff now because you're looking for it and know it's there,' he said as the tour went on and I got sharper. 'Most people ain't looking and don't see. Even if flunkies filed a report on their suspicions, the Bloods wouldn't react. Too speculative.'

'So, how does it work?' I asked. 'Why are they all doing this separately?'

'That Bloods' "who-meets-who" data analysis method you told us about?'

'Yeah?'

'We decided that bringing people together every day is not smart. We limit meet-ups to just a few people when we still do them. Here, come see. A little surprise.'

He led me along an old runway access road, and along the side of a bomb-blasted hangar, then we took a looping stretch of concrete that petered out at a cluster of broken brick walls. The concrete sloped down into a hollow: some kind of storage shelter.

'Welcome to our firing range,' said Pharaoh.

I heard them before I saw them: the *thwack* of weapons being fired. Dune's voice, calling out.

'Get your elbow to your anchor point! You fire from there, every time. You need to go there again and again until you build the muscle memory!'

We went round the last wall. It was a concrete-floored sloping quadrangle with a makeshift roof of steel panels. Straw bales lined the walls. Recruits were in a line, with catapults, at shooting distance from the bales.

'Do I breathe out when I shoot?' a recruit asked Dune.

'No,' Dune admonished. 'Breathe out before you shoot. Then you hold your lungs. The shot comes in the stillness. Breathing is movement. Be still. Watch.'

Dune let fly with their catapult. Their missile hit dead centre on a paper target on a straw bale.

'Got it?'

Dune saw us, nodded, carried on.

'My arm's sore,' someone complained.

'A little sore is good. Sore so you can't extend your arm is not good. OK. Let's wrap this session up!'

The recruits dropped their catapults into a bucket. Dune gathered the team around for a final talk. 'There's no wind in this shelter, so you've had it easy. Out there, you'll need to gauge wind speed. Some of you, your shooting hip juts out, messing up your stance. It's a weakness in the hips that causes it, so do the exercises I've given you in your own time to train the weakness out. That's it for today. Well done. Disperse.'

It was my first sight of Dune the captain. They fitted the part like a glove.

13

Negroes, Sunbathing

Next day, after Dune had gone off, Elizabeth X and Beta signalled and I went with them into the bog zone. We sat in silence until Elizabeth X was satisfied we hadn't been followed. Then she spoke.

'Resistance has contacted us. We need to rehearse the drone landing. We only get once chance. A lot of things could go wrong.'

Elizabeth X nudged Beta.

'Right,' said Beta. 'Think of this camp as Mars.'

'What?'

'Yeah. The Resistance has got hardware that scientists used to land things on Mars, and they're going to use it with their drone. It's called Terrain Relative Navigation.'

'And it works how?'

'Photo-matching. We've taken a set of photos of where we want the drone to land and sent them to the Resistance. The Resistance will upload them to their drone. On the day, when the drone goes up in the air, it will compare the camp terrain with the photos it has stored, until it identifies the correct place to land.'

Elizabeth X took it up. 'The system doesn't always work. It can be blocked by fog and smoke.'

'Yes. And rain and cloud and image processing failure. Any number of things,' Beta added. 'So they'll be using lidar laser as well, as back-up.'

I was out of my depth times two. They saw it.

'It's what operates driverless cars,' Beta said. 'Remember them? A set of light lasers. They supply their own energy so they can operate in light or dark, unlike Terrain Relative Navigation. The lasers bounce light and measure the return speed to gauge location and speed of craft.'

I got it. Just about.

'They need reflective surfaces to work best,' Beta added.

'Such as?'

'Anything reflective. Road markings are great. Licence plates. Cat's eyes.'

'Cat's eyes?'

'Not actual cats. Glass beads. Like in the middle of roads.'

Duh.

'But lidar lasers don't like water because it absorbs laser energy,' said Elizabeth X.

'So if it rains . . . ?'

'Yeah, problem of scattering,' said Beta. 'And bright sunlight can haze the retro-reflective data and the drone would need to switch to terrain tech.'

I looked at these two tech-heads. 'What do you want with me?' I asked. 'I only know code.'

'You're the one who's going to get the phone,' Elizabeth X said. 'So you need to know the various plays that might occur. We've gathered reflectors. Old licence plates. Road signs. Ripped-out Cat's eyes from runways, where we could find them. And a team have been in rehearsal. Grab your beret and come watch. Tell us what you think.'

*

There was a light drizzle coming down as we made it through the bog zone hinterlands, the kind of rain that smeared everything. It blurred the edges of figures who came into focus slowly, in glints of blue. Road sign blue. Elizabeth X had me sit in the long grass and watch as the figures made a formation from the reflective pieces they'd pulled out of the tip. The reflective squares kept rotating. Appearing then disappearing. I guessed they were flipping the material between reflective and ordinary surface. They were getting pretty good at moving into and out of the square formation.

An alert whistle blew. A quick blast. Flunkies on patrol.

The vision vanished. The figures scattered.

Then Elizabeth X was scrambling through the grass to me, lugging road signs, and Beta came stumbling with car plates and they told me we had to move fast.

Visibility was still low because of the drizzle. We'd almost made it to the edge of tent city, when two flunkies stopped us on a path. They looked cheerful, though their robes were sodden. They both had the Peace Committee-approved, double-knot hair.

'Negroes, hold up. What do you have there?'

They gestured to Elizabeth X, and the six road signs she was carrying on her head.

'Panels,' said Elizabeth X.

'What for?'

'Sunbathing,' said Beta.

'In this rain?'

Beta nodded coolly.

They didn't seem that concerned. 'Why is it all blue?' one of the flunkies asked.

'Because blue is the coolest colour! I have the bluest eyes, don't you think? Bluer than yours. So, which of us is the negro?' Beta said.

They laughed.

Beta gave it to them large. 'We are the worshippers of blue, embracing every drop of our whiteness.' Beta was a good actor. She sounded completely Whited.

One of the flunkies got busy tapping stuff into their tablets and we knew a report would get filed. But they let us go without further questions.

Back at tent city, Beta and Elizabeth X disappeared to hide the reflectors. Dune was elsewhere and the tent was empty, but not for long. Elizabeth X and Beta soon came back.

'What do you think, then,' asked Elizabeth X, knees crossed, 'about the reflector plan?'

I spoke my truth.

'Lugging that stuff around is slow and suspicious. What if the Bloods' drones spot them? Or the flunkies find where they're stored?'

'It's the best plan we have so far.'

'What about paint?' I said.

'How do you mean?' asked Elizabeth X.

'We already use reflective paint on our faces. Why not have a circle of people with paint daubed all over their bodies or clothes.'

'And the centre of the circle is the landing spot?' Beta asked.

'That's it.'

Elizabeth X sucked her teeth. 'Can that work?'

'Don't see why not,' said Beta.

'Wouldn't it be suspicious?'

'No. It makes total sense,' said Beta, now totally keen. 'We're already using paint. We wouldn't need all the signs. Just body paint.

161

We can store it more easily. If the drone has a light source, it will pick up the bodies in a circle.'

'OK. Why a circle?' said Elizabeth.

'So our drone doesn't confuse it with the straight lines of the airbase runways and stuff. Right, Ax?'

'That's it.'

Elizabeth X finally came round. 'OK. Blue reflective body paint. They could wave in a pattern, directing the drone where to land.'

A whistle sounded from outside the tent. Elizabeth X stood up.

'We'll talk some more,' she said, 'and rehearse this refinement of the plan. But yep. Idea adopted. Let's do it.'

'Pharaoh? Did the Scavengers ID him?'

Elizabeth X didn't answer.

'They probably got partials, right?'

Elizabeth X nodded. Then she was gone.

Much later in the day, when it was just me and Dune in the tent, and the wind had dropped and cooking fires were being lit, Horse came and said he had a message from Pharaoh.

'He's holding a special dinner this evening and you're invited.'

'When?' I asked.

'Now.'

We followed Horse over.

It was an ordinary fire outside an ordinary tent. There was no Elizabeth X, but Beta was there with her tentmate, Footsy, and I recognised a few others from artillery. Storm. Sly. Wires. There were twelve of us in all. It was a big group, but we didn't stand out. Everywhere people were gathered in groups at fires for the day's final meal. People talked. I kept an eye out for flunkies.

With a *psst,* Pharaoh beckoned me and Dune to come with him to the standpipe to fill a max-size water container. I could tell he had something on his mind and when we were out of earshot of the others he spoke.

'Dune?'

He'd thrown an arm around them.

'Yes?'

'You're training the recruits great. Keep it up. You're one brave soul. I respect you for that. I respect all of the trainees. They will carry the fight. If my eyesight goes. If my fight leaves me. If they wipe me, God forbid, or if Scavengers take me.'

'Don't say that,' said Dune, 'you'll keep on. Isn't that what you say to us? Keep on?'

Pharaoh grimaced. 'That's true. But I don't know.' He paused. The container was filling up fast. 'Axel, the targets list you sent in.'

'Yes?'

'I'm number one on that list inside camp. They'll be coming for me. Just a matter of when.'

'The list isn't science,' I said, 'it's guesswork. And they got to get you first.'

The container was full, the water slopping off its mouth now. Pharaoh turned off the tap and screwed the cap on. 'Let's go back there and sit down and have this meal together. Forget this conversation. I just wanted you two to know how much I appreciate you.'

We nodded. Dune looked across at me. I shrugged.

The fire was roaring by the time we got back and the cooking

163

was giving off smells that suggested this time the goop was going to be edible. Bowls were handed around and the stew scooped and as we ate it was quiet for a while. Only Pharaoh didn't eat. He leaned back and turned to us two again.

'Sing for me, Dune.'

'What?'

'Go ahead.'

'How do you know I sing?'

'The Resistance wrote it up in your notes that you can sing. I need something to feed my soul.'

In a distant tent, two people were having a shouting match. A man came stumbling by, his face caked in grey powder, glitching and mumbling, dragging a set of freshly dead brown rats on strings. He cursed us as he passed.

After the rat man passed, as the argument in the faraway tent kept on, Dune sang. For the first time in ERAC. It was a song that was soft and yet somehow wrapped in strength:

> *'Don't go, Pharaoh. Don't fade.*
> *Don't dim your light, don't fade.*
> *Don't go. Don't fade.*
> *You're the fire this time, and next.*
> *Reaching for us to be saved.*
> *Don't go. Don't fade.'*

All the pain and sadness and Dune's golden voice.

Everyone had stopped eating and gone silent.

'That was good,' said Pharaoh. He leaned across and hugged Dune. He wiped his eyes. 'Thanks.'

'You're welcome.'

'But why d'you choose that mournful tune though, making out like I'm fading? Pharaoh is not fading. Pharaoh goes on. Eat. Eat! You too, Horse, you too. Wires. Everybody eat.'

As the eating resumed, I caught Pharaoh looking at his hands. I knew the tattoos were there. He was holding his hands to his good eye, and I saw a smile install itself on his face.

'You seeing your kids?' I murmured.

He nodded and spoke to me quietly. 'They come back to me every time I hold my hands this way. Not always the whole of them, but I *see* them. They come back. Racing along streets. Across beaches. Me and my babies. *Carry me! Carry me too!* they'd say. And I'd have them both on my hips. *Throw me in the air, Daddy! Higher! Higher!* They never thought I'd let them fall, but I did. They fell. But not you here. You will go on and have lives and children and thrive and the Bloods will have to kill me before I allow them to get you.'

Pharaoh's hands came down from his face and his voice changed as he addressed us all. 'Remember to storify tonight. That's how I've kept on, that's what you have to do. It's the last thing I'll say. Now let's eat and live in this moment.'

14

The Howling Night

I woke into darkness. Deep night in the camp. An alert was sounding: a shrill whistle that ripped right across the tent zone again and again. Dune stirred too, staring blankly. I shook them and they seemed OK. We went to the tent flaps. Beams of light jumped from Peace Committee tents, raking the dark. They landed on a black-cloaked figure, moving low. The figure stumbled over guy ropes. Tent fronts zipped down to block the figure every time it passed. I glimpsed a beret. Heard the low, ear-popping hum then, from an armed night drone, hanging as low as it had ever been, its malevolent energy radiating, a gun arm dropped and extended.

'Get the catapult,' Dune hissed. 'That's Pharaoh out there!'

The figure got up on its feet again. Came spinning round. We called out. Waved and waved. In the end it stumbled over and we dragged the figure into our tent.

I could see the drone was close, so they'd know real quick it was us harbouring him. Still.

Dune had called it right. It was Pharaoh, his beret rammed low. We closed the flaps fast.

'I don't have time,' he said. 'They've got me, they finally got me. Axel, take this.'

He shoved a piece of folded paper into my hand.

Suddenly he relaxed, as if he'd stopped by on one of his litter-picking strolls. 'Tell Elizabeth I always loved her, OK? Say, even to the end.'

A smile of resignation spread across his face.

'Don't talk stupid,' said Dune. 'We'll keep them out, Pharaoh.' Dune had their catapult now, and was loading it, reaching for the tent flaps.

Pharaoh pulled Dune back. 'That's not gonna work. It would compromise both of you. Don't let me down now. Our hopes rest with you. You're the revolution now. Ax, those are the signal codes I gave you, on a grid. Do your jobs. Keep on. We nearly free. Keep on.'

'But . . .'

All the while that Pharaoh was talking, alert after alert had blared. Now the ground was drumming. Scavengers.

'I gotta step,' said Pharaoh.

'No!' Dune blocked him.

'Hey, Dune, I love the fight you got, I love everything about you. Both of you. You my kids now. And I'm not losing two sets of kids. Bloods not going to take me alive. My secrets die with me.' Pharaoh looked at the palms of his hands. 'You two keep on. That's a command. Now I'm going to see my boy, my girl. So step aside, in the name of Black Jesus.'

'No!'

But Pharaoh brushed past Dune and was gone.

Lasers from Peace Committee tents shone, picking out his moving figure.

Peace Committee collaborators. *Fuckers.*

The night drone's search beam switched on and picked him up.

We watched, helplessly. Pharaoh was up fully now and running. *1U. 70. 1609.* Running for the fence. Into the fence. There was a blue flash as he hit the chain link. Little bursts of yellow silhouetted him. A small explosion, head height. Then Scavengers were pulling at his charred body.

'Jeez,' said Dune. 'What the fuck.'

I hugged Dune close to me, closing my arms round their waist.

'Why?' Dune was saying. 'Why not risk the Reeducation Centre?'

'The volts would've destroyed his head chip. That way they can't download anything from him. No secrets. It all dies with him. He died to keep the Underground safe. Right?'

'Yeah.'

I lay back, raging. This world destroyed you. Even someone as capable as Pharaoh got taken down. He'd cared for us, risked everything.

Dune had my head in their chest, and I let my tears roll till I couldn't see any more. I felt Dune too, breathing heavy. Gasps and shudders. We coiled into each other. I remembered Pharaoh's last command to us – *keep on.*

Next morning, I was weirdly good. Hardly stuttered. I remembered something bad had happened in the night. *The night drone. Pharaoh's arm pressing into my neck. 'Keep on.' Pharaoh, running. The fence.*

The image blanked.

Dune hardly glitched. Just a couple of you *no-good negros*, and the maidenhair sorted that fast. They had recollection too, of Pharaoh last night. Like maybe the drones hadn't attempted rewrites then because they'd been too busy tracking Pharaoh.

When we walked past the gate on the way to the fields, we saw him. Strung up in a metal cage. Pharaoh. Swinging high, there in the wind. The cage dangled from the sniper's cradle of the crane parked on the other side of the gates.

They were waving Pharaoh's body in our faces. The tattered remains of his black cloak. His face, all burned away. The SIM side of his head blown off. The only thing left of his beret was the mesh wire. It had curled into what looked like thorns, burnt solid into his skull.

Late that afternoon, we got back from the fields and there was a message grooved into a piece of wood by our tent.

1U 45. 70.

We gunked up, slid on our berets and followed the directions. At the location, we found another note. I used the signal code grid Pharaoh had given me last night to decrypt it. The note was from Elizabeth X.

> *Don't give up. Pharaoh would have hated that.*
> *Don't give up. Then he doesn't die in vain.*
> *Don't give up. Let your tears fall in secret, like mine.*
> *Power.*

The last cipher was a visual grid. It decrypted as a fist.

Me and Dune did a ceremony for Pharaoh on our own in the tent: burning incense, and saying his name.

15

Jet Black

Grief burned slowly, the smoke of it coating everything.

It hit Dune hardest and they deteriorated fast. It quickened the work of their SIM, as if it had found a smart combination to worm its way deeper into Dune's psyche.

Artillery training was postponed. Stream decoding could wait, too. I was told to do whatever I could to get Dune back on their feet.

Dune had moments of lucidity. Times they could speak to me as the Dune I knew. It was maddening because you never knew which Dune was sitting next to you in the tent. The half-Blanked zombie or the lucid soulmate.

Dune was chewing marrow rinds one morning, when they jumped from silence to rambling.

'Everything's bleached, Ax. Like I'm half blind, know what I'm saying? To the past. I can only see now, not *then*. I'm already half Blanked.'

Pretty good, right? OK, it's bleak, but you knew it was Dune. Then next breath they'd be saying, 'You zero negro.'

Or, this one, their finest diss so far, done with a hard stare at me: 'The lighter the skin, the better. And you're dark, Ax. Dark. Dark. Dark.'

Sometimes, I put a blanket over my head and cried.

It wasn't just Dune that was having stuff wiped. My mind was melting too, at least the memory part. You'd think you'd know your parents' faces like the back of your hand. Their faces were all gone now. For sure, their faces had been flickering since arrival in this camp, but now they were totally wiped. Eyes, nose, mouth, all gone. The SIM had moved on to their hands. I could no longer see them. Which hands held mine in theirs? Which hands rocked me to sleep? Which threw me up and caught me? Which hands wiped my brow when I was ill? Which hands pinned up all my cat and dog drawings? You get the idea.

I must have been speaking aloud or at least muttering. Dune had put their arm around me.

'That was poetry. You always were the poet, Ax.'

I thought I was under the blanket during this, but it must have slipped off. I snuggled into Dune. The Dune I knew. They were in a reflective mood. Lucid.

'What about the memories we storified? They're meant to still be in there now, right?' Dune tapped their skull. 'Burned in. Can you find them, Ax? I can't find anything.'

It was faint, but I could see something. Driving up. A double wide door. A figure. The preacher. 'The American preacher?' I said. 'Remember him?'

Dune just stared into the tent's ceiling, remembering nothing.

'I can see you there, Dune. Chewing gum. The preacher's moving his mouth but the words don't line up with his lips. He's saying, "White is better. The negro is the carrier of water and the hewer of wood."'

'And then?'

'We reply. Like in a chant. We're saying, "I worship the one drop of white blood in my veins." Did we say that?'

171

'I don't know, Ax. I don't know.'

'Hey. It's OK, I got you. There's another memory sliding around. A paddling pool. A shed in a back garden. You got that?'

'No. But keep going. Maybe it will come.'

'It's a baby, being held up to the sky by one of three Bloods. They've got Bibles and are holding them up to the sun too, with the baby. The baby has a golden aura around it. So does the Bloods' worshippers. They're Witnesses. They're in a back garden. And the mother. Her name's Charlotte, I remember that. The baby's mother is draped in blue and white sheets and she's standing like the statues in Catholic churches.'

'Like a nun?'

'Yeah. And her hands are pressed together in prayer at her chest and her head tilts up to the sky. She's thanking God for the Bloods taking her baby. She's saying, "Blessed are the Bloods. Blessed is Mara. Blessed am I that I may donate my baby." You remember any of this?'

'Nope.'

'Nothing at all?'

Maybe they heard my disappointment because they squeezed my hand and said, 'It's all right. I don't need thousands of memories. I only need to hear your voice, Ax. Everything's in your voice. I hear you and I know I'm alive, I know I'm safe and loved. You make me. You define me. You hold me. You keep my shape.'

Damn. Sometimes Dune said the nicest things. I kissed them on the nose.

They smiled back. Then: 'What you do that for, you no-good negro?'

You see the way it went? The Dune I knew was gone again and

I was sobbing in a corner of the tent till the canvas there was wet with my snot as Dune cursed both their skin and mine.

A couple of minutes of sobbing and it got boring. I decided to go see Beta.

As I approached her tent, I saw Sly and Wires hanging at a standpipe nearby. They both scooted as I walked up, Wires with a little nod to me. Footsy wasn't there. It was just me and Beta inside the tent. Beta had spent the morning in the bog zone, shovelling shit on a wagon to be spread on the fields. The smell had got into every pore of her body. She asked what was up.

'I'm losing Dune, Beta, you understand? Ever since Pharaoh died, Dune's in bits and pieces. Their memory's crumbling. They don't wash. They stare out of the tent most days and their eyes are all vacant. Try to get them to do anything, and they mouth at you, "Ugly negro. Step and fetch it yourself." Or they duck under the blanket. Each night I lose a little more of them. And I'm scared.'

'So it's Beta to the rescue again?'

She sounded prickly. I ignored it. 'You managed it last time,' I said.

'Do I hear a thank you?'

'Don't make me beg.'

Beta shifted on her bum, her eyes closed and she steepled her fingers in that way she had. 'Here's how I see it with Dune,' she said. 'Pharaoh was last seen at Dune's tent. That was a mistake. Dune was in the zone when Scavengers raided. Dune was there too when the drone was downed by catapult. Also, Dune's been leading the artillery training and the flunkies are bound to have picked up something about it. Together, it puts Dune, even more than you, in the drones' crosshairs. Add to that, Dune's grief over

Pharaoh, which is likely inhibiting the efficiency of their bio-memory network so the bio-memory struggles to take back control from the Bloods' SIM. End result is, Dune's head is fucked.'

She opened her eyes at that conclusion.

'Can't you do anything?'

To give her credit, Beta came back with me to the tent to see Dune. And she worked her guts off. She tried all the feelgood stuff, dancing, singing, storifying. Through it all, Dune sat in a corner of the tent in a blank state. Nothing worked. Occasionally they'd look at me or Beta and say, 'This ugly negro needs shooting,' even as they wiped the eyebrows that one of those *ugly negro*s had styled for them.

Beta gave up eventually. It says something when Beta gives up, she doesn't give up. We were standing outside the tent and she had an arm around me. I thought it was the wrong way round and I should be doing the arms-around bit, seeing as it was her who had done stories and stuff and got nothing by way of reaction from the lump inside the tent formerly known as Dune.

'Hey, don't lose hope,' Beta said, her forehead almost touching mine. 'What did Dune like doing outside? Before camp?'

'Skateboarding. But we already told a skateboard story and nothing.'

'Something else?'

'Shooting rabbits.'

Yeah. It had been a useful skill when the shortages started. Nobody noticed or cared because there were plenty of other shots being fired in the fens: by the New Militia Army, the Pure English Army, the New English Army, the English Regulars, the Brotherhood of the Blood of Jesus, the Knights of the Cross, The Daughters of

174

the Second Coming and all the others. The countryside was bouncing with bullets, and Dune out there, bagging rabbits with a 12 bore, was just another gun sound among many.

'Let me think,' said Beta.

Three days later, Beta resurfaced with Sly. Sly knocked fists with Beta and walked off. Beta slipped into the tent. Dune was asleep. She slung a bag at me so fast it slapped into my belly. I looked inside. A freshly killed rabbit. Of the four of us, the rabbit was the least smelly. It smelled good the way warm edible flesh smelled good. The little pool of blood in the bottom of the bag looked drinkable.

'It's beautiful,' I said.

'Just snared by bogside.'

'To eat?' I asked her.

'Show it to Dune. Might snag a thread of memory to pull them back with. The touch and feel of it. If Dune liked shooting, the dead rabbit might wake something.'

I was sceptical. 'Right. But what?'

Beta missed my scepticism. 'Grief? It might help Dune deal with their feelings of loss around Pharaoh's death. If not, then it's supper. Courtesy of the bogside sewage team.'

'Thanks.'

There was a pause.

I looked at her with admiration. She was so smart. She indicated her cheek with a finger. Maybe it was because Dune was no longer keen on shagging, maybe something else. Whatever it was, despite the smell that was rolling off her, I found myself thinking a kiss wouldn't matter. So, I did what I shouldn't have done and I leaned in to kiss. And though Beta had tapped her cheek, she turned her face round at the last moment and I ended up kissing her mouth. She held my face when this happened and before you knew it, we were sucking away. Then we broke. And she left without another word.

Had I been unfaithful to Dune? My body told me it was right because I'd enjoyed it, I'd felt things wetting up, you know what I mean. And I didn't even feel guilty. I told myself I did it for Dune. To say thanks for the rabbit. I owed Beta at least that. Which I did, right? And anyway, Dune was zonked and under the blankets all the time that me and Beta were sucking each other's faces off. And what you didn't see, couldn't hurt you, not so?

I got Dune awake and upright and placed the rabbit in their hands and made them look at it and feel it. Maybe it's because humans have a deep connection with animals. Maybe Dune was self-healing and it was just coincidence. Maybe that 'death is beautiful' line was true. Whatever the reason, finally, after Dune had flatlined for close to a week, the dead rabbit in their lap stirred something. They picked it up and inspected its eyes.

'Fresh,' they said. They examined the ears and tail and neck. 'Been caught in wire. Died slow. It's less cruel to shoot them.' Dune mimed holding the moving barrel of a shotgun and pulling the trigger, mimicked the kickback to their shoulder from the blast.

'Remember how you used to go out and shoot them?' I said.

'Yeah,' Dune said slowly, tugging at the thought, gathering in a memory. 'Ax. You remember that day I bagged three? And we came back and ran into the checkpoint? Your mum got us through. Your mum was a star. Can you see that day?'

'I can see the car,' I said. 'My mum was driving.'

And it was true. I could see my mum in the car. Most of her was just outline, but some parts started to fill in. I felt a wave of joy and fear. 'I see it,' I said again. 'I see it.'

'Tell it me,' said Dune, still holding the rabbit.

I lay on their stomach, the fur of the rabbit brushing my face, and tried to summon it all up.

We were in the car, Mum was driving. *Her hands. I could see her hands on the wheel.* The wipers were going. A figure all in blue was standing in the middle of the road, holding something up, pointing it at us. As we got closer, I could see it was some kind of soldier, holding up a gun as long as his arm. Behind him, two other soldier types, both with rifles. They were in shiny blue workwear trousers, camo hip bags, and black vests with pockets all over.

'Leave this to me,' my mum said. *Her voice.* Me and Dune were on the back seat. 'Don't say a word,' she said.

The car stopped. Mum wound down the driver's side window. It must have been raining because the rain flew in on her though she acted like she didn't even feel it. 'What's going on?' she asked the man who strode up. He had a long ponytail, blonde eyebrows and short moustache. His voice was officious.

'We believe this vehicle is registered, owned or being driven by a black person.'

Mum did her *No shit, Sherlock* face.

'And?' Mum said.

'That gives us the power to stop it.'

'Since when? Why?'

'Driving while Black decree. It's a routine inspection. Can you open the boot then step out please?'

As he spoke, the man reached in and took Mum's keys from the car in one swift move, like he'd done it plenty of times before.

Mum looked furious. She made no move to get out. She kept her hands on the steering wheel and this fixed grin came onto her face, like her brain had frozen and she was trying to figure out what to do. I stayed *shtum* like Dune, we just stared into the front seat headrests and listened.

The man had moved back and levelled his gun at Mum. We all heard the click as he flipped the gun's safety. 'Step out!' he called out. 'We have a resistor!' Two other gunmen began to stride over, rifles high.

Something shifted in Mum's brain and she picked up the dead rabbits Dune had shot that were on the passenger seat and lifted them slowly up so the militia could see them through the windscreen. She shouted through the driver's side window, all cheerful: 'You the New Militia guys? *I have one drop of white blood and that is the drop I worship.*'

The first gunman lifted his head slightly off the gun's sights and approached the car again.

'We snared these,' she said. 'You like rabbit?'

The first gunman laughed, keen. One of the rabbits spasmed. 'You want to finish that one off before it makes a break for it,' he said.

Mum pulled at the jerking rabbit's neck. Bones cracked. The rabbit flopped like the other two. She looked up again at the gunman. 'Done. Would you like one? A gift from me, for all the good work you do.'

'These folks are one drops? They're with us?' asked one of the other gunmen, leaning right into the car now, curious about the rabbits.

'It's a sign of the times,' said the third soldier.

'Eh?' asked the first, the one who had stopped us.

'The rebirth. The Second Coming. Mary, Mara, coming again. Rabbits are a sign of the Resurrection,' the third soldier said.

As the other two nodded patiently, guns still cocked, the third soldier went large about how two days ago there had been hailstones falling out of the sky as big as his fist and it was a sign of the times. How three sets of traffics lights had frozen with all three red lights blinking in unison and it was sign of the times. And this, the arrival of rabbits at a checkpoint was a sign of the times.

His sermon ended.

'Right,' said the first gunman.

'Take two,' said my mum. 'One's plenty for us.'

The first gunman allowed the preacher soldier to take two rabbits off her.

'OK. You're good. But we still need to check your boot.' He nodded by way of explanation at me and Dune in the back of the car, but his gaze lingered on Mum.

'No,' said Mum, 'we're bona fide one drops. Can you give us a pass that says this? We've been waiting and they still haven't arrived.'

Car horns blared away behind us. The rain was lashing down.

'There's mail problems. Send a complaint,' the preacher soldier said.

'OK,' said Mum. 'About you and this stop?'

'About the passes. We stopped you. You haven't produced them.'

The preacher-soldier seemed to have taken delayed offence at Mum's use of the word 'you' while looking at him. He ducked his head into the window again, explaining.

'We're here to protect and serve. More and more are joining since things went *boom* in London. A people's militia. It's a sign of the times. It's all legal. My son and daughter-in-law joined. They're on the Prepare and Preempt Programme right now.'

'Prepare and Preempt what?' asked Mum calmly. You should never debate with my mum. You never win.

'It's about getting to the sources of trouble before they get out of control and rampage through the country, destroying everything we're used to. Our customs and traditions. Violating our women. Burning our churches. It's about nipping it all in the bud.'

'Oh, I see,' said Mum, slumping back. 'And who exactly is "they"?'

'Malcontents. Migrants. Misbelievers. Misbehavers. You know, the usual suspects.'

'Ah, the usual suspects,' said Mum. 'Is that the *usual* usual suspects or a different bunch of usual suspects?'

Mum was pushing it. The other two soldiers had wandered off a little to the queue of cars that had built up behind us. The preacher-soldier answered indignantly.

'Our job is to nip it in the bud. Either by getting intelligence to the relevant authorities, or, if it's a clear and present danger, acting ourselves, with roadblocks, gunstops, citizens' arrests and the like. All legal under the Bloods' new regulations. It's giving power back to the people instead of leaving it to the elites. The dark times are coming, we have to prepare. You understand?'

'Yes, I think so,' said Mum. 'Enjoy the rabbits.'

The first gunman was back. He tapped the preacher soldier to get out of the window, then gave one last sweep of us with his rifle. Mum's fingers clenched tighter round the steering wheel.

Finally, he backed away.

The car horns behind us had gone nuts.

He chucked the car keys through the open window. Mum caught them.

'*Fnarr fnarr*,' went Mum as she moved off.

We cleared the roadblock fully.

'*Fnarr fnaar*,' Mum went again, her eyes glued to the rear-view mirror.

Everything was quiet in the car for a bit. Then Dune began singing, softly. Doing the 'Sign o' the Times' hook, mocking the soldier. We all joined in.

A minute later, we were back.

Dune ducked into their house, told their grandpa what had happened, then came back across to mine.

Mum told Dad. Dad swore. 'Fascists!' he shouted at the walls. At the fridge. At the carpet. Finally, he said, 'What are we going to do about this?'

'We march,' Mum told him. She was standing in the middle of the living room.

'Aren't marches banned now?'

'Not yet. They get stewards assigned to them.'

'You mean thugs,' Dad muttered.

'There comes a time when you've got to stand up and be counted,' said Mum firmly. 'Get that transmitter of yours active, Herbie. Work the lines while we still have signal. We need to organise. Push back. Show them this won't be taken lying down, that there is a resistance.'

'It's either that or head north with all the others,' said Dad. 'Cut and run.'

'No.' Mum was resolute. 'We shall not be moved.'

It was a good moment in the tent. Dune was fully back.

'I lived next door to you, didn't I?' Dune said slowly, 'with my grandpa, only he wasn't my biological grandpa. I didn't have a mum and dad, right? I never did. I was adopted.'

I was quiet. The roadblock memory had brought my mum back while I'd told it. I'd seen her hands, even her face. Dad's face. I was shaking.

I tried to hold on to the images, but their faces started fading again. I told Dune this.

'I know how you feel,' Dune said. 'It's how it's been all my life. I've never seen my parents. Never will. It tastes bitter, right, when you can't see them? It tastes bitter.'

That evening in ERAC, we cooked and ate the rabbit Beta had brought us. There were jokes, hugs, laughter. And we told the story again, the one about the three-rabbits roadblock, the one that brought Dune fully into their true self, the one that gave me back my mum and parts of my dad. We storified it hard.

Then night hit and the alarms sounded, and the drones came.

Next morning, I woke and touched my face. Tears. I forced open my eyes. I was Axel. I was in the Bloods' Huntingdon ERAC camp. *The Bloods.* I hated the Bloods.

I smelled Dune by my side even before I touched their thigh with mine. The length of their body was stiff. I turned to them and shook them gently.

Dune stirred but some night terror was still running through their mind, their breathing jerky. When they stopped breathing altogether for way, way too long, I shook them: 'Wake up, Dune. Come back. Come on.'

I held them in my arms and they bucked at the hips, thrashed their limbs. Their eyes were shut tight, holding in some nameless terror.

And this was OK, it didn't panic me because, more than the terrors, what I feared most for Dune was the Blanked state, the plain emotionless face that you saw sometimes on the early morning risers out there along the paths. Once they got you in total Blanked state, they could do whatever they wanted with you. Converts. Scavengers. Whatever.

'Fuck. Shit. Fuck. No-good negro.'

I didn't mind. Not the curses rolling off Dune's tongue. Nor the shower of spit they sprayed out with those words.

I held their face with both my hands. Dune's eyes, open but unseeing, the thick eyelashes fluttering. Dune took my face in their hands and held me in a grip so tight that I got scared my cheekbones would crack. Then slowly their head came forward and their lips pressed into my neck and their face went so far into my flesh, I could feel Dune's nosebone. All the while they were whimpering, like a chained, beaten dog.

Worse. I had no maidenhair. We'd run out. I held them through the trembles.

Beta came checking on us, and when she saw the situation, she dashed and returned with her last handful of maidenhair. 'This is good stuff,' she said, 'the best. Get it in Dune, then get them up and about, walking.'

Yes, I kissed her. Just on the cheek.

She left for a dig shift and I brewed the maidenhair and forced a cupful of it into Dune's mouth.

Their body leaned into mine for support, then they took a deep breath and pulled themselves away, sat up and looked over.

'Fuck this shit, Ax,' was the first thing Dune said when they finally came through. 'Fuck this . . .'

It caught me by surprise. I had been expecting a *no-good negro*.

'I'm here. Dune, it's me, Axel.'

'I'm so done with this shit.'

'Drink more.'

Dune drank the lot. I knew then I'd have to find more, else I'd lose them. And I could take everything except losing Dune.

The maidenhair did its work. Dune was still sweating, little trembles running the length of their body, but they were lying beside me now, and stuttering last night's story as I went back through it with them.

'The rabbits. The roadblock. I shot those rabbits, right?'

'You did. And we got away. Even though the shotgun was in the boot of the car, they never found it. And we drove off. Remember the song?' I hummed the 'Sign o' the Times' song. Dune picked it up, joined in, and within three bars was soloing, then they were back, almost complete, only their eyes still blunted with some primitive fear.

I tried to console them. 'The night drones must have ramped up their attack on you last night.'

Dune shrugged. 'I'm exhausted and I only just woke up.'

'But you woke. You woke.'

Throughout that morning, a torpor held Dune and didn't let

go. The Peace Committee sent messengers to ask why we weren't on our field work shift. I told them we were ill with a fever and we couldn't work that day, and they could fine us all the food rations they liked.

We sat in the tent, Dune more subdued than I'd ever seen them before. The Underground left a message. I read it and absorbed it. Meanwhile, Dune talked about us in the past tense.

'You gave me all the tingles, Ax. Thanks for that.'

'Cool.'

'You straightened my back too. You whacked right between my shoulder blades and lifted my chin. With you by my side, I could see a future for me. You did that. You made me feel worthy, Ax. You were my miracle.'

'Still am.'

'I can't recall it all, but we had times, right? There are days I forget who you are, like, your name, what we did. I forget everything except this feeling, this glow that stays with me and is somewhere inside me, folded into your name. Yeah, all the warm tingles, Ax, that was you.'

'Still is.'

Dune took my hand. 'No, this is important, let me finish. Ax, I feel you now. But it's fading, all the memories of me and you. I got so little left.'

'I hear you, Dune.' I hugged them until their body stopped trembling.

'Listen, the Underground has arranged something for us. Something special. Let's make some new memories.'

'How you mean?' asked Dune.

'Shh. You'll see. They sent a message. It's ready.'

'What?'

'You'll see.'

I got Dune gunked and dressed and fetched breakfast. It was a cold beetroot soup with oat grains and pea husks, and a drizzle of dried apple flakes. I smuggled two bowls back to our tent. I bulked it up with some corn mash we'd saved. After we ate, we set off, following the Underground's directions.

It was hot outside. Flies were dropping, green leaves wilting, even the main stinking tent city creek that sucked up the standpipe runoff and sewage pits' waste, was drying up. I took us beyond the crop fields to the north-east edge where the land dipped. *U1. 50. 235.* This was far enough away that we couldn't be seen by Peace Committee snitches.

I looked it over. Neat work. They'd tied plastic guttering along the tree's boughs so that when it rained, water ran along the guttering into buckets and from there into tubes that fed into a blue plastic food waste barrel, covered up in bindweed and brambles. The barrel sat at the foot of the tree. Stuck to the inside wall of the barrel was a hand-held pump made of scrap plastic that pushed water from the barrel along a green hose coiling up into the lower branches of the tree. It ended in a shower rose hidden in the foliage. Neat, right?

'Know what it is?' I asked Dune.

Dune scratched their face. 'Maybe, maybe.' Dune clocked the barrel. I saw their eyes light up.

'Is that the Underground's magic fountain tree?'

'Sure is.'

'Boom, I'm gone!'

Dune crashed through brambles and bracken and thorn bushes,

not caring about cuts. They beat me to it fair and square and shed their clothes and got under the shower.

Although Dune was shy with everyone else, with me, they didn't care. They shed their clothes in a second and stood waiting, hands held high in expectation for the showerhead to do its thing.

I looked at Dune buck naked and thought about how I never understood what it was that made people get so intense about knowing who had what bits where, anatomy-wise.

'Stop gawping, get pumping!' yelled Dune.

I smiled to myself and cranked the pump handle and water began flowing through the apparatus. It took time to work through the system though, so Dune stood there, alternately stamping their feet and looking up into the tree canopy, head rocked back, waiting for the waterfall.

When it came, it came in a giant gush and Dune splashed about, rubbing their armpits and bits. Dune's bits were male, and they joked about, playing with them as the shower water splashed down. Thing with Dune was, they had no issue with their body, they simply didn't see themselves as male. Or female. 'I am what I am,' they would say. 'Deal with *your* issues.'

Dune's legs and crotch were hairy, and their back and chest wasn't, and somehow the whole of it together was beautiful. I pumped the water and their head hair turned all white in the water because of the gunk turning solid in the cold, making Dune look like a frost-dunked bear. They began singing into a pretend mic. I pumped till the tank was half empty. Then it was my turn, so I stopped.

'Hey, keep going!' Dune called over.

'What about me? I'm under nothing but sun here, I'm close to passing out,' I complained.

187

'This isn't half.'

'It is.'

Scowling, they stomped over to take a look at the barrel.

'That's a third.'

'It's a half.'

'Half's up to my hip, right?'

'Yeah.'

In one bound, Dune'd vaulted into the barrel itself and stood there in it. I tried to measure the levels as the water sloshed about.

'See?' I told them.

'But that's cos I'm in it. My body's displacing water, making the level rise.'

'Right, and that means I'm being robbed. If it's still up to your hip when you're in it. By rights, I should have more liquid than is remaining.'

'You want more liquid?'

Dune had that look on their face.

'Don't you dare.'

'Dare what?'

'Don't you dare pee in *my* water.'

'Would I do that to you?'

'Yes.'

'Ha. Give me a kiss then.'

Damn Dune. I laughed. We kissed, Dune vaulted back out and worked the pump and I got myself all soaked and glistening and cool under the shower. And right in that moment, in that count-them-on-your-hands number of seconds, we were happy.

We must have lay down and dozed off then, because next thing, I was woken by Dune jumping in the grass and flapping their

T-shirt at a cloud of mosquitoes. The mozzies got us good. But Dune was back. We lay in the grass up there. Then my mind did a handbrake turn and images of Pharaoh with his skull half blown off pitched up, and Pharaoh dangling up there on the crane, all burned in the wind. How did I remember this, yet not my mum's face? Was this the SIM deciding which memories played in my head, forcing me to see Pharaoh like this, all blown up? When I looked across, Dune murmured, 'Go easy on yourself, Ax.'

And we lay there, sprawled out together, in silence. Somehow, in those moments, despite the electric fence, despite the explosives in our heads, despite the rewrites, despite all of the shit thrown at us, we found strength to carry on.

16

Tell Nobody

When Beta next came by, Elizabeth X was at her side and I had to follow them to Beta's tent. Footsy wasn't there. We had the tent to ourselves. 'What's this about,' I said, when we were all sat down.

Beta tapped her skull.

'How we escape the threat of these SIMs in our heads, is what it's about. That's always been the question. We need the handshake protocol to get inside the SIM code.'

'Like the door to the SIM code.'

'Right. Once we can unlock that door, we can look around the SIM, see how it works.'

'Agreed. The handshake is the key to unlocking the door to the SIM code. So?' I asked.

'We think we've got it. We've made a key. Here.'

Beta dug into one of her pockets and pulled something out. A boxy thing.

'Another of your gizmos?'

'Yup.'

This one was like a TV remote control but with a big LCD screen that looked like it had been prised off a car satnav system.

'Does it work?'

'If it does, the SIM code will leap up here on the screen.'

Elizabeth X nodded. 'We're going to find out. If the reader's near-field sensors get past the handshake protocol, we can access the SIM code.'

Beta turned the gizmo on.

Elizabeth X screwed her lips in a half smile.

Beta pressed the reader gizmo to her head. I jerked and grabbed it.

'What are you doing?' I pushed her hand back down.

'What do you think? It uses near-field sensors.'

'Not so fast. Her SIM could explode. Is there no way of testing this other than . . . ?' I asked.

Elizabeth X shrugged, 'If we had time, we could explore but . . .' Then she said, 'You good?' to Beta.

Beta nodded. 'Beta by name, Beta by nature. Let's test this.'

'Wait,' I said. 'Go wash your face, Beats. Get all the reflective paint bits off it, in case that interferes.'

'Good call,' Beta said. She left for the standpipe.

Neither of us spoke in the tent. Elizabeth X sat, arms folded and still, her face impassive. But her earring was shaking.

'This is necessary,' she said eventually into my silence. 'We need to crack the digital handshake for the SIM. It will give us access to the SIM, and from there, to the night drone code. Without that, our escape plans are useless.'

Then she clammed up, like she'd spoken too much.

'Why can't it be me instead of Beta?' I said, 'I'll . . .'

'No,' Elizabeth X said. 'It's decided. Underground orders.'

Then Beta was back, face scrubbed and shining.

'Let's do this.' She dropped to her sitting space inside the tent again.

'What if it doesn't work?' I asked. I spoke softly, making clear

PETER KALU

I was speaking to Beta alone. 'I mean the risks, Beats. What are the risks?'

'Yada, yada, yada,' said Beta. 'Everything's a risk.'

I turned to Elizabeth X. 'You tell me then.'

Elizabeth X's voice was even. 'Possibility one, it simply doesn't work. For instance, we haven't cracked the handshake. Possibility two, it works but incompletely. So, it lets us in but only for a brief moment then the door slides shut, locks again.'

'And three?' I asked.

Elizabeth X sucked air through her teeth. 'If the SIM has anti-tamper code and that's aggressive, it could either reset Beta's SIM to "factory" or else throw a kill-switch and shut her SIM down completely.'

'And if either of those happens?'

It wasn't Elizabeth X who answered. It was Beta.

'Then maybe the fat lady sings, you know, the SIM blows and I'm dead!' Beta leaned into me and put on her prettiest face. 'Hey, Axel, ease up, it's a remote chance. From all we've seen of the Bloods' SIM, it's primitive. Most will happen is the handshake isn't hacked and we're still locked out and we'll all three look stupid. Let's go. What are you? Scared?'

'I dunno,' I said.

'C'mon, let's do this,' Beta insisted.

'Right,' said Elizabeth X. 'We going in. Beta, you may feel a little funny as the reader activates and starts interrogating your SIM. We'll look out for you.'

Elizabeth X slipped on her beret and patted the protective wiring through its felt. She handed me a beret and I put it on. 'Axel, back off a bit, just in case. I want this kit to read Beta's SIM, not yours

192

or mine, you know? Just watch the kit screen and let me know if any code that you recognise shows. Could be SIM code.'

I shuffled back. Beta's eyes stared upwards, hard, bright. There was a flicker of fear in them.

'I love you, Axel. More than you know.'

'I love you too,' I murmured. I kissed her.

'Everybody good?' asked Elizabeth X. 'OK, deep breath,' she said. 'Take up the reader now, Beta, and get it close.'

Beta raised the reader, held it by her SIM bump, pressed something on the reader handle. The reader's LCD screen powered up. It glowed blank for twelve long seconds. Then code began scrolling on the screen.

'I see it,' I said slowly. I was figuring it out. 'Yes, that's Bloods' code.'

Elizabeth made a fist. 'We're through the encryption!'

'Hang on,' I said. 'It's in compressed state. Probably it only unzips when the night drones activate it. You're right that we're in, though. Congratulations. We've got the decrypt key. You've worked out the handshake. Wow.'

Then Elizabeth X was mumbling to herself.

'What d'you say?' I asked.

'I said now, finally, we can hack those fucking night drones.'

What she'd first said as quiet statement, she was now saying as prayer.

'And then we break out of camp?' I said.

'A breakout gets closer. We're still waiting on the Resistance's drone to fly in. When that does, we use this handshake protocol, and upload the new hack code to the drones. Then, if it all works, these SIMs are safely deactivated and we're free.'

If.

'And if it doesn't?'

Elizabeth X abruptly switched her focus. 'Look at me,' she said to Beta.

Beta raised her eyes. It was a weird gaze between the two of them, like two opticians in a stare-out.

Elizabeth raised two fingers either side of Beta's eyes. Beta followed them. Then she held out only one finger and moved it right up to touching her nose. She did the out-wide gaze test again, with eyes locked. The weird one.

'Tell me your name?'

'Beta.'

'Where are you?'

'Bloods' prison camp. ERAC.' Beta answered with aplomb.

'All right, she's fine,' Elizabeth X said finally. 'She's fine, we done.'

Then Beta was pulling me into a hug that lasted till my ribs ached.

'Is it stored?' Beta asked. 'Can I see it? The SIM code?'

I handed her the reader and brought up the code on the screen.

'Dang,' Beta said, 'dang to the double. Is this the real thing, Ax?'

'Sure is,' I said, 'compressed, but real.'

She hugged me again.

Elizabeth X squeezed Beta's shoulder with a hand. 'It's looking good. We've got the handshake. We can hack their night drones now. We just need the hack code delivered.'

Tiredness had broken out across Elizabeth X's face. She had one arm lashed across Beta, holding her close as if suddenly the risk of losing Beta had hit home.

'We've done more than enough for today,' said Elizabeth X. 'It's time for you two to storify yourselves. Tell nobody about this, OK?' she said.

We both nodded.

'Nobody knows we were doing this, right?'

'I . . . I mentioned it to Horse,' Beta stuttered.

Elizabeth X's voice went cold: 'What did you say to him?'

'I only told him we were having a look at the head chips. Nothing more. Nothing about handshake protocols. He came by my tent. We were just chatting, really.'

'Nothing more?'

Beta shook her head.

Elizabeth X squeezed Beta's shoulder, but I could see she wasn't happy.

'Listen,' she said to both of us, her arms on our shoulders. 'This is the highest level, what we're doing. It's the last step for when the hack code flies in. Don't talk about this work. To anybody.'

'I'm sorry,' Beta said again softly. She wiped a tear.

'Today's done. You worked hard,' Elizabeth X said, easing off.

17

Under the Heavenly Sky

That evening I got back and Dune had cooked, and we ate and then I lay down and talked dozens to Dune about the slant of the sun, the thickness of the soup and the quality of the air. But I said nothing about the handshake code work I'd been doing.

Dune said they'd done some good work but didn't elaborate. We both knew they'd been out training catapulters.

The conversation dried.

It was strange, lying there in the tent with secrets between us for the first time.

We had the flaps half folded back and I said to Dune that wasn't it funny how at night when the sky was clear you could see the sweep of the Milky Way, yet here we were, captives on this tiny spot on Earth.

'Yeah,' said Dune, 'that's about right.'

We held each other tighter.

After a while, I could feel them sniffing me. Sniff, sniff. 'What's on your mind, Ax? Spill it.'

I smiled. 'It's deep. You ready for this?'

'Sure. Hit me up.'

'I'm wondering whether you could like, reduce someone down to a set of memory chips. Is there something beyond memory that is the essence of who you are? Like, when you're born, you have no memory, yet you're still you, a you that existed before you laid down any memories. Like the first you, the you that was whole, and didn't need memory to know who that person was?'

'I'd agree with you if I understood you,' Dune said.

We laughed softly at this. And my tongue was so tempted to talk about what we'd been doing. But I bit my tongue.

We watched the sky a little longer, three straggling birds making for trees just beyond the fence lines, the drifts of smoke far away in the south that I thought meant they were bombing there again, though Dune, who had the sharper hearing, said it sounded more like road-launched mortars, on account of the recoil sound made by the mortars' metal plates on tarmac when they fired. Other than the birds and the smoke, the sky was empty. Darkness gathered.

'How's Beta?' Dune said.

'You're not supposed to know.'

'About what?'

'Nothing.'

I'd thought Dune was talking about the experiment. Of course they might be talking about *that kiss*. The one when, after bringing the rabbit, Beta had turned and tricked me and . . . Had Dune seen it? It wasn't possible. Surely. Dune read my hesitation.

'You're seeing her again?'

'It's work.'

'How is she?'

'Are you jealous?'

'Nope.'

'You're not meant to ask about work.'

197

When I didn't say anything more, they said, 'I can tell from your eyes.'

'You've nothing to worry about,' I said. 'I got eyes only for you.'

'That so?'

'You know it's so.'

A distant whistle.

'I made a song up for you. While I was waiting here for you.'

'Sing it then.'

'It's called "Under the Heavenly Sky".'

'Good title.'

'It's late. Where are you, Ax? Did you make it out of here? Did you find freedom or did it all pitch and slide?'

'What are you talking about? I'm right here.'

I worried Dune's chip was starting to mess with them again.

'No, no, no, that's the talking part of the song, the intro,' Dune said, eating their upper arm to stop themselves from laughing. 'Till the melody kicks in.'

'Duh. I gotcha. Cut to the melody though, honey.'

Softly, without once looking at me, Dune sang:

'Ax, is this my last day, my last sky?
Did we gather up our dreams only to throw them away?
Was it all – the oaths, the plans, the maps of our souls –
Was it all a waste . . . of time?
Now we'll go into the burning night
Into the wire, the waves, the flames,
Let the wax melt cos we'll still fly:

Skittering on ice, tumbling down stairs, seeing stars,
Locking hearts – me and you, Ax – under the heavenly sky . . .'

It was a sweet sweet song that Dune sang ballad-style, more gently than I'd ever heard them sing before.

And the fact it made no sense didn't bother me.

The curfew caterwaul sounded.

'Storify for me now,' Dune said.

So I did. *Gauge your strength.* I didn't feel I had the strength to go into any pain, so I searched for joy, and found something.

'Remember the pillow fight in the city centre?'

'How did that go?'

'You were on fine form.'

'That sounds like me. With mighty blows I whacked you down, right?'

'Hundreds turned up. An evening flash mob. Pillows flying. Little sponge pieces everywhere from the insides of them. You remember? You called it bouncing snow.'

'I see a clock. A big old clock.'

'That's the town hall clock. That's where we had the pillow fight. We organised it on our phones. Midnight pillow fight. Flash mob.'

I could see the memory digging its way into Dune's mind from underneath all the SIM rubble.

'Right. We did some big licks, didn't we, with our pillows? Madness till midnight. Then in the shop doorway, among all the bits of pillow foam and feathers, we got fresh.'

That's right, Dune, you're remembering.

Dune ran a hand into my hair and I placed my thigh across

them, and the inevitable happened. We fucked in a frenzy, like in that shop doorway.

Then we lay there, remembering.

And braced for the night drones.

I was vaguely aware it was morning. My eyes were open. The tent. I looked across. Dune was fitting a little. I woke them and got them upright. They glowered at me through tight eyes, so I knew they didn't recognise me yet. You know what's coming now, don't you? Well done. Yeah. They said it: 'You no-good negro.'

I got the maidenhair down them. We'd been given a new ration of it. 'Who am I, Dune, who am I? Remember the pillow fight? The bouncing foam snow? Fucking in the doorway? The big clock?'

It took five minutes of prompting and maidenhair drinks before they could answer.

'You're Axel,' they said, and rolled over and asked me to massage their skull because their SIM was hot and their whole head felt tense.

It was while I was giving them a head massage that I heard it. This shout from outside.

'Holy! Holy!'

Shit. Even from far, I knew the voice: the high joyousness of it. I piled out of the tent and looked.

'Holy! Holy!'

Beta. Shouting 'Holy! Holy!' The call sign of the Blanked.

There were cries. Sobs as others picked up her shouts.

Shit. Beta, of all people. Why her? She had seemed so together only yesterday. For the Bloods to have done this, they must have launched a hard attack on her. Why now? Was this because of the

SIM hack she'd developed? Were the Bloods onto us? Onto the whole hack plot?

I watched. Most of the Blanked started shouting *Holy! Holy!* and headed straight north to the Hallelujah Barracks. Some wasped around first, betraying people by tapping their tent as Bloods' spy drones watched above, before they beelined north. Beta neared our tent. She saw me standing guard and our eyes locked. She startled away.

There was no time for permissions from the Underground. I gunked my hair, slid on my beret and followed.

I caught up with her in the tent zone, north-east. She was on a direct route north. People called out to her, but their shouts didn't register. She bounced along, a rictus grin on her face. *Holy! Holy!*

The sun blazed. Breakfast fires were burning. Smoke trails laced the air.

'Holy! Holy!'

She'd reached the tent city's edge.

I wanted to drag her down, stop her. But stopping the Blanked was tough. Like Scavengers, they felt no pain.

There was a line of tiny static reception drones ahead in the sky now. I had to break off in case their profile recognition sensors picked me up. Nobody headed this far north except for one reason. Nobody shouted *Holy! Holy!* except for one reason. The Bloods had definitely Blanked her.

Then *thunk*. A crossbow bolt flew. Another. Beta fell face first, two bolts through the back of her skull, two into her chest.

I never saw who took the shots. Blood spurted like tiny fountains from her chest. My legs gave way. Breathless. I didn't want to see any more. I retched into the grass.

I heard Undergound alarms but ignored them. An explosion. *Beta's head SIM*. Carnage.

Numb, I slipped away and went back to my tent.

Beta. Who hadn't a malevolent bone in her body. Slain by Underground crossbow bolts. I was mad and afraid and trembling. I needed to put what I'd just seen out of my mind and I thought Dune didn't need to know right now. I was finding it hard to absorb myself; it might blow Dune's mind entirely.

'What's my name?' Dune was asking, 'What's my name?'

I knew I shouldn't have left them. It never went well if they were only half awake and I wasn't there.

I made more of the maidenhair tea. 'You're Dune and I'm Axel and you'll be just fine. Keep sipping that.'

'Why are you here, you dopey negro? Do you sleep here? Are we like, in a relationship? Eww.'

I was still trembling at what I'd just seen. I couldn't tell Dune. Not while their head was mashed. And I had little patience right now for their white ramblings.

'Both those things are correct,' I replied in a flat voice.

'Um. OK. You're cute, you know?'

'Thank you.'

'For a blackie.'

And so we got to it. You know the routine by now. I talked over the story we told last night. I got them in the zone. All the while, I was trembling. And I must have hidden it well, because Dune didn't notice. I did what I had to do. Went through the story. Even faked the enthusiasm with it: 'The biggest pillow fight you ever saw, right, Dune? You're whacking away with your pillow. Then me and you in the shop doorway. Amazing that shop door's glass didn't break.'

202

I rammed a chunk of maidenhair into Dune's cheek. Dune dredged the story up and rescued themselves with it. They pressed into me, saying, 'Strawberry soap bombs in the shop window? That sounds good.'

'What's my name?'

'Ax, baby.'

'Where are we?'

'The shithole known as ERAC. Bloods' prison camp.'

Dune was back.

Only when I was sure they were back fully, did I tell them about Beta.

Dune shook from the news. I wanted to say more but they hushed me.

We were silent in the tent for a long while.

Elizabeth X came by and I dragged her into the tent and asked her why. Dune was in a corner, rocking, listening and not listening.

'It's the rule,' Elizabeth X said. 'To destroy anything and anyone that endangers the cause.'

'No!'

'Sometimes we have to do things none of us wants to happen.'

'No!'

I hit Elizabeth X in the chest. She caught my hands, but I kept hitting her and telling her no. I didn't even know what I was saying *no* to any more. Beta's death? The Bloods' SIM chip experiment? The whole escape plan? The entire situation? To living itself?

'Leave us,' I said to Elizabeth X when my energy was all spent. Dune was still rocking in a corner. 'We have to deal with this on our own.'

'There's a ceremony for her. It's happening right now. Come outside, both of you.'

We dragged ourselves out.

The sky was a uniform grey. Wind lifted the smell of grass to my nose, and the dank odour of moat water.

Me and Dune and Elizabeth X stood together outside our tent with a bunch of dried-out, smouldering gorse branches. Smoke signals.

Even as I stood next to her, I thought, *Bastards. Bunch of sadists.* The Underground had killed Beta. If this was what the revolution meant, I was not a revolutionary.

Elizabeth X nudged me, prompting. 'For Beta. Respect,' she said. We raised the gorse to the air. Drifts of smoke across tent zone.

I saw a rank of figures behind our tent. Elizabeth X often had people around her like this. I recognised Wires and Sly among them. Others, standing silently by their own tents, were dotted across the camp.

We did the Underground fist salute into the indifferent grey sky.

That was it. The whole of Beta's ceremony.

Then came the *whoop whoops* of Bloods' guard vehicles on the roads beyond the moat, and rabid barking and I heard dogs racing along the enclosure between the two fences. More alarms. They'd picked up on the ceremony and this was their reaction. Underground drums began beating hard and low, warning everyone in camp to be on guard.

18

Starless Night

The Peace Committee posted appeals at each of the crossroads for Beta's killers to give themselves up for the good of all. They should confess so the camp population could avoid collective punishment.

The expectation in tent city was that the crossbow shooters who'd killed Beta were going to be hunted by the Bloods as never before. Rumours rippled out. They'd be blasted. They'd be hanged. They'd be publicly executed. As would everyone with any Underground connection to Beta.

Flunkies rushed around, their batons charged and armed. They were going to random tents and searching them. For crossbows, arrows, any weapons. Peace Committee loudspeakers ramped up the Bloods' slogans: *Might is White, Resistance is Futile* and *Bloods Supremacy is God's Will* rang out through the morning across tent city.

The Underground drumbeats kept on, which infuriated the flunkies. They rushed around confiscating anything that could double as a drum. Still the drums talked: everybody must steer clear of the weapons stores. Go on with normal camp life.

I tugged Dune along with me and we did a work shift in the clothes tent and watched the flunkies circle tents. Pulling up groundsheets. Beating anybody without a clear work-study chit. Up high, spy drones hovered.

It was from the clothes tent that I picked up on a weird scene.

It began with a *boom*. I rushed to the tent's opening and looked. Something had exploded into the sky. A big fire had started up in the east, and flunkies were diverted to it, the spy drones following them.

The explosion had all the signs of a decoy manoeuvre by the Underground. The Resistance did this on the outside too. I watched and saw it. A swift infiltration of berets in the outlying west of tent city.

Elizabeth X was among them, I knew from her gait, the way she held her shoulders, the slight hitch of the left leg, the tight guard around her.

They were by Horse's tent. Had it surrounded.

'What you staring at?' asked Dune.

'Nothing. Look away,' I said.

There was some scuffling. Horse was being pulled from the tent. A hand over his mouth. He was bundled into some large container, and then the berets were gone further west.

It didn't look good for Horse, whatever had gone down.

'What?' asked Dune.

'What?'

'You're muttering "*What the fuck*",' said Dune.

I sucked my lips over my teeth and bit down.

'Let's just sort clothes, OK?'

I kept what had gone down with Horse to myself all through the work shift. Dune didn't need to know. They were still too fragile. Dune got the hint and stopped asking.

By the time me and Dune were back inside our tent, I was shaking.

Dune's eyes asked again but they read my face and didn't press it.

Beta. Horse. It was like the Underground was eating itself. The sheer randomness of it was terrifying. Who next? Me? Dune?

Dune nudged me, they wanted to walk, so we walked around for a bit. Rumours flowed at the standpipes. Horse had been shot like Beta by the Underground. I saw Sly and asked him. Something about him told me he was closer to the Resistance leadership than us, but he said nothing.

As far as I could tell, Horse was the only new casualty. Even that was a surprise. Speculation about him washed through the camp.

Here and there, a lamp flickered. A child cried.

Evening thickened into night. Not one Scavenger crew had entered the camp. Maybe the Bloods were busy with other things.

Elizabeth X called at our tent late and had me step outside.

She spoke in an urgent whisper. 'Horse was a spy,' she said. 'He was the common denominator. He was implicated in what happened to Beta and what happened to Pharaoh. He sold out several more too. We took him out. I'll tell you the details in time, not now.'

'So you killed Horse? Just like that?'

'We are *so* close. But we will not tolerate traitors. Not even if they're as likeable as Horse. Revolution requires discipline.'

So that was that. The Underground had killed Beta. And now they'd killed Horse.

We stood in silence a while.

'It's been tense. Events have been unfortunate,' Elizabeth X said finally.

I didn't reply.

'Everything rests on the hack code flying in now. Whoever wrote that hack code needs to have been on their game, because it's our last chance.'

As I took all this in, there was a familiar clicking behind us.

'I'm needed elsewhere. Make sure you storify tonight,' Elizabeth X said. Then she pressed something into my hand. 'Ax, take this. It's maidenhair. Distilled, so it's strong. We don't have much. Use it for Dune when you're desperate. We've got intelligence and we know the drones will keep targeting Dune. Their pattern analysis is putting Dune close to the top of their Wipe list. We need Dune. This is one vial of distillate. Holds four cubes.'

Elizabeth X took her hand from mine. Then more clicking and she melted away.

Night thickened. I lay with Dune. I cried into their shoulder. I was scared, and not only of the Bloods. The Underground was more ruthless than we'd imagined. They'd killed Beta. They'd killed Horse. Pharaoh had warned us of the price of betrayal, but still. Maybe the Underground was as sick as the Peace Committee.

We drank maidenhair, the ordinary stuff. Deep night came, heavy with fog, sealing us in our tent.

Dune wiped tears from my face. They cradled my head in their armpit and we listened to night sounds. Low sobs. High cries.

'We have to clear our minds,' I said to Dune.

Dune asked me to storify for us both and make it a story about fighting back, and that I had to try to think of my mum and dad again because they knew how much I hurt not picturing them.

'It's time,' Dune repeated. 'Find something. You need them now.'

So I dug. And found a memory.

19

Fire Doors

We were in the house. Dad was speaking from up high.

'It's only time before a mob arrives, we need to move,' Dad shouted. He came thundering down from the loft. 'BloodChan channels are supplying Resistance addresses to all the Alt-Right mobs.'

'We don't run,' said Mum. 'We stand and fight them. Fight till we drop.' Yet Mum had busted her foot badly in a running battle with Bloods' hecklers on a march last week, and she couldn't stand at all. She was sitting on the sofa, sucking on a morphine tube.

A couple of talking heads on TV were going on about 'The question of white Muslims'. Mum flipped channels. Channel 27 was showing a parade of handcuffed Resistance members. They were confessing the error of their ways to a reporter who moved across them with a mic. Mum gasped. 'I know him. That's Marcel, that's Marcel!'

'We need to get out now, head north. Find the Free Northern Army. We'd have some protection if we made it north,' said Dad.

'I'm not saying we don't go north,' Mum said. 'I'm needed here a few days longer, is all.'

'What if they knock here tomorrow and pick us all up in one swoop?'

'You head north then, if that helps. Take Axel. Take Dune.'

'No. We stand together. We stand up and fight them.'

'I'll tell them to hurry,' said Mum, 'the painters and decorators. We need to go fast, to get out.'

The painters and decorators was code for some unit in the Resistance. Did you notice something else that happened there? The polarities reversed. It started with Mum wanting to stand up and fight, and Dad saying run. Then, when it came to heading north or staying put, it was Dad saying stand, and Mum saying go. They did that a lot. It was like they couldn't think anything through except by opposing each other. It didn't matter who took which position, their favourite thinking style was antagonism. Deep, right?

'Come here, Ax, come here, darling,' my mum said.

I let her smother me. She was woozy from the morphine. 'Gentleness,' she said as she stroked my forehead. 'We need to tell gentler stories. That's why it's called civilisation. People should be civil. Gentle. I'll never let them get you, Ax, nor you, Dune. Now, about you and Dune . . .'

'Yes, Mum?'

Mum necked a bit more of her morphine tube.

'You need to get out more. Go run in a field or something, burn off your energy.'

I laughed through Mum's loving chokehold of me. 'Do you know what it's like out there, Mum? Looting parties. Hold ups. Burnings. Lynchings. Drive-bys. Everybody with a gun?'

'No, no, no. It's up to us, the good people, to stop it happening. To say no, to remain civil.'

Dad walked by and kissed me.

'Dad, why did you just kiss me? And why's Mum strangle-hugging me?'

'Because we're proud of you and we love you. You've done vital work for the Resistance, both of you. You've been very brave. We're proud of you.'

This is deeply weird, I thought, they must be seriously worried about something.

Deep night came. Dune stayed over and fell asleep just like that on the sofa. Me? That night, I couldn't catch a zed even if I'd turned to the back end of a dictionary.

It was a good thing I stayed awake. It was the dead of the night when it happened. At first, I heard nothing. Just smelled smoke. The bitter, black, wispy smoke you get when a plastic cup burns. The smell got stronger and I started hearing crackles too. Suddenly, I knew I wasn't dreaming. I scrambled up. I saw this soft yellow glow. Almost like a sunrise. Except it was deep night. Noise. Like someone shelling walnuts. I got up into the hallway and saw the sun push its tongue through the front door letterbox. Only then did it click. Fire.

'Fire!' I shouted. I shook Dune and they got up, complaining. They never liked being pulled out of their sleep. I rushed to the stairs and that set off the burglar alarm. Mum was up first and calling my name. She made it into the living room in her dressing gown, shouting. The window frames were on fire now, outside. The glass had already cracked.

'Petrol, Mum,' I said, 'it's petrol, I can smell it.'

Dad dashed into the kitchen in his undies. He came back with a bucket of water and chucked it at the inside of the door.

Mum went screaming up the stairs for something. The door was buckling as it blazed. More glass panes shattering. The little drumming sound of debris falling at the feet of the door. Bits of

211

PETER KALU

the frame breaking off and sticking to the hallway carpet floor. Smouldering.

We did a bucket chain. Then Mum came through with a fire extinguisher. She whacked the guard off it and sprayed. Flung open the front door and sprayed some more. The powder smothered the fire at the door. She carried on. Did the windows. Some of the neighbours came out. They brought things. Buckets of water. Then biscuits. Tea. Blankets. A first aid kit. We were lucky, they said, that we'd caught it early. There was hardly a burn between us. The fire brigade didn't come out, nor any emergency services. None of us slept for the rest of that night. We stayed downstairs and talked. We all agreed. We had to leave Stukeley. We had to head north.

I was awake. I was in the Bloods' ERAC, in a tent that moaned lightly in the wind. The pictures were fading but I could still see them. My mum and dad. At home. Outside. *My mum and dad came back, I'd seen them*. In our house. As it burned. Not their faces but everything else. Their voices. Their clothes, their bodies. Their hands. I turned. 'You still awake, Dune?'

They were gone deep. I wasn't even drowsy. Too much had happened, and my head was full of it. I looked at Dune the way I liked to when they slept: I could inspect them without interruption. Every single skin cell. The thin film of moisture on their cheeks and the tiny, downy hair follicles there. The bunching where the mini-whirlpool dimple showed. The flop and pout of the hanging lower lip. The cupid's bow of the upper lip, pricked with silky black hair. I called up a memory. How we first met. I liked remembering it because it was still there, in full. Dune the new kid, freshly adopted

212

from a care home, moving in next door with a double-strap shoulder bag bigger than their entire body. Little Dune, all on their own, in the upstairs house window, smiling. I'd called Dune *Smiler* at first, and every time I went past, I smiled back. Dune told me later, kids who smiled got adopted faster so the care home gave them lessons in how to smile. But no care kid ever trusted anyone because all through their life the only thing anybody had ever done was let them down, and they had no reason to think that was ever going to change, smile or no smile. Dune was right too. The Everetts, Dune's new parents next door, quickly decided they didn't like their adopted kid. They put up a good front because they wanted to keep the fostering-and-adoption money rolling in, and Dune fronted up too because, Dune said, anything was better than the care home. Dune spent most of those early days on their own, locked in their room while their parents went off on long religious training courses. Dune's gramps was meant to be looking after them, but Dune and their gramps never got on. Mum was the hero. She marched right into the Everett house one day, unlocked Dune from their room and led them out, leaving the gramps speechless. After that, me and Dune played every day, all summer. One time, much much later, Dune turned to me and said, 'It was the first time I could see a future, Ax. You did that, your mum and you, you made me feel worthy of life, Ax. You were my miracle.'

Now Dune was my miracle. Amid all this misery, lying here with me. I waited in a doze to hear the shrill of the drones' motors overhead. I listened to the concert of cries across the tent city. They'd mostly been stifled now, just one kid who couldn't stop. And we were all that kid. What a mess we were in, I thought, what a mind-numbing, colossal pile of shitfuckery.

20

Aftermath

I woke. Light had crept into the tent.

I was Axel.

I was holding a hand.

Dune's. I knew Dune. Their body was floppy.

I got them sat up, crushed maidenhair leaf and brewed it then pressed the drink to their lips. They took a sip. 'Come on, look at me. Look at me, Dune. What's my name?'

They were gone. As close to Blanked as made no difference. Flashes of Beta hit my mind. Her fixed grin as she called out, 'Holy! Holy!' The crossbow bolts that flew into her. Dune knew too much. Was Dune going to go that way too?

I rubbed their cheeks and forced them to drink more. They looked at me with some momentary glimmer of recognition. Their teeth bit into their lower lip.

'What's my name?' I asked again.

I let them feel my face. I knew I had to give the drink time to work.

Sly was at the tent flaps. 'Any news?' I asked him.

'More guards been seen over at the main gate. They might be preparing for a big snatch. But nothing big happened overnight. No artillery. No tanks. No planes. Peace Committee say they sent a big apology letter about the crossbow death and took the remains of Beta's body to the Bloods' guards at the gates and that was what fixed it.'

'Believe that?'

Sly rolled his eyes. 'Underground say Bloods are getting sucked out of Huntingdon to go up north. There was a big battle outside Birmingham last night. The Free Northern Army regrouping and giving them a fight. Most Bloods' drones are redeployed there.'

'That's good.'

'They've hung Beta on the crane with Pharaoh.'

'Right,' I said quietly.

'And there's some abnormal movement of Scavengers but nothing to set off alarms. Yet.'

I signalled to Sly that Dune didn't need to hear any more of this or about Beta right now.

'OK,' said Sly, hanging there. I could see him thinking I seemed indifferent, but it was the opposite. I couldn't speak about Beta because if I spoke, I might blub, and what use would that be for Dune?

'Anything I can do?' Sly asked, nodding at Dune's half-here, half-not stare.

'Nah,' I said, 'leave us. I'll get them back. The maidenhair'll kick in.'

'Right.'

Sly left.

I told last night's story to Dune again. They didn't want to hear and held their hands to their ears. But I got it through. The heat of the fire. The door buckling. 'Can you hear the glass shattering? You cut your hand on the broken glass right here.' I dug into Dune's hand at the web between the left thumb and index finger.

I knew the exact spot. Yes, it hurt them. No, I didn't care. You see, I do what I got to do. I know I come across as kind and altruistic and all that. But I've got an evil streak like everybody else. And I wasn't losing Dune. Not now. Not here. I needed them. So I dug the wound. I forced them to picture themselves in the house, close to burning, as flames shot up the front door. I kept going till I got a reaction. And I got one.

'What are you saying, you no-good negro? You empty Afros deserve to burn.'

I never felt so happy being called a no-good negro. It meant they were talking. It was a starting point.

'Don't you *no-good negro* me. This is Ax. I got you out of that fire. I woke you first, remember?'

While I was wrenching Dune free from the latest Bloods' attempt to wipe them, I heard people charging about outside our tent. There were shouts. Some kind of rallying cry. Footfall. Scavenger boots? Drums. The shouts fading.

I stayed with Dune.

I made more maidenhair tea. Used a precious cube of the strong stuff. By afternoon, Dune was as good as recovered. They glanced over and made to say thanks. I shut them down. 'Hush. Now stay with me, OK?'

I sat quietly in a corner of the tent for a while and watched Dune come together, the tics ebbing, the puzzlement on their face softening. I was exhausted with the struggle of it. Each morning was harder. Each time I felt I might not make it this time.

I'd consolidated Dune's morning recovery with the story of the house fire. It was a jumble of sounds. Snatches of flames stitched together with pain and with many stitches missing. Somehow, I pieced it together, as best I could. And the biggest hole in it all for me was that my mum and dad were gone from it again. Yet I knew they'd been there, in the house. They had to have been.

I said nothing about my own memory loss to Dune. They didn't need the extra grief. Yet it weighed in my stomach, gave me this tingling numbness that spread.

I watched Dune find their makeshift Afro comb and go about unknotting their hair and gunking it. A flicker of gladness must have come through my haze.

'Who you looking at, dude?' Dune said, smiling. 'Either you got it, or you don't.'

I got them fed. When I knew they were good and smoothed out enough to be alone, I rose to my haunches. 'I'm going for a walk for a while. I'll be back soon. Rest here. Understand?'

Dune nodded as I left, even did a finger wave as I went.

I wandered across the tent zone, letting the wind smack my face. I was going nowhere, just walking. The sky was flashing, and the surrounding fields went blue as an electrical storm hit not far away.

I lost direction, crisscrossing the tent city, crop fields, bunker zone, the field by the gate.

I felt the wind separating the hairs on my arms. I was aware of the snatch of burrs in the tall grass, attaching to my legs, and clouds of little yellow flies leaping for my calves. The curl of the bullrush fronds mirrored exactly the curl of Beta's fingers when she wore those half mittens. The wind called her name. The sparking blue of the sky was her energy being rewired. The wind blew fiercer.

A sudden rip and boom in the sky. A jet. I ducked down, watched it waggle grey wings as it rolled beyond the horizon. The rumble of a distant bomb, unloaded.

217

I saw the fence, glinting. Deadly. I turned and turned. The fence was on every horizon, a metal noose that squeezed everyone in the camp tighter every day, slowly strangling us.

I crossed into the south-west fields. I tried not to think about the gaps in my memory. I tried to think about immediate stuff. Thinking stuff through. The Underground had killed Beta. I thought about Horse too. They killed him. Alone in the fields, I cursed the Underground aloud. I cursed Elizabeth X because Beta did not deserve that. If Bloods had got her alive, Bloods interrogators would have asked her, 'Who are you working with?' 'What are their names?' 'Pick them out from this video.' If she'd betrayed us all but she'd lived, was that worse than her dying? Maybe she would not have said anything. There again, she'd been Blanked. She'd have given us up because her SIM would have given them all they needed for that. Beta. They killed her. Did they do the right thing? It was all a moral mess.

'Fuck!' I shouted into the wind.

Rain bit its reply into my face.

I must have sat down. A shadow fell on me, blocking the sky's light. Boots in the grass. Dune's.

'What are you doing here?' I asked.

A grunt.

When I didn't stir, Dune sat beside me. Still, I said nothing. I let them stroke my hair.

'Don't give up,' Dune said quietly.

They didn't say anything more. Instead, they started singing. The song was from the car in summer. That tearjerker. *The bastard.* They had only gone and somehow fished out of their busted-up, broken-down memory the one song they knew would slay me.

When they hit the line, 'Change is a-coming', they popped the shoulder I was leaning on, for me to join in. I tried but I couldn't, it was too much, I just collapsed into them.

'You bastard,' I said, 'keep singing.'

And they did.

Back inside our tent, as night grew outside, we did routine things, folding clothes, straightening the groundsheet, wiping down the inside of the canvas. Dune's head rested on my belly and I stroked their eyebrows. *The eyebrows that Beta had styled.* The Bloods' wailing curfew alarm sounded from north, meaning night drones were on their way. I had to clear Beta from my mind, clear away all that had happened, all my anger at the Underground.

'Storify me something new,' murmured Dune.

I dragged up something.

'Remember that time we'd gone to the Odeon and there was a pair to the left of us, snogging, and a pair to the right, snogging?'

'Tell me.'

'And behind us too, was the sound of four lips smacking together. And there we were, me and you, wedged in the middle, and we looked at each other and . . . ?'

'Haha, yeah,' said Dune, feeling it. 'That was that the first time we kissed, like full smooch-kissed? I had retainers then. The metal ones. And your tongue snagged on them.'

I curled my tongue, pressing its underside, could still feel the healed ridge there.

'Yup. Blood everywhere, but we kept on. Like two vampires, slurping away.'

'Yeah, I'm remembering,' said Dune. Then, 'Your mum and dad, Ax, bring me them. I know you're hurting about them.

Bring them. They were mine as well as yours. As good as, by the end.'

By the end? I looked across.

The small smile from Dune. Then a tear in a streak from their eye that dinked the rim of their whirlpool dimple. I sighed but Dune was right. I had to go there. Unblock whatever it was. *Gauge your strength,* Elizabeth X had said. There was something really bad there. Yet I had to go in. Mum and Dad.

I willed their likenesses to come to me. I kept going. As I spoke, Dune's eyelids fell.

When it came, the memory of Mum and Dad was stained with blood. Overhead, faintly, a soft whine sounded, which meant the night drones were back.

21

Like a Dead Horse

The door was still charred. Dad said whoever did it, it was their shame, not ours. Mum was busy on the roof, plotting coordinates of where bombs were falling, from Huntingdon all the way north to York. Using sonar to ping the bombers and missile launchers. Working out delivery mechanisms from missile trajectories and sound prints. Then compressing the data and sending it in VHF radio packets to the Resistance.

Downstairs, Dad was calling Mum a fool for taking all that risk on the roof and there was a time for everything and now was the time to put one foot in front of the other, to pack and flee, it had been agreed last night, so what was she now actually doing? Dad hauled Mum off the roof and they had an argument before we got the bags loaded into the car and piled in. It wouldn't start. Me and Dune got back out. Someone had messed with it, Mum swore, after poking around the fuse panel. She started it using wires she cut from the old phone lines that were now all dead, as dead as Stukeley's internet and mobile phones. We got back in.

Then Dune's gramps sped out from their house, ran all the way along the path to the rickety gate, shouting to us it wasn't bombs, it was food parcels they were dropping over north Huntingdon, no need to flee, only the guilty and undesirables had to flee, he'd heard it on the Bloods' official radio. He gave me the cut-eye when he said 'undesirables'. Dune had ducked down into the rear footwell. And I have to admit, Gramps' hate vibes made me laugh in the back seat, even with Dad trying to nudge me to be quiet. And all these lyrics about why you should never fall in love with the girl or boy next door began to drop into my mind, because Dune knew what was up and they just hung there in the back seat footwell looking up at me, their lips glossed, their eyebrows freshly trimmed, their ear jewel sparkling in the noon sun. They were mouthing curses at their gramps. Then they whisper-begged Mum to *Start off, get it in gear, please, I swear I'll be your best passenger ever and won't even sing or nothing if you get us moving before Gramps' mouth goes full Bloods Apocalypse.*

Mum popped the car locks and said a cheery *goodbyeee*. Gramps went bitter and said good riddance because a new world was coming and our type wasn't wanted in it anyway, and Mum popped the radio on and it said everything was going to be clean, white and new and true, soon. Dad gave Dune's gramps the thumbs-up, but he switched to the middle finger when we were safely out of shotgun blast range, and said, 'You can get up now, Dune. What a nasty piece of work your gramps is.' And all this time he hadn't known his true colours. And we all cheered as the car finally pulled out of the close.

We hit the Stukeley roads. Mum steered round craters as Dad watched the sky and swept the streets ahead with the scanner. For a while, all we heard was his scanner blip and the music of a burst of spring rain on the car roof.

I caught my mum's face in the rear-view mirror.

My mum's face.

A squat nose. Like mine. Heavy eyes, good for reading and dreaming. A mouth constantly in motion, the lips quick and full, and waxy with what in the car smelled like apricot lip blossom. A news reporter once came to our house and he wrote afterwards, *She may cut you with her words, but her breath will smell sweet and her face will be radiant.* Sexist rubbish, don't you think?

'Axel, you OK? You look tired.'

'I'm fine, Mum. Just zoned out. These last days have been mad.'

'Things will get better,' she said. 'Always believe that.'

And she reached back and curled a finger around one of mine for a moment even as she drove.

'I love you, Ax,' said Dad, turning in his seat to look back at me as he said it.

I stared right back at him. 'Why are you saying that?' I said. 'Don't say that.'

'Why?'

'Last time you said that, our house got burned down. Say the opposite. Say "I hate you". Then maybe something good might happen.'

Dad's brow did its thinking sideways frown. 'But wouldn't that be the most awful thing if I died and those were the last words you heard from me, "I hate you"?'

Mum interrupted. 'Can you two stop arguing? Nothing bad is going to happen and we love you. Both of you. I love all three of you. End of.'

So that settled it.

Hedgerows and crop fields flicked by. Then a river with small white boats. We covered a good six miles and Dune was totally behaving, mainly because they had fallen asleep on me. We were doing fifty on the A17 going north and had almost made the fens by Holbeach when a Bloods' patrol caught us.

223

The red laser dot hit Dad's chest and Mum whacked the brakes hard and the car skidded to a stop. There were four of them. Bloods Militia soldiers. You could tell from the kind of khaki they wore and the insignia. They kept their guns sighted on us, and waved for us to get out. We had to place our hands on the roof of the car. They frisked us. They wanted the boot opened next. Mum did that. All the bags had to be unzipped and tipped out and we had to do it ourselves while they stood back. They kicked through the contents of the bags until everything was strewn out on the road, then one nudged the other and they started looking at Mum. I saw now they were either drunk or high or both. Mum kept her eyes down. The short one went to Mum and patted her down again for belts and pulls. Then he placed a hand on her crotch and left it there. Dad protested and the leader struck him with his rifle butt so Dad fell like a chopped tree. Mum gasped. They put a gun on me.

'Tell us the Bloods' Four Commandments,' the short one said to Mum. 'Tell us,' he repeated. Mum refused. He took his hand off her crotch and grabbed the front of her dress and tore it so the back of the dress ripped and the dress fell to the road. Mum was doing these little short breaths. 'Maybe I can help your memory,' he said. He felt for the flies of his trousers.

I sprang across to Mum before the one with the pistol to my head knew what was happening.

I made it halfway before I felt a thud to my neck and even then, I kept going.

Mum had made her own move and the short young one with the open flies was on his back, howling by the time I reached her. Another hit between my shoulder blades. As I fell, a gun fired, and

Mum was lying there. I spreadeagled across her, trying to cover every part of her so they couldn't shoot her again. Her blood was soaking into me.

'What is this?' one of them said. He was above me, but he wasn't talking about me, his voice was directed elsewhere.

I looked over my shoulder.

They had a gun to Dune's head now. Dad was still lying there on the road, and hadn't moved through all this, his limbs scattered like he was a dead horse.

'Is it a boy or a girl?' one of them asked, poking at Dune. 'Umm. Should we find out?'

They were enjoying themselves, spinning Dune round, the oldest one with the short white hair, prodding with his rifle, telling Dune to unfasten their dungaree buttons. Dune was shaking.

'No!'

I leaped off Mum. Then the soldier lying next to her, who she had been holding in an arm lock, rolled free and shot her again. Blood spewed out of Mum's stomach. I froze in the middle of the road. Which was stupid of me, because there, in the middle, I was useless to either of them. The blood on the road pooled in some pothole. Dune stood rooted, shaking noiselessly. Mum sighed and leaked blood.

The crewcut, white-haired one who was the leader whipped his rifle butt across Dune's face. Dune fell to their knees.

I went for Dune's assailant, aiming low. His rifle rose up, but I crashed past it and fell into him, taking him down with me. Then blows to my shoulders, my back, my legs. My lungs exploded and my head cracked.

They sat on my back and used plastic cable ties to fasten my wrists together and then rope that looped round my neck and they tethered me with it to the far side car door window frame. I couldn't move. But I saw and heard everything.

One of them casually shot Dad in the head with a handgun. I jerked forward and the rope throttled me. I tore at my limbs to free them from the ties, but they held fast, tightened. 'Fucking ape!' I said. He turned to me, raised his gun. 'Do it, do it!' I screamed. He pulled back the trigger. Then changed his mind. He uncocked the gun, came round the car, closed the gap and slapped me.

'Stop your yelling,' he said. He took a hand to my throat and started squeezing and pressed his handgun to my temple at the same time. I could feel the pressure in my eyeballs building. I heard a gasp. My mother's body rose and made a lurch towards me, even as her guts dangled out of her body. She made two floundering steps and fell at the soldier's feet and he shot her in the neck and then the head quickly with the handgun. All the while he stayed in front of me, his hand on my throat. He smiled. I gulped air. He holstered the gun, then used the free hand to tear open my top and feel around with one hand. He found my left nipple and squeezed it. I gasped. This pleased him and he did it again and ducked his head into my top and licked my skin, then came up, grinning. I wanted to spit in his face, but my mouth was dry. There was a shout from Dune. The soldier leaned in and whispered in my ear: 'One moment, I'll be back, cutie.' Then he stepped away and strolled round to join the other soldiers circling Dune.

'Run, Dune, run!' I cried.

On their knees, surrounded, dungarees already ripped off, Dune wasn't running anywhere. The soldiers hoisted Dune up. Two of them swung them to the grass verge and flung them down there. The short one fell on top of Dune.

Eventually, Dune's screams became halting sobs and then I knew it had stopped. They dragged Dune over to the car, to the same side where I was tethered, and tied them there. I thought it would be my turn next because they had begun to gather round me, hands to their groins, but a call came in on their radio that frightened them and they shifted from the car fast and started looking up at the sky. Dune shook on the rope that tethered them, their hips knocking into the car's side panels, lips twitching, a milky green and red liquid coming from them. I bent as low as I could and stroked their face, and they looked at me, uncomprehending. I sobbed with them. A plane shot across the sky and there was an explosion close enough you saw the earth throw up a cloud. A tree toppled. Everywhere on the road that you placed your eyes there was blood and spilled guts and lungs and brains and luggage. Mum and Dad. Mum's hair lay in a mess of blood. She hated dirty hair.

'Mum!' I reached down and managed just to touch one of Mum's fingers. It was cold and straight and didn't curl round mine. Her eyes were still open, and she was staring across to where Dad lay in the road minus the back of his head. A gas bubble came up out of Dad's skull and grew there like a washing-up bubble. It expanded and burst. I passed out then.

For the rest of that day, I woke and passed out. I knew they'd loaded me and Dune onto an open-top flatbed wagon. I saw fields flitting by. A radio was playing in the wagon cab. Dune was there alongside me, in a heap by my side. Sometimes I imagined my parents were there riding in the back of the wagon with us, chatting to each other about petrol supplies and the price of tomatoes, but

227

I knew also they were both shot dead and every time I realised they were dead, I woke to just me and Dune in the back of the wagon, and this voice screaming. Mine.

Then some clinic place. A week there at least. And then ERAC – and living hell.

22

Tribulations

'No. Please no!'

'Wake up, Dune. C'mon.'

Dune's eyes were blank, the irises frozen, the pupils two dots. They'd been thrashing in the tent all morning. I held them in my arms, rocking them. The vial. I had to use the last of the distilled maidenhair fern. I added it to the dregs of maidenhair we had, made two balls of it and forced one ball into the pocket of Dune's cheek and only then let them close their mouth. I kissed their lips. They looked at me. Their eyes were still marble. Then the filaments of the irises stopped trembling. The pupils widened.

Slowly, in twitches, clutches of breath, Dune came round.

'You OK, star?' I asked.

They sat up, staring into the tent roof, unmoving as a Buddha. I took the last maidenhair ball, added water and brewed it and forced the cup into their hands. They drank in sputters. It killed me to see Dune like this.

'More.'

'No.'

'Yes.' I forced it into their hands again. Motioned. Dune drank.

Their shoulders relaxed a little and their breathing grew regular. I got up to start tidying.

'Axel?'

'That's me.'

They shook their head, mute with fear, watching every move I made inside the tent.

I came over and took their hands in mine and kissed them. They shook their head, as if throwing off pain, and looked at me with pooling eyes.

'When I try to wake, my brain gets slaughtered ... You understand, it kills me. Kills me. Kills me.'

The repetition. It would go.

'I was ... stuck. I was stuck there.'

A flicker.

'What?'

'I can't bring anything into my mind. No memories, no feelings, nothing. But I'm awake. It's a living death. You managed to wake me and I'm struggling to even know who I am.'

'It will fade. Drink. I've got your back, OK?'

'Ax. I'm tired. I want it to end. I've been like this too long. I look at knives and I think about stabbing myself. I see a tent peg and part of me wants to drive it through my skull.'

There was a noise from Dune's mouth. Their teeth grinding. It was the first time I'd heard that. Their head shook.

'Come on, Dune,' I said, 'you know what's going on. It's the Bloods' SIM, messing with you. Hang in there. They must have downloaded a big attack on you last night. It will pass. I will love you back to who you are, to your true self.'

I put my arms around Dune. They unlocked their mouth and talked into my shoulder.

'I see my skin and hate it. I see my reflection and I want to smash the surface that shows it. I hate my hair, my legs, the sound of my voice, everything. I don't know who I am any more. It kills me to remember stuff from more than a week back. I can do it, but to stop the memory from playing hide and seek, you know? That shit is draining. I'm not living any more, Ax, you understand? I've got to break free. I've got to get out. Or I'm finished.'

I hugged them.

'It will pass. We always find a way, nuh? We gonna break out soon, the Underground promised.'

'They've been saying that since for ever. But what have they done? Nothing. Is that right?'

I had to nod. Dune was right.

'We got to do something more direct. Like, just me and you. Why can't we climb the fence?'

'Serious? You know why, we'd fry. You know how many people have tried that before and got fried? Besides, the SIM explosives up here in our skulls might detonate if we leave.'

Dune's head dropped. 'I won't last much longer, Ax, I'm not as tough as you. Each morning, it's chaos in my mind. I got an escape plan and I'm gathering stuff for it. It's what I do some afternoons when you're away. I've hidden stuff. Out there, by the fence.'

Dune shuffled around on their knees, smoothing the bedding.

'What stuff?'

'Gloves. Insulators. Bolt cutters for the fence . . .'

I laughed. 'Bolt cutters? Come on. Where would you find those?'

'Where d'you think?'

'The tip?'

'Was in the sides of a mangled cleaning truck. One of those Billy Goat things with big brushes at the front. All crushed up, but the cutting head still works, the jaw bites fine.'

231

PETER KALU

'Good spot, then.'

'I'm making ladders.'

I knew now that Dune was serious. 'Dune, come on. Even if we broke free of here, the SIMs in our heads would get us, remember? You saw what happened in the tent when we arrived? That explosion, right?'

'Makes no difference. Ax, I can't hold on much more. If you weren't here, I'd just go straight for the fence, you know? You're the only one holding me back.'

'Shush.'

'If the Underground don't call it in the next couple days, I'm breaking out.'

'We can get through this. The Underground say the breakout is soon. Keep believing. We talawa, right?'

'We talawa? Yeah, I remember that. And keep going. Yeah. For you, Ax. For you.'

They said it, but Dune's voice wavered. And we lost something between us in that moment, me and Dune. It was the first time I'd seen the lights dim on them. It wrecked my heart and bunched my fists.

When Elizabeth X came round, I told her outside the tent that, whatever plans they had, they must move them forward if they wanted Dune with us.

She went away and when she came back, she handed me a two-cube vial.

'This is all we have,' she said. 'Scavengers found our distillation equipment and smashed it. We can't make any more till we rebuild and that could take weeks. This is it. The last. For Dune. Use it wisely.'

I thanked her. She left, but not before saying that there would be a big meeting of artillery this afternoon, Dune was to be there if they could, and, breaking the rules of isolation, I was invited.

Late afternoon, I had Dune swallow a half of a maidenhair cube then we made it to the artillery meeting. It was in the sloping bunker. Elizabeth X was there. Dune stepped in with no trembles; they were proud even at what they were going to be showing me. They looked around. 'Where's Horse?' Dune said. 'We're missing Horse.'

Maybe I should have told Dune earlier. They were going to learn now anyway.

All eyes came to rest on Elizabeth X. Truth time.

'Horse is dead,' she said.

So some didn't know. I watched them react.

'What do you mean, dead?' asked Storm, her voice as clear and firm as when I'd first heard her.

'We ... We killed him.'

'What the fuck?' said Dune.

Elizabeth X picked her head up and looked right at Dune. When she spoke, her voice held a hardness I'd not heard before: 'Horse betrayed Pharaoh to the Bloods. He betrayed Beta. He betrayed two others, we're sure. He was leaking information. We worked it out and set a trap. And Horse fell into it. He was a traitor.'

'What trap?' Dune again, as sharp now as this morning they had been blurry.

'I can't tell you. But we caught him carrying what he thought was sensitive Underground information to the Peace Committee.'

233

'But why?' said Sly.

'Who knows why?' said Elizabeth X. 'It's irrelevant.'

'What d'you mean, you *killed* him?' Storm said. She was wiping her eyes.

'We took him from his tent. We told him what we knew. He confessed. We gave him two options. Either we shot him and threw him onto the fence. Or he walked into the fence himself. He walked. Scavengers collected him.'

'But he's not up there at the gate, hanging like Beta and Pharaoh,' said Sly.

'And doesn't that tell you something?' Elizabeth X said. 'He was one of theirs. That's why he's not swinging.'

'I liked Horse,' Storm insisted.

'We all did. But the struggle goes on. Nobody is bigger than the cause. I did warn you all.'

'OK, Horse is gone,' said Storm. She stood up. I could see that inside, she was raging.

Elizabeth X kept her voice low and calm. 'Don't leave, Storm. We need you. We need everybody. We've lost Horse. I understand it's a hard thing. The punishment. We explained when you signed up. Still. If anybody wants to step away because of this, you can do, right now. And you'll be OK so long as you don't talk. We are *this* close to breaking out.'

On the word *this*, Elizabeth X snapped her fingers. It made some of us jump.

'We simply need a little more time,' Elizabeth X continued. 'And to hold discipline. We're at a critical stage. We've made big progress. We need to know only two things. That we can hit the Bloods' drones effectively, and that we can shut down the chips in

234

our heads, so they don't explode on us. We solve those two problems, and we'll be out of here. Are we all onboard? Storm?'

Slowly, almost reluctantly, Storm sat down again. Nobody asked to leave.

'Dune, can you take over?' Elizabeth X said. 'For the artillery briefing.'

'I don't know,' I said, speaking for Dune.

'It's OK, Ax, I'm good,' Dune said.

And they were. The mood remained subdued as Dune went calmly and competently through the day's artillery training plan and then answered questions. Dune spoke well, without glitches. Elizabeth X listened carefully throughout.

'Remember,' Dune finished up, 'from now, when on operations, keep the berets on. And the drones may pick up audio, so the less said, the better.'

Elizabeth X stood and silent-clapped Dune. It seemed Dune had passed some kind of test. 'Let's get on with it,' she said.

We set about donning face masks, berets, and gunking up.

'What's this?' I asked Storm. She had pepper-rowed her hair, instead of Afroing it.

'I wanna try it,' she said, 'see if it works. Don't it look good?' She threw a coy look at me.

I saw Dune roll their eyes.

'You're losing the full head cover, styling it like that,' I replied.

'Nah, it's covered,' she said. 'I wanna try it anyway. And it's all tucked under the beret. The beret will protect me.'

With Storm's feelings as raw as they were, I knew it wasn't good timing to argue it out with her. I let it go.

Elizabeth X bumped fists with us all as we made our way out

again. When she bumped mine, she held me a second. 'Is Dune back fully?' she asked.

'They're back, they're good.'

'Be ready to step in. I'm not far away. Any problem, send for me.'

Then she was gone, leaving Dune in charge.

I wondered where Elizabeth X got her information on Dune from. Dune's memory was a strange thing: things they remembered, things they didn't. It made me realise the things you loved the most, you forgot the least. Like those who'd loved music all their life, if they got dementia when they grew old, the last thing they would lose was their memory of music. The catapults and everything about them were Dune's music. But some things were lost for other reasons. Like my mum and my dad. I was sure that was not the SIM, that was me. The real me, who couldn't cope with seeing what happened to them again. Was that right? My head was a mess. But Dune's head, right now, was clear.

'C'mon now, down to the shooting ranges,' said Dune.

'There's more than one?' I asked.

'Yeah,' Dune said to me. 'It's like a multiplex. A shooter's dream.'

We scrambled. Dune didn't glitch once as they led the squad, sliding confidently through rubble holes in the bombed buildings. Everyone had to keep up as best they could.

We reached a partial clearing in the underground rubble, then snuck down a hole that widened and widened into some kind of silo that had maybe once housed an intercontinental nuclear bomber. It was surrounded by the shells of broken-up concrete barracks. The silo walls were lined with straw bales.

'Armour up!' Dune ordered, talking to everyone but looking right at me. I almost saluted.

Everyone began tooling up.

The silo was sunk deep, well hidden from drones and carbon monoxide detectors and vibration monitors. I looked around. Three mounds of stone missiles, sorted by size. A heap of roughly smelted knives. *All the metal we'd collected. All those tin cans.* A triple box of spears. There was a bustle as everyone chose their weapons.

'Spotters up and out to watch the skies!' Dune cried.

Three departures from the silo.

Then the teams dragged old doors into place. And plastic panels from car wash enclosures. And sheets of metal from white goods. And the shooting practice began. The silo's air filled with the sound of missiles whistling above and the clatter of strikes and ricochets. Spears thrummed into straw. Panels split and splintered. Metal targets howled. I took a spear up. It was light in body, with a shaft of wood, and a bluish, triangular iron tip. I aimed, took three fast steps, then, whipping my arm down fast, chucked it. The spear flew smooth as a javelin, and straight over the wooden house door I'd aimed for.

Dune laughed. 'Watch me. See the door's letterbox?'

They stepped up. With hardly a run-up at all, Dune launched their spear. *Bam.* It spiked right through the letterbox. The half-buried shaft dangled there. People clapped.

'Show off,' I muttered to Dune.

'Jealous.' Dune grinned. Then, turning to the onlookers, 'You can all do it! Practise!'

And they did. Practise. Throwing until they were dripping sweat.

'Come,' Dune beckoned to me. There was a high-ceilinged catapult range deeper inside the silo.

I watched silently as three rows of catapulters launched stones high. There was some cussing and calling of names. Dune stayed calm. 'They're trying to get their angles right,' they explained to me, 'to pull off a cloudburst, where the stones hit each other and ricochet. That would take out more drones than just shooting at them individually. Get it?'

I nodded. It sounded smart. But I'd believe it was possible only if I saw it. The argument among the shooters intensified.

'It can't be done!'

'It can!'

Dune intervened. 'Front row, aim high! And tilt!'

They got to it again. It looked OK. The cloudburst didn't happen though. It became two volleys of interlacing stones arcing down.

A whistle blew hard. Everyone froze.

Waited.

Listened.

'A sky crew alert,' Dune whispered to me.

'All clear!' a voice called.

Dune was back in charge. 'False alarm. OK. I need to see you crawl-shoot. Now!'

Immediately, the catapulters dropped on all fours, loosed off shots from this position, then crawled forwards, stopped, loosed off another barrage of shots. It had a military efficiency to it.

'What are the knives for?' I asked Dune.

'Scavenger combat, if they get close to us. We have knives and spears. The spears have a range from ten metres to thirty metres max. They have special barbs, so once a spear goes into you, you're not pulling it back out.'

The catapult squad practised hard. I joined in at the back row, Dune telling me where to stand, how to drop, how to roll, how they were visualising their enemy's position at each point. This was a Dune as I hadn't witnessed in a long time. Composed, decisive, clear-headed.

When finally Dune called time on training, we placed the weapons in the store boxes and started making our way in ones and twos up out of the silo and back to the tent zone. As I walked with Dune, I told them how calm they'd looked down there in the silo.

'It's a kind of zen, maybe,' Dune replied, their eyes not leaving the sky. 'When I draw a catapult or aim a spear, in that moment, I'm at one with the equipment and the world itself . . . I can't explain it.'

'It's good. I didn't see a single flicker on you. Not one.'

Dune shook their head. 'I don't have time to be thinking about myself out there, I'm thinking about them. I owe it them to keep them alive by making sure they do the best drills, make the right moves.'

I nodded. I believed Dune. But I also believed in the power of the distilled cubes.

We made it into our tent. The light dipped. Curfew time was close. I had Dune take the second half of the maidenhair cube. Despite the calmness they'd shown in the day and now, Dune couldn't find much by way of memory. They told me they remembered a tree and the tree had mossy downturned branches.

'I know that tree. It's in Stukeley Park.'

'Stukeley? Where's that?'

I talked softly as they lay on me, choosing the one park incident Dune never forgot: 'Hey, Dune, remember that time the snow was a metre high across the entire park, and we built Snowman, Snowwoman and Snowperson?'

'Tell it.'

'And we got the idea of building an igloo. We made bricks using your gramps' old mop bucket to press the snow into shape and stacked the bricks in a curve. You dived in first. I got in too and it was snug. The light inside was all pinky-orange and eerie like a grotto and it was warm because no wind, but still cold. Then the roof collapsed, and we were trapped. No way you'd imagine snow could weigh that much. We couldn't get out, remember?'

'Yeah,' said Dune, 'it's coming to me. The dark whiteness. I went numb. You too. Your lips turned blue. We tried shouting, but it was hard with the cold and the weight of the ice on us. I thought we'd freeze to death.'

'I know. I passed out and you told me you wriggled across to lie on top of me to keep me warm.'

'Your eyes were closed and you didn't talk,' Dune murmured. 'I thought you were dead.'

'Right. And we were saved by a dog. It found us and barked like hell. The owner dug us out with her bare hands and we ended up in hospital and in the local news next day.'

'And because the dog bit me, I had to have the jab in my arse and I've still got the mark there.'

'Yeah. You remember, Dune, that's good. That was a good day. Snow. *Let it snow, let it snow.* Ever since, I've always hated that song. You remember that day?'

Dune lay there in the orange glow of the tent and nodded, tears streaking their face. 'Every time, buddy,' Dune said to me. 'You find me every time.'

23

The Scavenger Raid

I woke early in the morning. Dune was under the blanket, breathing but lifeless. I dressed, went to the standpipe and met Sly there. He said the night drones had hit hard overnight, targeting individuals. We should expect more difficulties than usual with those affected.

I got back to find Dune with their left hand in their mouth, head pushed into the tent sides. I tilted a bottle and put it to their lips, and got three swigs of maidenhair brew down them and waited. Dune made to say something but stuttered.

'You're Dune, I'm Axel. Don't cry. I got you, I got you.'

'Axel, where's my towel?'

They took it and shuffled off to the standpipe to wash.

I was so busy in the morning with Dune, I didn't notice when Sly slipped into the tent. He suggested walking Dune, the Underground had found it helped. We took a route through the tent zone. As the world of the camp refreshed itself in Dune's memory, Sly told me word from the Underground was that the Bloods had managed to boost their night drone code and it had become much more aggressive.

'It's not only Dune struggling, then?'

'No. Across the camp, twice the usual amount of people have been Blanked. A couple of them went into the fence last night. Everyone's restless.'

'Any news on the breakout?'

'There's an update tomorrow.'

'Can you help me get more raw maidenhair? We need the best there is, the stuff out deep west, in the rocks out there, where the ground's warm, that's where you find the best stuff. Dune would be defragged in an hour with that.'

We'd stopped at a standpipe. 'Wait here,' Sly said. He went off.

I drank from the standpipe and helped a kid with a left hand that was missing two fingers wash clothes.

In five minutes, Sly was back. 'They say fine,' Sly said. 'We can do it now. I'm to go with you.'

So we did.

The Peace Committee had put a makeshift wire fence over by the western outcrop of maidenhair, but the fence was weak and we slipped beyond it without problem.

Me and Sly found and plucked the best, greenest, ferniest, chewiest leaves, and bundled them into our sleeves. While we worked, Dune stood around, shivering, mumbling, not making sense but somehow knowing they were among friends and safe.

Footsy met us back at the tent zone and Sly and Footsy took off with most of the maidenhair for other Underground cells. They left me and Dune two big bunches. I boiled water and dropped in a large fern. I soon had a potent brew. I added the last cube from the vial.

'What the dang?' Dune announced, spluttering, as I prodded them to keep drinking. The pupils of their eyes blew wide and a full-width grin spread across their face.

'You good? You back?'

'Slap me one more time and you'll know about it, bitch.'

242

I smiled. 'OK, you're back.'

'Tell me, Ax, baby, how long I been gone? Did you miss me? I bet you missed me, right?'

'You're so vain,' I said. 'Maybe one day I won't bring you back.'

'That so?' They came at me, leaning forwards, lips pouting. I backed away till I hit a tent corner pole.

'Come on,' I said, breaking if off, 'we got to shift. Artillery meeting.'

'I'm hungry though.'

'We can eat later. We got to link with them now.'

By the time we had made it to the silo, most of the cell had already gathered. Elizabeth X said there had been a big training exercise on the cards, the Underground had been planning to test the Bloods' forces around the camp, but it was all off.

'It's too dangerous now,' Elizabeth X added. 'Our sources say the Bloods have these new flamethrower drones, and right now we don't have a defence against them. We have to pause operations until we do.'

The news was absorbed in silence. It was the same old: we wait.

I watched Dune, and they seemed to be taking everything in. Elizabeth X glanced over at them a couple of times too.

We ate right there in the silo, bowls of oat bread, pulses and a salty marrow sauce. The food had cooled on its journey to us, but still tasted good, and we wiped the pan clean with our fingers. Then we dispersed back to our tents.

Dune took off on their own for a while. I let them. I knew they had to be working on their ladders and pliers and gloves and all the other stuff in their crazy scheme to break out alone, but I said nothing. If it gave Dune hope, let them do it.

When Dune returned to the tent I didn't ask where they'd been and, once they'd settled, I brought up the news of the new delay. Dune wasn't convinced by the original tactic.

'We'd have lost the element of surprise by attacking the Bloods before the breakout, so why was it even being considered?'

Dune was venting. I paid them no mind.

The curfew caterwaul hit the air. 'We got to storify,' I said. 'You got anything?'

Dune sucked their teeth. 'I can . . . I saw a birthday cake, it flashed up when we were at the silo. Don't know why.'

'How old were you?'

'I'm not higher than the table. At your place. Candles on it.'

'All right, I know it. That was your sixth birthday.'

'Yeah?' Dune lay down and spread themselves on the blankets, their hands behind their head as I talked on.

'You had the party at my place because your parents were arguing at the time. Gramps bundled you over to mine. My mum baked a cake and found candles while I played with you. She called us down and tugged your hair as we all counted to six and sang *Happy Birthday*. You didn't even know the words to *Happy Birthday*. You stood there, miming. Then, as you were sucking in air, I nipped in and blew the candles out. Remember that? You cried and cried because it was your cake, your birthday, your candles. You went to pull my hair out and gouge my eyes and my dad bundled you up in his arms and held you as you thrashed. Mum got up and found new candles because you didn't want the blown-out ones, and this next time Dad held me back just in case, and you got to blow out all the candles. Then you stood there, happy-crying.'

'Yeah,' said Dune, remembering, 'I was laughing and crying at the same time. Good times.'

Dune stayed quiet for a while, then said, 'I forgive you, Axel, for blowing out my candles. You must have been only just turned six yourself and all, and there's me, this strange kid you hardly knew, walking into your house, taking up all the attention. I forgive you, Ax, you don't need to carry that guilt about blowing out my candles no more.'

'Thanks. Just so you know though, if I was six, probably I'd do it all again.'

'Keep going,' Dune said. 'Tell me more good times, whatever you remember.'

I settled into it, waiting for something to float up from memory. 'How about that night we ran off and stayed out in the park two nights running, with everyone looking for us because you'd broken the humungous TV screen and you couldn't face going back to your gramps?'

'That was our first night together,' said Dune. 'Funny I can remember all that now, after all this time and all this SIM shit . . . You never forget love, right? Love can't be wiped . . . Right?'

Dune was drifting. Soon they were out like a light.

Early morning crept in. I put some maidenhair brew to Dune's lips. They stuttered and mumbled, refused to drink any more and went back to sleep. Then an Underground alarm. The ground started shaking. Our canvas shook. 'Open up!'

I knew the voice. Footsy. I unzipped the flaps.

'Take these. Underground says Scavengers are coming for a

snatch. They've intercepted Bloods' comms: Scavengers being sent in for a big hit on the Underground leaders. Elizabeth X's a target for sure. You might be too, Ax. They've crunched Beta's heatmap showing who she met with most in the camp.'

'What's our plan?'

Footsy jerked her head to outside the tent. 'We target the Scavengers as they come in.'

Footsy looked past me to the heap in the blankets.

'Dune's not here yet.'

'You can't wake them?'

I shook my head. 'They're iced. And no more vials.'

'What about the fresh stuff you gathered yesterday?'

'I tried it on them. It's stopped working or not got through yet. Dune hardly flickered.'

'All right, leave them. You're in second row. Aim at a hundred metres. The Scavengers' lower torsos may be unprotected.'

Footsy slid two large-scale catapults into my hands and a pack of ammo, then was off.

I shook Dune, trying to wake them, but it was useless.

The ground-shake grew fiercer. I gunked my hair, daubed on camo paint fast, pulled on my beret.

I left the tent. The tent zone was heaving. The air rang with whistles and shouts. People slithering in the mud. Wailing. Hurrying away from the Scavenger threat.

I weaved through the mayhem to the edge of the tent zone to join the catapult squad. We arranged ourselves in three rows, loaded, test-flexed the catapult bands, then waited for the noise that signalled the Scavengers' squad. I saw Storm, Footsy, Sly in the rows of catapulters. Footsy was in charge.

They came.

There were maybe thirty. They marched off the lip of Runway One and cut onto the main road that was the artery into the tent zone. They were a cluster of grey armour amid the grass and concrete. We heard their grunts, a kind of barking of the lungs. *Harh! Harh! Harh!*

Lasers hit the Scavengers from all sides: some Underground cell helping with range targeting. The Scavengers wore full kits. Helmets. Chest guards. Thigh pads. They had electric batons. They were coming into range.

Footsy raised her arm. 'Row one. Ready . . . Fire!'

They drew hard and fast. The whistle of airborne flint shards. The rattle of stone on Scavenger armour. The shatter of their helmets' visors. The soft *thump* of stone on flesh. Row two let loose, then three. No Scavenger cried out. But the *Harh! Harh! Harh!* stopped. The thud of their boots stuttered. Two Scavengers dropped to their knees, faces gargoyling behind steamed-up visors as they sucked for air. The mass of Scavengers kept going. We were already reloading.

Volleys of stone and flint thudded into them again. Another two dropped. Then the Scavengers were close enough to us they could charge, and we had to retreat. I expected to hear the scurry of chasing boots. But they didn't chase us. They stayed locked together in formation. Pushing hard into the swirling rain over the tents, homing in on their targets.

Suddenly, the Scavengers split. Two gangs, heading in different directions. Footsy had no plan for this. She scrambled to give orders.

'Artillery rows one and two, follow that Scav squad eastwards. Row three, target the Scav squad heading west. Move! Move!'

I moved with artillery one and two, following the Scav squad across the tent zone. The Scavenger gang we were following was going fast. They had to be using spy drone info relays, because they kept skilfully repositioning, zigzagging round obstacles. We loosed off catapult shots on the go, but the ammunition bounced off their armour.

The Scavs halted. They spread out into a semicircle around a particular tent.

Footsy shouted: 'That's Elizabeth X's hide! Burst through. Defend that tent!'

We charged forward and manoeuvred round the Scavenger line, forming a defensive circle around the tent. The Scavs held their positions. There were no more than thirty metres between us. I'd reloaded. Our catapults were ready. Their batons had enough volts to kill. It was a standoff.

'As soon as they take a step, fire at will,' Footsy called. 'Aim for the neck and lower torso.'

Drums sounded. A call for reinforcements for a battle elsewhere in the camp.

We stood solid.

Then it happened. A Bloods' attack drone swung above us. It had an armoured undercarriage.

'Attack drone!' Footsy cried. 'Target! Target!'

We fired upward but our ammunition bounced off it. The drone retreated higher. There was a hum. A telescopic arm emerged from the drone. A column of flames came lancing down. Elizabeth X's tent ignited. There were shouts from inside. We tried to beat the flames with our hands. A further burst of fumes, up high. A ball of fire falling, ripping into the tent. Storm and

Sly, closest to the tent, were coated in fire. We fell on them, beating out the flames. Three people scrambled from the engulfed tent, Elizabeth X among them, each on fire. Another flamethrower attack. Storm screaming as liquid, then flames, engulfed her. Sly crumpled down on his knees, his back, his hair on fire. We beat at the flames. We rolled Storm to smother the fire. And managed it. But the fuel they were covered in, whatever it was, kept reigniting. Another column of fire shot down over Storm and Sly. The roar of flames.

'Back! Back!' cried Footsy.

The explosion of SIMs.

Storm and Sly's last screams.

The attack drone lifting away, veering off.

'X! X!' Footsy was shouting.

Someone had doused Elizabeth X. She stood by Footsy, shaken but alive. The Scavenger squad pressed forward. We formed a guard around her. Reinforcements arrived. The Scavs charged. We fought back. Spears sliced the air. Crossbow bolts. Outnumbered, outweaponed, the Scavenger squad retreated, marching in a defensive array, shields high. They backed out of the tent zone, across the grass expanse. On the runway, they turned and marched for the camp gates.

Elizabeth X was gone. We didn't know where she was, but we did know she was alive and the Scavengers had failed to snatch her.

Then Footsy was redirecting us. We were needed in the western tent zone.

The second artillery group had run out of ammunition and was fighting hand to hand, too close for us to use our catapults. Footsy pointed to a hessian sack she'd flung down in the field. It spilled knives.

'Grab!' she called.

We took up the knives.

The second Scavenger squad had surrounded one tent.

'Is that . . . ?' I asked.

Footsy nodded. 'Yours.'

Dune. They were still in there. They'd take Dune over my dead body.

A howl erupted from the tent. Dune, waking. They came out barely clothed, wild. Leaped straight at the row of Scavengers, landing in the middle of them, knife high, plunging.

The Scavengers broke formation, piling onto Dune.

What now? The speed of Dune's attack had caught us out.

I cried, 'No!' and waded in.

Curses. Cries.

The *thuck* of knives and batons. A thud on the ground next to me. *Dune.* Blood pouring from Dune's mouth.

'Fuckers. Fuckers!' I flung myself into the *Harh! Harh! Harh!* A hand ripped at my face, another flung me down. Boots. I fought back. Clawing helmets. Kicking a Scavenger's arm. Stamping down.

Harh! Harh! Harh!

I felt Dune's arm at my waist. A *whup* of metal through air. I ducked. A crossbow bolt tore through a Scavenger's breastplate. I threw myself to the ground, dragging Dune with me. I listened.

Harh!

Our sheer numbers were overwhelming the Scavs.

They backed off. I hauled Dune up and stood in front of them.

My knife hand was trembling. Blood had slicked up all the way to the hilt.

A shadow in the sky above us.

Another flamethrower drone. This time it didn't get the chance to ignite us. Footsy called it and crossbow bolts flew up straight and true. They pierced its armour.

The drone lurched low. Its flamethrower arm was only half retracted. Then there came a spill of liquid, the downdraught of a heavy object plummeting. Its dark energy pushing out waves of air. The drone smashed to earth in a bare field behind us. It ignited. The orange glow of flames illuminating us all.

We held fast together.

The Scavenger squad grabbed their wounded and dragged them and themselves out of the tent zone, scuttling across Runway Two for the north camp gates. Some of the catapulters fired at their backs.

A long continuous whistle. The battle was over. For now.

A crew of berets were at the fallen drone already, dousing it, examining it.

Bloodied arms helped me carry Dune into the tent. The same arms found water for us.

Dune's chest rasped. Their lungs stuttered. I bandaged their shoulder, dabbed blood, got them to drink water. There was nothing more I could do.

Dune's breathing smoothed out. We stayed in the tent and I told Dune what had happened while they'd been asleep: the attempt to snatch Elizabeth X, the casualties. They took it well, but by dusk, they were jittering, their hands as unsteady as they had been rock-solid when they'd attacked the Scavs. I made them lie on me and we watched the sky a while, then Dune whispered: 'The Underground got this all messed up.'

They said it in a strange tone. A lamentation.

'How so?' I asked.

'How many dead so far, that you've told me of?' Dune asked. 'Beta. Storm. Sly . . . ?'

'Pharaoh, Horse,' I added for them.

'That's the ones we know. I don't trust the Underground and their plan no more, you know what I'm saying? Sly and Storm burned to death, you told me. Can you imagine how that feels?'

'Shh,' I said. 'Stop thinking on it. We got to storify now. Drink, then storify.'

'I got nothing, Ax,' Dune sighed. 'You're on your own.'

'I'll storify for us both.'

I stroked Dune's raggedy eyebrows until the trembles steadied.

'How about the first time I bit your neck? Remember that?' I said. 'You had to hide that hickey for days, going around town in a fluffed-up outsize scarf, styling it out, saying it was the New Harlem look.'

Dune hardly engaged. They were zoned out. But I continued.

'Yup. And at school, you were all buttoned-up and wearing the school tie tight as fuck to hide it. You got compliments from the teachers. "Dune's looking all dapper and scholarly." They actually said that.'

'The light I was seeing was you, Ax. And that light won't never go out.'

'You remember, then? The hickey?'

'No, but keep going. Maybe it will come through later. Keep on with the story. You revive me, Ax. I was dapper? Damn. Betcha I was.'

I storified for Dune until my tongue was tired. By then, they had stopped twitching, and they'd turned, face down, into sleep. I turned into the covers myself.

In the morning, my shoulders were stiff with bruises. There were stitches in my upper left arm. *Who had stitched me up?*

Dune was unconscious, their mouth open, face blank.

I went out of the tent. The usual queues snaked around the standpipes. The usual people were shaking bedding and piling twigs together to make fires. The usual smoke blew. The usual cries and sighs. Yet there were signs. Patches of blood, dried brown on the ground. In the mud, the blurred prints of Scavenger boots. I looked out west. Nothing remained of the Bloods' flamethrower drone that had crashed in the field, only a burned crown of brown in trampled green grass, and the taint of petrol in the air.

I checked round the edges of our tent. There were no messages, Underground had left no news or instructions.

Back inside the tent, I tried to rouse Dune but they were deep gone.

I found the fresh maidenhair from the outcrop. Already, there was so little left. I got Dune upright.

'Open your fucking eyes, Dune. This is Ax, who loves you like nobody else. Damnit, come to me. It's Ax, Ax.'

I kept cajoling, cursing them every way I could think of. I applied kisses to their brow, a bite to their arm.

Eventually, the eyelids drew themselves up. They saw me. They felt my face. Wiped my tears. Smiled. 'Hey, Axel. Wassup?'

I pressed my forehead against theirs for a moment. Then

hauled in a breath. 'Why you keep me waiting longer and longer, Dune?'

Dune's hands wandered around me, scouting my bruises. 'The Scavengers came, didn't they? They beat you. They didn't get us. Did they get anybody?'

'We beat them back. We used the catapults and knives. You did too.'

'I did?'

'Yes.'

'Umm. We done good then . . .'

The eyelids shuttered down. Opened again. Incomprehension.

'Who are you?'

'I'm Ax. Drink.'

And so I began the process I'd done so many times before, of getting Dune back.

And I got them functioning.

Whistles started. An artillery debrief was being called at an outer standpipe.

When we got there, Elizabeth X arrived with three Underground medics. All four of them handed out bandages and cleaned wounds.

'Great work repelling the Scavengers,' Elizabeth X said to us as she worked. 'Downing the drone too.'

'We downed a drone?' Dune asked.

'A flamethrower drone,' she replied to Dune.

'Storm? Sly?' I asked.

'The Scavengers took their bodies,' Elizabeth X said. 'They came back in and took the bodies.'

'Why?' Dune's face went all *What the fuck*.

Murmurs.

254

'They died protecting me from the Scavenger squad,' Elizabeth X said. 'They died for the cause, for all of us.'

'Fuck the cause,' Dune said.

Elizabeth X looked to me, quizzical.

I winced an apology. Dune was not fully there.

'When are we breaking out?' said Dune, as a medic bandaged their right thigh. Others picked up Dune's question, calling out the same thing. There was a wild energy in the air.

Elizabeth X called for hush. 'Be patient. We need to adjust tactics because of the Bloods' flamethrower drones. We're almost ready.'

Dune kissed their teeth. '*Almost?* Sounds like excuses.'

There were callouts in support of Dune.

Dune scowled right into Elizabeth X's face as she dabbed their head wounds. She was unfazed by the anger and doubt. She inspected my shoulder's bruises and let them be. 'Be patient,' she repeated. 'Everybody has to show patience. And discipline. OK. Well done, everyone. That's it. Debrief over. Disperse.'

Then she and the medics were gone.

On the way to the fields later that day, I saw new bodies swinging from the crane. I tried to distract Dune, but they saw them. The charred remains of Sly and Storm, dangling there with the others.

A numbness spread over me.

The Peace Committee put out on their PA system that life had to go on, routines kept to. Adversity was a blessing. The Bloods were kind people. Without crops, we would starve. The PA speakers went on to blast out another message: because the Bloods were no longer supplying more than rice and vegetable stock, we would soon be eating a gruel so thin that there was likely to be widespread severe malnutrition unless we tended to the crops. We should report to the fields at all costs.

'Come on,' Dune said, 'let's get to these precious fucking Peace Committee fields.'

In the fields, very few were digging. People didn't care much about Peace Committee work schedules any more. Me and Dune dug a little, then quit.

After the field work, Dune disappeared again. When they came back late to the tent, I asked where they'd been, and they didn't say anything except, 'Gathering things.'

We sat in silence, Dune morose.

'What's up?'

'Elizabeth X. "Later. Almost. Be patient." I mean, Sly and Storm are dead. Like, burned to death, and she's still all "be patient".'

I remembered how it was those two, Sly and Storm, who had been the fiercest about how the Underground had killed Horse, they'd had the strongest misgivings. Yet, when it mattered, they'd saved Elizabeth X, died for her. Was that irony?

Dune was continuing with their own thoughts. 'X. She's started to sound like the Peace Committee. Notice how she always disappears when there's danger?'

'That's normal for leadership. They can't lead us if they're dead.'

I made to oil Dune's hair, but they shrugged me off. They were acting like it was the wounds and the drone attacks that were causing their silence and tetchiness, but I knew their moods better than they knew them themself. So, when Dune slipped out of the tent as I pretended to doze, I got up and followed them.

24

Laying It All on the Line

One thing the Resistance Youth Corps taught us well was how to follow someone. Anyone. Dune took a mazy line across the two runways, then crossed through the bog zone, skirted the bunker zone and angled off further east, out and beyond the cornfields. I scurried behind, keeping the gap between us, moving from boulders to brambles to saplings. They kept going for at least a mile and a half. Closing in on the perimeter fence.

Would they?

Finally, Dune stopped. Turned. Did that Resistance countersurveillance sweep. I slid down. When I raised my head again, they'd disappeared.

The land was flat. Dune could only have gone low.

I put my ear to the ground. Tapping. Nothing on the surface explained it. I crawled my way closer to where Dune had disappeared, through wild grass and dandelions, horsetails and rushes. I kept stopping to listen, homing in on the sound.

The tapping stopped. But I'd got the location now.

Two metres ahead, I saw a grey shadow, breaking the line of meadow grass stalks. The clean circle of a manhole or concrete trench. I crawled to it.

It was a buried concrete culvert. Dune was there, inside.

'Nice yard,' I said, shuffling in. 'Any room?'

'Damn, Ax. You ain't meant to be here.'

They let me in anyway.

It was long and narrow and low enough that our bodies were curved into C-shapes. Dune had two long poles inside, nails, a hammer, a pile of short planks. It would make a ladder. They also had rubber gloves, boltcutters. I put it all together. Dune was planning to cut through the first fence, straddle the moat with the ladder, go across it, cut through the second fence, then make a run for it.

'Why, Dune?'

'I told you already.'

'I didn't think you were serious.'

'I've been planning this a long time.'

I fumed. 'You know the Underground breakout is close. This is bad timing. Really stupid. I won't let you.'

'We've been hearing that stuff from Elizabeth X since . . . since time. I don't trust the Underground. Neither should you. All they managed so far is to one by one get us killed, Ax. Am I remembering right? Pharaoh, dead. Beta. Storm. All dead. And those are the ones I remember. We stay here any longer, we'll be swinging from that crane too. I won't let the Bloods do that to me. It's all right for you, Ax, but this Bloods' SIM has been drilling my head, big time. It never lets up. They'll get me wiped or Blanked or just plain dead. They'll get me. Like they got Beta. And the Underground will let me go. Or kill me, how they killed Beta. Put a bolt through me to help the Bloods out. 'For the cause.' Didn't they do that to Beta? Didn't they?'

I nodded. I couldn't lie to Dune.

Dune's head dropped into their knees.

'I thought I got that right. The Underground will give me up, saying we're not ready for a breakout yet. They'll time me out. It's a sick dream thinking the U are going to break us free. By the time they're ready, we'll all be dead.'

I flew at them, took them in an armlock, flattened them against the pipe. 'It's suicide. You're gonna get yourself killed!'

I pinned their neck with one arm and I beat them in the stomach with my fist. I took their head in my hands and kneed them in the stomach and . . .

Dune didn't fight back. They let me hit them as much as I wanted. Free shots. Till I couldn't hit them any more. I let them go and crumpled. I beat the sides of the concrete tube we were trapped in. 'Dune, don't you see? It's a fucked-up idea.'

Then Dune was stroking my arm, saying, 'C'mon, Ax, it's OK.'

'Please, Dune. You can't get past that fence. Nobody has.'

'There's always a first time for everything.'

'Fine. What if you do get beyond the fence? It'll activate the SIM and blow your head off.'

'Nobody knows that for sure, though, do they? That the SIM explodes beyond the fence? The Blanked don't get blown up when they go through the gates. So there could be a way past the fence.'

'Everybody who's hit the fence has had their head blown. Case closed.'

'But that might not be true in all circumstances. They hit the fence. Set off an alarm. Take volts into their body. Like maybe I can get past the fence without triggering it.'

Dune snapped the boltcutter as they spoke on. 'You notice the electricity to the fence has started switching off at times in the evenings. Did so yesterday. The hum of it stops.'

'Serious?'

'Yeah. They must have problems with supply or be doing repairs or something.'

The electric fence stuttering wasn't completely new to me. The Underground had noticed too, and put out a message that this was an encouraging sign but not to act on it. The Underground's position had remained the same. No breakout was to be attempted until the head SIMs were deactivated.

'That's in our favour,' said Dune. 'Makes the fence more like a gate.'

I calmed my breathing and thought about it, like it was a debug routine. Dune's plan relied on the SIM not exploding. It made some sense. The SIM explosive arming switch might fail. Or might be only intermittently switched on. Or might rely on the roll-call drones being present within fifty metres of a straying SIM and activating the explode switch. Software could fail. If *Explode* was reliant on a kill signal from the drones, the Faraday cages – in the berets – could work. And the berets might also block GPS tracking. Of course, there were other technologies, the Bloods might have engineered other ways of activating the SIM explosives. But getting as far away from camp as possible as fast as possible was a good first step in minimising the chances of that outcome, whatever the tech. It was all still a long shot.

'I know it can work in theory,' Dune said, reading me.

'And you want to test the theory?'

Dune shrugged. They held me between their knees, their arms over my shoulders, and when I stopped sobbing, they spoke in a new voice, all rational. 'You don't understand, do you? I'm going, Ax, the drone attacks are getting through big time now. They're

260

wiping me serious. Every day, there's less of me. I can't remember anything. I can't remember your parents any more, nothing about them; I can't remember my life before this camp. You say I had a grandfather, and you remember him, but I can't. Most mornings I can't even remember you, Axel. I know you get me back every time. You put me together best as you can. But one day all your tricks aren't going to work. One morning that maidenhair trick's not gonna work. What's left of me if I can't remember you, Ax? I'd be dead already. Every day I'm in pieces. Every day it's worse. It's best I go now, take the chance I have, however small it is. I don't want to be the living dead and I know I'm close to that. You know it, too.'

'I won't let you go,' I murmured. 'I won't let you.'

'Shh. It's all right.'

We lay there in the culvert and cried.

Eventually I dried my tears and said to them calmly: 'I'm not as strong as you think, Dune. So long as there's someone else in this world who loves me, who needs me, I can carry on. But if you go, I don't know if I can pull through.'

'I'm sorry. I just . . . I have . . . I have to do this.'

'OK,' I said, 'Fine. Then I do it with you.'

Dune turned on me. 'No, no, no, Ax, that's not a good idea, you're not being gummed like me. You're—'

'Listen to me. If you go, I go. That's the deal.'

'But they may get the breakout right. There's a chance the Underground can break out in time. You should wait for that. It's just me, I can't hold it together no more. But you? You're strong. There's something inside you so strong. What I'm planning is *maaad* dangerous. Like you say, it's got next to no chance. The

Underground thing is dangerous, but there's a slim chance with it
for those who've got time . . .'

'Stop,' I said. 'You don't get it. It's me and you. We go together.
Or not at all.'

Dune sighed. 'All right, let's do this crazy thing together.'

It was like I was signing my death sentence. Dune's too. We'd
just written them in this tube of concrete.

'We wear the berets, yes?'

Dune nodded. 'We cut through the fence, cross the moat using
the ladder, and run. Split and run.'

'Split?'

'Yes. It's safer that way. Give us both a better chance.'

I thought about it. Dune was right about that and also I knew
that if one of us didn't make it, maybe the other would. That bit
was unspoken but I knew Dune had thought this through and
they also knew I would figure it out. I didn't speak it. Instead, I
agreed. Dune sighed at that.

'So?' I replied. 'When? Damn, Dune. What a mess. I'd hate
you for doing this if I didn't love you to bits.'

Dune didn't say anything. Just slid their arms tighter around
my neck.

I was sad and furious. And yet how come I was also happy? If
we had to die, at least we'd die together.

'What now then?' I said.

'We go back to the tent, wait till night. Then we go.'

Night couldn't come fast enough. We walked around the camp,
listening, observing, picking up snippets of information. Then

headed back to our tent and waited. And during that wait, Dune's plan began to look, well, possible. I'd picked up from the Underground networks that the Bloods were storming up north with their tanks and drones and planes so fast that they were leaving themselves stretched here in the south.

And I'd also learned that the Underground had received the phone with the hack code on it: the 'fool kid' had delivered. But they were still struggling to get a team in place to deliver it to us in the camp. If we received the hack code here, and uploaded it into the Bloods' system, then, if the Underground had got their calculations right, it would take down the Bloods' system, stop and reverse the rewrites, shut off both the SIM explosive and its GPS tracker. *If they had got their calculations right* was the key bit, and that bit involved me. It dawned on me that, if I left, that was my expertise gone. Would the Underground even be able to upload the code to hack the SIM without me? Maybe. Maybe not. If not, I was betraying them. Elizabeth X. Footsy. The little kid with two missing fingers at the standpipe. The girl who danced with the plastic chandelier on her head. The ratcatcher. Everyone. I pushed the thought away. Maybe they didn't need me. And anyway, when did I sign up to be the standout hero of the Underground? Elizabeth X could run the code in my place, I decided. Or she could delay, like she always did.

The waiting dragged and we wandered through the tents one last time, and I was thinking it all through. What if me and Dune's pretty little smartarse self-made escape plan worked? The best thing for me and Dune to do, I figured, once we broke out (and there was a big *if* in that), was to race as far as possible from the camp. Before any Bloods' reinforcements arrived, or in case the Bloods'

GPS tracker tech in our SIMs only worked close to the camp. There was a chance, if we could get out of range fast. If the tracker tech was limited. If our homemade escape equipment worked. A lot of *ifs*. But Dune's mind was set, so I didn't waver either. Our escape was possible, as a matter of logic.

'Sky's pink,' said Dune.

We were back in our tent.

'And?' Since we'd made the decision to escape through the fence, Dune had been sharper, less gummed, almost chilled. Still. Pink sky? Big deal.

'It's a good omen,' they said.

'Better be.'

'All right, it's time,' Dune said. 'It's time.'

I took a breath. If we were going to go, now looked as good a time as any.

25

The Ladder

Dune stared out of the tent in the direction we were going to take.
'We are going in one direction. Out. You feel that?' Dune asked.

'Yeah, I got all the feels on that. Still . . .'

'What?'

'We've not said goodbye to the others. Footsy. Wires . . .'

'We'll see them again. Don't do that face, Ax. We're not letting
them down, we're moving forward. Right? Showing a way.'

'Right.'

'Good,' continued Dune. 'Ain't no stopping now. If we hear
the dogs, we keep going. If we see lights coming on us, we keep
going. If there's shouting after us, we keep going. If drones drop
down on us, we keep going. We don't ever stop until we reach
the other side and taste freedom. Even then, we keep going.
Right?'

'Right.'

'OK.'

'Let's do this then.'

We slipped out of the tent. Our faces daubed, hair gunked,
berets on, clothes hazed in dark grey camouflage paint.

We moved in a trance through the tents: skirting the glow of
a tent here, avoiding a baby's cry there. I was hyper-alert to
everything. Figures moved in the tents' openings. There was a splash

of water as someone took a cold shower in the growing dark. We kept low, hugging shadows.

As we moved through the camp, I was checking everything for differences. Change meant danger. The road had the same busted-up shapes. The distant hangars were the same black crumpled winged shape. The lights of the gatehouse to the north were dotted in the same pattern. The pull of the wind at my back was the same. We kept going and I smelled the familiar bitter wet concrete and rich earth mingling with the sour slop of drainage channels.

I stopped and looked back. Across the tent city's flickering oil lamps, there was no unusual movement. No one following, that I could see. I checked the gatehouse's outline again, this time letting my eyes move above it to search the horizon, because when drones came, they always swept in from there. Nothing strange hung on that horizon. My eyes scanned from the north to the east, and I could only see the sway of the treetops in the east, which would be our first sanctuary when we broke out, and the ghostly flit of two birds in twilight, two beating curls of darkness, late to roost.

The wind was up but not so much that it buffeted us. I turned again after we'd crossed Runway Two. Did a shadow move? I held Dune down and we waited. The blotches of grey and black were immobile. I nodded. Dune surged forwards and we pushed on till the tents were specks, then gone. Dune's hand was suddenly soft in mine, pressing. We kneeled on our haunches, hand in hand, looking at the fence. There was no setting sun or moonlight, but there was absolute beauty in that wired horizon.

We made it to the culvert. Dune hauled out the cutters first. I took up the twin long wood poles and the bundle of rungs that would make up the ladder.

Then Dune's killing arms were around me and I held my breath. The scent of them, the bitter, oily, flowery, crushed grass, human scent of them. I squeezed Dune like I wanted to get every last essence out of them and into me.

Dune gasped.

I looked up into those pearlised autumn eyes. 'It's a fucked-up world, right?' I said.

'I'm gonna miss you too,' they said.

The plan remained that we'd split up once we got through the second fence, so we increased the chances of at least one of us making it. We both knew the odds.

'When all this shit is over, we'll meet again, I swear down.'

'All right, let's do this,' I whispered.

We rolled rubber gloves on. We pulled silicone covers over the soles of our footwear.

We knocked fists one last time.

In my chest was the jigger and lick and hop of a future life free from this. It was a freedom that smelled like pancakes dripping with honey. Something got through and I had a burst of longing for the smell of my mum. Daft, but I saw bacon too, a crunchy streaky slice of it, wrapped in bread and dripping in butter and my dad losing the race with me to the plate to grab it. These flashes of sudden, released memory made me feel giddy, weightless. Then anguish charged in. I saw the towering height of the fence, understood the voltage power that could be charging through it. Beyond that, the moat. The moat's width and depth. What if we got our calculations wrong and our ladder was too short to span the moat? What if we slipped off it and fell into the moat? It was too late for *what ifs*.

We closed in on the fence, hauling the equipment. Dune upped the pace, lugging the cutters low at their side, their Afro under the beret bobbing along, gleaming. They stepped it up again as we crossed more ground. And now the fence was close, its full height made real. We were maybe forty metres away. Dune stopped.

'You good?' they whispered.

'Sure.'

'You notice?' they said.

'What?'

'No hum.'

I listened. The fence was silent. It was a good sign.

They squeezed my arm, hefted the cutters up, and, in a running crouch, approached. We were so close, we could make out the fence's chainlinks. Dune turned, waved me forwards.

Then I was running. Forgetting worry. Forgetting pain. Forgetting sadness. I was a body in pure flight, as a howl of joy silently erupted inside me.

We got there, almost tumbling into the mesh. I rolled over and looked back. Blinks of light came from afar. Two short, one long; two long, one short:

$$** \underline{\quad} / \underline{\quad} \underline{\quad}*$$

U.G.

Morse for Underground. *So they knew we were out here. How?* I turned my back. I didn't wait to see if they sent any instructions. I didn't even tell Dune. We were too far gone with this plan to turn back now. This was it. I put my arm round Dune, to comfort them, and to shield their eyes from the morse message.

We took a few seconds to get our breath. I could feel the hairs on my forearms prickling up. I checked with Dune. They were ready. The cutter's big-nosed, steel head glinted. Dune's eyes gleamed too as they brought it down on the chainlink. The jaws of the thing snagged a wire. I'm sure Dune, crazy fucker that they were, actually winked at me, right then. Then the moment of truth. The cutter's jaws bit though the first wire.

No spark.

No leap of blue.

Nothing.

Dune squeezed the cutter's long arms together again and again. The quick sharp snap of the wires. They cut through six links before I tapped Dune's shoulder. We had enough space. We tugged the mesh apart. I went through, then Dune. We dragged the ladder pieces after us. We snapped the rungs in place and bolted them. We hauled the ladder upright, each held a side for a moment then, on my count of three, we let it fall. It made a neat, noiseless quarter arc down, like a giant protractor drawing in the sky. It landed with a *thunk* on the bank of the other side. It was a good alignment. And the right length. I stooped and stood on the base lightly, making sure it was sunk fast into the soil of the banks. Then, leaning low, transferring more of my weight, I placed my hands on the third and fourth rungs across and tested. There was a little give to the left, but then it held. Rock steady. It felt evenly embedded on both sides. Like a perfect landing on Mars.

A distant bark stopped me. I turned, retreated from the rungs, and looked over with Dune for any morse light of warning or unusual movement. Nothing. We listened and waited. The bark had been no different from any other bark at the gatehouse, no more frenzied or urgent. No closer either. And it didn't repeat.

'Let's move,' Dune whispered. They'd taken my place on the first rungs of the ladder, and they were crawling across, shuffling hands then knees, midway already. I turned for the cutters because we'd need them for the second fence.

Then it happened.

The ladder twisted.

Dune slipped. I heard them swear and saw their body slide with the wobble and twist of the ladder. The shadow of Dune's torso, shifting. The slow motion of it. The scrape of their shoe silicone on wooden rung as it lost its grip. They didn't fall fast. They fell slowly towards the water, their chest sliding low, one hand still holding onto a rung. I heard the splash as their feet hit water. They didn't shout. Nor lose the grip of their other hand on the rung. The effort of speaking would topple them.

Their free arm waved to me, frantically. Dune couldn't swim off to safety. The high sheer banks of the moat thwarted that. And if the dogs got in the water too they'd tear them up for sure. That dog howl came again now, and closer. I dropped the cutters and slithered along the twisted ladder, using my weight as a counterbalance to almost straighten it. I made it to the eighth rung before the swing of the ladder got too dangerous to go any further. I was fully over the water, close enough I could hear the jerk of Dune's breathing.

Spreadeagling myself flat across the ladder's rungs, I stretched down and out for Dune's hand with mine. I couldn't reach it. I went lower, slipped first my left shoulder then my head through a gap between the rungs. I wriggled the other shoulder through and slid down further, turned fully upside down, and wedged the back of my knees into the ladder. With an effort, Dune swung towards me. Through the dark, I could pick out the shadow of

270

their hand again. I twisted to align. Our hands met and Dune's fingers were briefly in mine, our rubber gloves sticking. Then the inertia from Dune's counterswing wrenched their hand from mine.

'Again,' I hissed to Dune. I couldn't reach them from here, I had no other way of getting to them: they *had* to swing again. Upside down in the dark, the broken ladder my trapeze, I stretched. 'Swing,' I said. 'Do it. Come on, Dune, do it.'

There was a sigh from Dune, a stir of the black mass where their shoulders were. Then their body heaved again. The free hand fluttered out to me. I stretched and stretched to meet it, the gap only a fingertip. In a last, desperate shift of my body down and outwards, I was there. But the hand had gone. The back swing was taking it away again. Then a sigh. And Dune's other hand slipped from the rung. I heard the simple splash of a body hitting water.

No. No. No.

The barking was frantic now. Louder.

Dune gasped from the void: 'Help me, Ax, help me!'

A low shadow tearing through the bank's undergrowth on the other side of the moat. Snarling.

The shadow slithered across to the moat wall's edge. Another shadow. More barking. The shape of something leaping into water. Another. The splash and churn of two dogs. Frenzied swimming.

A hum. Flashes of electricity. The sensors in the fence posts, reactivating. A change of note from one of the dogs.

Dune's scream. 'Help me! Help me!'

Ripping.

More snarls. Churning water. The bared teeth of a dog, leaping for me.

271

I twisted and it bit onto a rung of the ladder. Hung there. I
didn't retreat. But I looked back. Saw morse flickering. I didn't
need to watch more to know what it said. *Get out.* But I couldn't
leave Dune. I would never leave Dune. I smashed the dog's head
with my hand. Again and again. I aimed for the eyes. Smashed a
thumb into an eyeball. Finally, in a howl, it released the rung from
its jaw and dropped down. I heard the splash and its frantic
paddling.

I listened. A tearing sound. Dogs. Ripping away.

'Dune,' I called out, 'Dune! Where are you?'

'Help me, Ax, help!'

They were in the water still.

'Dune?'

Quiet now. Except the paddle of dogs.

Then someone in a beret was clambering onto the ladder from
the camp side. They grabbed my foot, wrenched at it, got both
my legs.

'No! No!'

They ignored my pleas. Hauled me along the ladder and away
from Dune. They were too strong. I let go and allowed myself to
be pulled. On the moat's bank, they flipped me up easily and they
were carrying me now. My rescuer's earring caught the light from
somewhere. I remembered the rapid rise and fall of their chest. Morse
flashing.

From afar, an order in the rasp of a Scavenger's voice: 'Halt!'

A cluster of whispering voices, close around us. The *thuck* of
catapults firing. Stones hitting Scavenger armour. More whispers.
I was pushed down onto a stretcher and carried somewhere
underground and pitch black.

26

What Do You Fear?

Daylight pushed furiously at the canvas. I clamped my eyes shut, trying to will myself back to sleep. None came. *Of course they'd have strung up the body.* I got dressed and went north, skirting close enough to the gate that I could see the crane.

Dune wasn't up there.

A thousand emotions shunted through me. Relief. Fear. Bafflement. Hope. Each feeling colliding with the next. I wiped away tears and stumbled into the crop fields and asked around, I didn't trust my eyes. The Underground said things were getting chaotic outside for the Bloods, all kinds of shit hitting their fan; it could be that, or it could be something else. Dune's body was not up there on the crane. I pulled weeds. I dug. My hands trembled.

Waves of disapproval of what we'd done came at me in the field. Sneers. Curses. Spit. I shrugged them off. 'Go ahead, put a bolt through me,' I said to one of the mutterers, because they didn't affect me. I only wanted to know about Dune. Then Elizabeth X arrived in the fields, and spoke to them, and they left me alone.

A weak sun hid behind sheets of clouds. Some small Bloods' reconnaissance drones crept low across the camp sky. Someone dinged one with a catapulted stone and hit its wing, and the drone nosedived into the bog zone. We waited. No Scavenger alert. No

Scavengers gathering at the gates, preparing to retrieve it. Two berets seized the drone and smuggled it away.

Midday and there was still no news of Dune. I dropped my rake and strolled right by the gate. The gate guards got antsy as I passed. *Go ahead, shoot me.* I checked again. Pharaoh, Beta, Sly and Storm there, swinging. No Dune.

I wandered away, ducked into the bunker zone and hunkered down as five attack drones whirred over the camp in star formation, undercarriages fully retracted, on their way someplace north.

I crossed Runway One and Two and crept low, past the culvert where we'd hidden the ladder and I got right up to the fence and found the section we'd cut through. It had been patch-wired by Scavengers and the electricity was coursing through it unevenly, causing sparks. I stayed back, wary of arcs, but I scanned the moat banks, my heart kicking my chest. I half expected to see Dune's body floating there, face down. Or else Dune sitting on the bank on the other side, chewing a grass stalk, looking up and waving as they hollered to me, 'Wassup, dude? What took you so long?'

The moat water was the same murky brown. One long limb of our ladder was dangling on the far bank. It had several bent iron reinforcers still attached. Like broken ribs. There was a smear of darkened blood on the dock leaves across there, and more blood splashed the nettles above the dockplants. And one shoe. *Dune's.*

I heard the ground shift behind me. Turned.

Footsy. Running low, her long limbs spidering. She was breathless, urging me to her.

'What?'

'Peace Committee turning over your tent. Come now.'

We scooted across both runways and took the approach road

back into the tent zone. No one was in the tent, but it had been ransacked. The maidenhair pot was in shards. The battery lamp cable cut. Bedding turned upside down and slashed. The groundsheet pulled up and holes dug in the earth underneath. I sat down in the middle of the mess.

Wires showed up and Footsy nodded him in. I remembered when I'd first seen Wires in the base bunker. He was wearing the same shirt. The collar was frayed now. 'We can fix this,' said Footsy, a hand on my shoulder. I let Footsy and Wires do whatever. The Peace Committee had been looking for something, the decrypt codes for Underground signals most likely. If so, they were way too late: I'd long ago memorised them all and eaten the guide. I knew the Peace Committee had found nothing because nothing was here. Dune's clothes were all scattered about, though.

Footsy worked her way through it methodically, putting things back in place, folding clothes into piles, but really carefully, using zone-searching to check there were no devices planted, the way the Underground had taught us.

I held my sides and closed my eyes. A storm of thoughts knocked around in my head about last night and Dune. The ladder hadn't held. Why had I let Dune go first? *It should have been me falling off that ladder, not Dune.* When Dune dropped, why didn't I catch their hand that first time?

'Don't be pulling yourself apart.'

It was Footsy. I must have been speaking aloud. She was standing over me, her hands in my hair, now combing the 'fro with a pick, worrying out knots, then gliding her fingers through, gunking it.

'Your ends need trimming,' she said. 'Want me to do that?'

It was what Dune would say.

275

'Stupid stunt they pulled.'

This from Wires, talking low, maybe to himself, but loud enough that I heard.

'Not now,' said Footsy.

'Shh,' said Wires, this time from somewhere else in the tent.

Footsy again: 'Actually, cry all you like, I'll just keep teasing these knots out.'

'You know what's a joke, Foots?' I said.

'Tell me.'

'What the drones and the SIM couldn't do all this time, the Bloods have finally managed. Without Dune, I'm numb. I . . . I don't feel anything.'

Silence.

'Dune would be here now if it wasn't for me. I let them slip. I let them go.'

'Hush.'

It was Wires again, iron-faced in a corner of the tent.

Footsy nudged my head, on the SIM. She stroked oil into the skin there then began dabbing at my forehead with a cold cloth.

'. . . The only reason I stay alive is so I can sleep. Last night, Dune came to me in my sleep. Their voice called to me there. That's where they are. When I'm awake, all I want to do is crawl under the blankets and sink into Dune again, get right into the tang of them, feel the heat of them. It's a drag to be with other people, it's a drag to be awake, it's a drag to talk.'

'It's OK, baby,' Footsy said. 'I got you. I feel you.'

Wires had come from his corner of the tent and kneeled low to face me.

'C'mon, Ax. You can't mope like this.'

'No?'

Wires stared back. His opal brown eyes glittered fiercely.

'How about I mope like this then?' I said.

He didn't see it coming. I busted Wire's lip good.

He stayed where he'd slumped after I'd hit him, blood dribbling through his fingers.

I was standing now.

'Fuck you, Axel,' Wires said. He got up, ducked out of the tent and was gone. I didn't care.

Footsy had been kissing her teeth. Now she dropped the cloth and hair pick onto the groundsheet and followed Wires out of the tent.

Fuck them both. Who invited them here anyway?

I turned. Too much stuff was running in my mind, and there was not enough bandwidth in my brain to cope with it. One question kept on and on: *What do you fear? What do you fear? What do you fear?*

The question demanded answers. It screeched inside my head till I yielded. I gave in. I gave it answers.

I fear having my teeth wired together and my throat stitched.

I fear being forced to stare at the drone light.

I fear the buttery, sweet smell of my mum's clothes when I fell on her after she'd been shot.

I fear bleach of any sort.

I fear soldiers. Shots.

I fear Bloods' wastepaper baskets holding Underground fingernails.

I fear trying to delete my SIM only to find the SIM is all I am.

I fear the earth tilting, everything sliding off it.

I fear the Second Coming.

I fear crossing water, I know I can't swim.

I fear burning doors.

I fear you.

'Wake up, Axel.'

What do you fear? What do you fear? What do you fear? What do you fear?

I fear crossing the moat.

I fear the creak of the ladder as it comes apart.

I fear the dogs. The noise of flesh ripping as they tear at Dune.

I fear Dune's voice calling out: 'Help me, Ax, help me.'

I fear I let Dune down.

I woke, sweating. I was in a tent. It was dark. The canvas thrumming from rain. Nobody here but me. I crawled to the front and opened the flaps. The sky above was black.

Who was I?

No recall. No idea.

Only one word. One word I knew from a smell in the blankets. That word?

Dune.

Dune.

Dune. Dune. Dune.

I couldn't see them. Not Dune's face. Not their voice. Nothing. Only knew the name.

I sat in the void, saying the name until daylight came in.

'Wake up! It's me, Footsy.'

She tried to make me drink a foul maidenhair tea. I sent her away.

I emptied my pockets. A knife. A ball bearing. A catapult. What use? I left the tent and walked. People called out to me, I ignored them. I heard only the fence.

Two birds sat cawing on the stump of a concrete pillar and on a wall in bunker zone. Wind surged through rusting steel. Concrete debris rattled. The cold in my feet. Corpse blue. My legs drained of power. The mud sucking.

Maybe it was sweet and right to stop struggling, to sink.

I wanted to nestle myself into the broken concrete and mud. To not wake again.

I stumbled, fell to my knees. Here was as good a place as any to lie down one last time, lie down and die.

'Ax!'

Someone was shaking me.

27

Badseed

It was night again.

I was in the tent. Pulling at old stitches in my left arm. A red welt there, running across. Stuff running through my head. I tried to hold it back. But the stuff installed.

What do you fear? What do you fear? What do you fear? What do you fear?

Your friend Dune who was evil. You were both badseed.

You are here in the prison camp because you have been on a wrong path.

We tried to reason with you.

But your habits of thought, your books, the stories you told yourselves, misled you and made you ignore the truth.

You were the wrong civilisation.

Your historians' erroneous interpretation of progress had you living under a dangerous illusion.

You were stubborn.

We tried hard.

We were merciful.

But you shot at us. You repelled our attempts to help you.

Our bombs were used with precision and only when you could not be pacified by reason.

Our troops were merciful.

We Bloods have been kind. We will fix you.

You are being given help with your thinking through the Bloods'
SIM programme.

Accept it.

You will be held here until your thoughts are satisfactorily cleaned.
You can build the foundations of a bright new future here.

Your target should be to think clean for an entire day. We will help
you do that.

If you listen to this voice, all will be fine.

Your memories of Dune won't help you. We will erase Dune for
you. Accept this.

'No!'

Daylight.

Someone pushing me upright. Holding a drink to my lips.

'Ax, wake up. It's Footsy. How are you feeling?'

'I'm . . . I'm Ax?'

'That's right. Drink. It's the best there is.'

'Dune.'

'What?'

'Where's Dune?'

'Dune died, Ax. But we won't ever forget them. And we won't
let you forget them either. Look. There's Dune's clothes. It's OK.
Sniff them all you like. Drink some more. Dune's coming back to
you. *Let's do it. I got an idea, let's do it!* Remember that? Dune was
always saying that. *Let's do it!* Go ahead, smile. You're allowed.
Dune loved it when you smiled.'

'Dune's dead? They drowned in the moat. Right? Have they
hung the body on the crane yet?'

'C'mon. I need to show you something. You need to see it with your own eyes. C'mon.'

Footsy dragged the bedcovers off me.

'Bitch.'

She laughed.

'Cuss me some more, let it out.'

She pulled on my socks, found my shoes, got me clothed, drinking. I remembered things. It trickled in. Where I was and why. The SIM madness installed in our heads. The fence holding us in. The Underground. Dune. *Dune.* This surge in my heart at every mention of the name. Dune. That word alone could kill me. I put the drink down.

Footsy took my hand and led me out.

'You know where you are?'

I was looking at hundreds of tents, extending almost as far as the eye could see. People milling about.

'Yes. They put SIMs in our heads. What's been happening to me, Footsy?'

'You've been refusing the maidenhair. Don't do that again.'

'They killed Dune, didn't they? The dogs.'

'Follow me, I need to show you something.'

Footsy led me through tents, out into the field and across until we neared the gate. There, in a field at the far north end of the camp, she had me crouch down.

'OK, deep breath. OK. Look in this direction. See?'

She was pointing at the crane by the gate.

Dead people, dangling there. 'You mean ... *What the fuck? Why Footsy? Why are you showing me this?'*

'No, no, no, I'm sorry, Ax, it's not Dune up there. Come on, let's get closer.'

I followed her till we were close enough we could pick out the guards, the Interrogation and Reception centre, the drawbridge, the warning lights on the pillars of the gates.

'Now can you see?' said Footsy. 'Not Dune. The one with the wig? It's one of the Peace Committee, up there, swinging. His face is blown off, but the wig is still there. Only Dolphus had a wig that big.'

'You took me all the way out here for that?'

Footsy looked at me strangely. When we got back to the tent, she made more maidenhair tea, had me drink it. Watched me.

I thought about what I'd just seen. 'Since when did the Bloods attack the Peace Committee?'

'Exactly. It went off last night, Ax. You missed it, you were asleep. The Underground said to ensure you rested. They put berets around your tent to make sure you didn't get snatched. Scavengers stormed the camp. We shot them up till a flamethrower drone came across, the ones that shoot fireballs. You remember those?'

I nodded.

'We scattered then.'

It came to me. How Sly and Storm had burned.

'The Scavengers surrounded the Peace Committee tent and yanked out Dolphus. You remember him? The one who liked to wear the long-tressed judge's wig and sit there giving out food punishments: "Late arrival at the field work site." "Not weeding efficiently." "Tent flaps improperly tied." Scavengers took him and the Peace Committee just gave him up. Allowed the Scavengers to

283

drag him out of the camp. Soon after, we heard a single shot, and the crane arm lowered, went up again.'

'They strung Dolphus up there and then. In the night?'

'Yeah.'

'What did they do that for?'

'We don't know. But it's got the Peace Committee panicked. One by one they're quitting. Peace Committee's finished.'

Footsy had her hands in mine now. 'Ax. What I'm trying to say is, Dune *isn't* up there. On the crane.'

'The moat and the dogs. The dogs got them.'

'We don't know. Dune might have got away. Their body's not up there, and that's weird. Usually, they put them on show quick.'

I thought about what Footsy was saying. There was some sense to it.

Footsy spoke softly. 'Even if Dune didn't make it, don't let Dune have died for no reason. Work with us again. Ax. The Underground still needs you.'

'I don't know if I can help any more, Foots. They've wiped my memory something bad. And they took everything from me when they took Dune. It's like I try to remember me and Dune but everything's been erased. Like they've worked out the best way to kill me is to attack my memory of Dune. They've left me the name. *Dune.* And a song. I remember Dune's song. Everything else, I have to work to remember. And it hurts. It hurts so bad.'

'I know it hurts, Ax. But your love for Dune, you can still feel it, right? Then channel it as rage against the Bloods. We need you, Axel, the fighting you. That's who Dune knew and loved, that's who we need. Dune wouldn't want you to give up. And the memories will come back. You two were too tight for the SIM to hold all that back from you.'

Footsy was squeezing my hands. I couldn't talk because I knew that if I did, I'd cry.

'Can we hug?' Footsy said.

When we stopped hugging, she said, 'Also, bathing.'

'What?'

'Get to the standpipe and scrub, yeah?'

'I smell?'

'A little. You've not bathed in how many days? We still love you though.'

Footsy left and I went out to the standpipe. As I passed them, some people did that Black nod thing at me. It was early evening and I saw the white and orange canvas of tents. The paths of dark brown mud between the rows. Foam in the soil by the standpipes, from soap suds. Someone bathing a brown toddler at one standpipe, swishing their hands round the child's body. I found a free standpipe, went between the canvas screens, took my clothes off, let my bucket fill and soaped myself, then poured the bucket of water over my head. My arm stung where the stitches were. I liked the water's coldness. When I was done, I dressed again, then stepped out and looked around. The camp was calm. A few people standing about, watching the purple-black sky. No drones. No Peace Committee watchers. It was weird. I slipped back into my tent.

Footsy and Wires came later on, and Footsy made me drink. After, she began dabbing my face again, to clean the cuts, she said.

'I'm sorry,' Wires mumbled. 'I said some bad things last time.'

I couldn't tell if Wires was mumbling because he hated saying sorry, or if it was his swollen lip which caused him to mumble. I remembered my punch.

'I'm sorry about your lip.'

'S'OK.'

'We all cool now?' asked Footsy.

Me and Wires did a handshake, pressed shoulders.

Wires said: 'Don't regret. If you got anything wrong or made a mistake of any kind out there that night, Dune would forgive you like you'd have forgiven them, right?'

'I guess,' I said. I didn't really understand what Wires was talking about.

'How you feeling now?' said Footsy, smoothing my cheeks. 'You're all scrubbed up and squeaky clean.' She sniffed me then. She actually sniffed me. It made me smile. Then came a memory. *Dune used to sniff me.*

I took a breath. 'I'm good.'

'Look at me. Your eyes can't hide, Ax.'

I let her see the tears spill, let her wipe them with the flats of her thumbs.

'You all know Dune more than me now. How can I live with that?'

'Dune will come back to you in full, I guarantee,' Footsy murmured. 'Wait and see. They'll come back to you, and in a good way.'

The light in the sky was fully extinguished now. Wires left and came back with some food: two bowls. It was a watery gruel with bits at the bottom that were clearly spaghetti and peas. Other than that, it might as well have been boiled salted water. I tasted it and put it down. Footsy raised it to my lips again. Insisted. I drank it all.

Then they began storifying Dune for me. I sat and listened and remembered and wept.

'I didn't know Dune from the outside,' Wires said, 'you know, from before camp, like you, but I remember them when we was all in the fields, and this afternoon sun was raging and the Peace Committee man was driving us on and on. And Dune got up this song. Don't know where they found it, some old slavery times song they started singing, like taking the piss, you know, done in the old negro voice:

> "Massa got us digging, sun up till sun down.
> Massa don't know our names, everyone got the same pronoun:
> You digging there,
> You go faster,
> You slacking,
> Go harder, all o' you, dig like you care!"

'Dune sang that and everyone started joining in, the whole field singing, and the Peace Committee dude couldn't take it and walked off and we all finished work early. After that day, Peace Committee folk tried hard to learn our names and they never called anyone *you* again. That was all Dune's doing.'

'Yeah,' I said, remembering, 'I was there. I was there.'

'I got one,' said Footsy. 'I mean it's nothing long, it's more of a vibe. Dune's voice was something else, even just when they were talking, there was something smooth in their voice, like they'd been born with honey in their throat. Whatever they said, you appreciated it, not just for what they said, but for the sound, too, you appreciated their voice. That make sense?'

'I get you,' said Wires. He leaned back. 'Remember the time Dune sneaked up on a bird in a little tree and caught it in their hands? Tell that one, Footsy.'

And Footsy did.

The two of them told stories, and they all sounded true. Yet none of them was the hot stink and sweet, sweet sweat of the real Dune. And even though I couldn't recall even the half of Dune, I knew somewhere inside me, Dune was fully there.

'I'm tired,' I said finally.

When they left me, I zipped the tent, pulled the blanket of night over me and let the tiredness emerge from my bones. I wanted deep sleep. That way Dune would come to me fully. Only I couldn't catch that kind of sleep. Once or twice, I glimpsed Dune's face, only for it to immediately fade from me.

Footsy was above me. Someone else: Wires. Footsy was talking.

'Listen, like Wires says, things are moving. The full set of night drones didn't come overhead last night. Some of us remembered new stuff last night, Ax. From before this prison camp time.'

'Too late for me,' I said. 'They're wiping Dune from me. I have nothing. Not even Dune's eyes. I was sleeping, trying to remember. What colour were they?'

'Dune's eyes were autumn leaf brown. And their smile could light a room. I know it's hard but don't worry about it. It'll all come back,' Footsy said. 'Your SIM is only attacking that specific memory because it knows that's what's important to you. Drink more. Get your maidenhair levels up. You can fight it.'

'It's happening soon, Ax,' said Wires. 'It's all gonna go off. We goin' in, we goin' in.'

Wires looked buzzed. How come I didn't care?

That afternoon, I went into the fields. It was good for me, they said, to get back into a routine. Elizabeth X came by. She squeezed my shoulder, let me rest in her arms. Her incense smell was strong and I remembered Pharaoh and how she'd lost him and how he had the same scent as her. She took my hands in hers. She was murmuring into my ear. 'We are so close, Ax. And we need you.'

'But I don't have anything left, Elizabeth,' I pleaded. 'I don't have anything to give you.' I sobbed into her.

She held me. 'We got you,' she whispered, 'we got you. Here. Take this earring. I know you been fangirling on them.' She pressed the miniature Afro comb earring into my hand. 'It's soon. The drone's coming in and we're counting on you, Axel. Don't quit on us now.'

Then, as I clutched the earring, Elizabeth X and Footsy and Wires talked softly together.

28

The Line Map

A fever held me. I kept waking to find Footsy at my side, now swabbing my forehead, now forcing me to eat, now pressing towels to my head. Gradually, the fog in my mind lifted. I saw daylight without it hurting. I went out and bathed at the standpipe, Footsy holding me up, now watching on. I went to fetch food from the Peace Committee tent. The queue was long. I shuffled in the line. The speaker inside the tent was playing. *You are special. You are loved. You are patient. You are good. You conform. You are peaceful.* I paid it no mind. When I got to the front of the queue, the stew was congealing. It was a mix of brown noodles and old carrot chunks. I sat in the food tent and swallowed it without letting it touch the sides of my mouth.

I went to the fields and tried to dig but they said I was too weak. A heavy rain fell. Footsy and Elizabeth X walked me back to my tent. She took my pulse and made me drink. She looked at my tongue and into my eyes, and asked me lots of questions, like who I was, how was I feeling and what did I remember about the dangers in camp.

Next day, Elizabeth X was in my tent again and she brought out some little box of tricks and scrolled through a page of code and asked me to tell her what it was. It was JavaScript. She pressed it close, so I actually looked. It was a live feed shell, taking weather data and transforming it into graphics, and it had an unexploited decision path subroutine, just waiting to be hacked.

She was happy with that.

'It's what I expected,' she said to Footsy.

'What?' I asked.

'Ax still reads code like nobody.'

A couple of days later, when I woke, my fever had completely gone. I turned and there was a diagram by my head on starch paper. It showed the Underground's delivery drone from three angles: side-on, top, bottom. The diagram had cutaways, and the sheet also listed the drone's dimensions, colouring and weight. A line map underneath showed where the drone was going to be landed. I studied it. A worm's eye view showed the undercarriage and the slot where the phone would be housed. I absorbed it all then I put the starch paper in my mouth and ate it.

Footsy came by and asked the usual questions. I passed the test. My head was fine, my lungs were better. I had good cognitive function. All through the questions, there was an edge of excitement in her throat, and in the end, I called her on it.

'What's got you so buzzed?'

'I've been put in charge of artillery. I'm the new captain.'

'Good for you. You'll make a good captain. Should I salute you from now on?'

She laughed at that.

29

Scratches in the Dirt

They were like a tag team. Shortly after Footsy left, Elizabeth X arrived at my tent.

'It's on. The delivery drone is coming.'

'When? Now?'

'Imminently. Here's how it's going to happen. Budge over.'

I shifted and Elizabeth X pulled the groundsheet up at one side and drew with a stick in the hard soil and dead grass exposed there.

'You are here. The runway cuts across here. You'll be looking for our drone marshals. They will guide you to the drone. They'll be in reflective paint, so shiny blue bodies, moving around randomly. They'll form a circle only when the drone has landed. That's your cue to run, get to the centre of the marshal circle, get the payload. From the diagram, you know exactly where on the drone undercarriage it will be. You'll have protection on your run. A team will be alongside you, in case of Blood guards. Or Scavengers. Or dogs. You pick up the drone. Pull out the phone. I'll be with you within five seconds of that. Else you smash it. Understand?'

'Smash the phone?'

'Yes. If I'm not at your side within five seconds. Rip the back off. Someone will hand you a rock. The SSD is a chip soldered to the motherboard, dead centre of the phone. Smash that and the

292

data automatically deletes. *If* I don't arrive by your side. It's damage limitation.'

'OK.' I absorbed the information. 'And if you do arrive?'

'You follow me, I'll take you to where we're going to upload the hack code.'

'The hack code and the handshake that gets us in so we can deploy it. I have to graft them together without any rehearsal?'

'If the code's good, it will be simple. You graft the handshake protocol to the code on the phone. Then execute upload to the Bloods' drone server. That's all.'

'Haha. I pray to Black Jesus it's as easy as that. Will it be in daylight or at night?'

'The Resistance is not saying. Timings are on a knife edge. Any other questions?'

'The marshals. How do they get the signal?'

'You don't need to know. Just run to them when they form the circle.'

'Why me, to do the run?'

'We want as short a chain as possible from the drone landing to getting that code uploaded. Chains have links. Links break.'

She scratched converging arrows into the soil diagram.

'There's plenty that could go wrong. We might be under attack from drones. Guards. Dogs. Scavengers. The Resistance drone may not land or could get hit out of the sky by Bloods' craft or friendly fire. Or the phone could drop out. Or is not there.'

'But I just concentrate on the marshals and the run?'

'Correct. Once I join you, you'll sprint with me, for some distance, with the phone,' Elizabeth X said. 'And after all that physical action, you'll need a cool mind for the code. You got it?'

'Yeah, I'm good, don't worry about me, worry about yourself,' I said.

For the first time, Elizabeth X smiled.

Then she began rubbing out all the mud drawings with her boots.

'Great. Get some rest. Footsy will call within the hour for a further briefing.'

I was ready for Footsy when she came through.

'Brief away,' I told her.

'You'll be embedded with artillery,' she said. 'And Elizabeth X insists you know what's happening around you while you're with us.'

'Fine.'

With her knees poking through her black trousers, and a needlepoint knife switching from fist to fist, Footsy ran through the plan. She explained the angle from which the squad had to fire the catapults, and what shots they would use when aiming at different drones. Then came the shooting distances and best firing sequences for the smaller drones. She laid out the anti-Scavenger strategy, and ways of avoiding ambushes. She went through whistle signals, hand signals, and the new defences against the Bloods' flamethrower drones, including the new rules on hair gunk and berets.

'There will be diversions planned,' Footsy said, 'to confuse Bloods' forces.'

'What diversions?'

'They haven't told me. For security reasons. But Elizabeth X says things will happen in the battlezone or beyond that we won't know about in advance and not to get sucked into them. That's all she'll say. We stick to our plan.'

'Got it.'

'There will be a smoke screen. When that goes up, that's the sign that the Resistance drone is set to fly in. The Resistance drone crew are in position already. The flight takes one hundred and sixty seconds. If the smoke gets cleared in that time by enemy drones and our drone hasn't landed, we shoot for the spy drones, take out the Bloods' eyes. When you run, you will have blockers tackling anyone or anything that attempts to intercept you. Just focus on getting to the drone. If the drone is captured by Scavengers, or anything else major, you will hear the "abandon mission" whistle. Then everyone heads to the gates. Your blockers will take you. There'll be a mass breakout attempt there, that's the Plan B. Again, no further details on that. If Plan A locks, the drone lands, you get the phone, and you go with Elizabeth X.'

'And if both me and Elizabeth X are killed enroute to wherever it is we're going with that phone?'

'I asked Elizabeth X that. She said we didn't need to know.'

'But they've planned for our deaths?'

'No one is bigger than the plan, Elizabeth X says. Not even her.'

'What if the camp gets restless and people start trying to break out early?'

'It won't happen.'

'People might see the Bloods' drones getting hit and fancy their chances?'

'Everyone has to wait for the code to upload to the Bloods' night drones so the hack code can brick our head SIMs. That means waiting for the night drones.'

'I know that. But restless is restless.'

'Not gonna lie here. There will be no early breakout. The Underground will impose discipline. For everyone's sakes.'

'And what if, after all this, the Resistance code doesn't work? What if our SIMs blow when we break out?'

'If the SIMs blow, then we're dead, end of. If they don't blow, and we survive, there are three surgery centres on the outside that the Resistance has set up. You can get the SIM hardware physically removed from your head at one of those. They're not saying where yet.'

'For security reasons?'

'Yup. But they exist. Elizabeth X swears.'

As we were talking, Wires came into the tent. Footsy greeted him and he palmed her a message. She glanced at it and went quiet for a moment, then she said, 'Look, I've got to go.'

'Sure,' I said.

Footsy glanced at Wires, then left.

'What are you doing?' Wires asked me after Footsy had gone and we'd sat in silence a while. I had a little metal prong in my hand and was scraping away.

'Carving Dune's name on these pieces of flint. If I get the chance to let loose with a catapult, I want Dune's name on everything I hit.'

'I feel you,' said Wires.

He left soon after.

I got the sense Footsy and Wires were both watching me, gauging how strong I was, how ready I was, and reporting back.

30

The Drop

'Wake up, Ax.'

It was Footsy. Patting my face. I caught her hand.

She grinned. 'Good reflexes. Drink this.'

'What's the news?' I asked.

'Who said there was news?'

'I can see it in your face.'

'The drop is on. Word from Elizabeth X. Bloods are seriously weakened. Last night there were only two night drones covering the entire camp. The gates opened this morning, but the Scavenger squad never moved. They backed away and disappeared into the Interrogation and Reception centre. An hour later, same thing. There's been no new arrivals. No deliveries. The guards are shouting at each other. It's chaos outside the I and R centre. Probably inside too. Pull on some clothes.'

The sky was the usual grey, the wind the usual blustery. Yet something was in the air. The lines of washing were gone. A kid, no older than ten, stood dressed to the nines with a packed bag, staring at us until an arm tugged her back into her tent. On paths, people were hanging about, shoes fully laced, talking; two carried catapults openly. Footsy nodded to them. They nodded back. Then went quiet as we passed.

Footprints in grass showed people had been busy in the early morning. Fresh piles of stones were heaped up along the pathways. We reached the tent zone's perimeter. I turned and looked. To casual eyes, we were a vast refugee camp under United Nations humanitarian relief canvas, pitched among rubble, piles of refuse, busted roads, boggy paths. We were scruffy, dirty, and SIM'd. We were a people beaten down and ready to rot.

Yet.

Footsy, tugging at me. I followed her and we hung low, following the lip of a road then slipping into the last grass expanse before the gates. It looked down at the I and R centre. Guards were standing around. Some of them didn't have uniforms on now. Two of them were having an argument that briefly became a scuffle. One side of the centre's steel door was hanging off its hinges. A flatbed wagon was reversed to those doors and boxes were being loaded by two men in courier uniforms. Even the fence was sounding different. You heard a stutter every five seconds in the hum. Something big was up.

Footsy absorbed all this. Then we were on the move again. We crossed east to the crop fields. Nobody was there and the crops were gone, only stalks left. Peace Committee orderlies were turning people away, advising them to chew remaining food more slowly and that the leaves of some grasses were edible.

All day, I had to stick with Footsy. She was my minder, she said.

We crisscrossed the tents, Footsy nodding to people, giving hand signs, occasionally she was palmed messages which she read and ate. All around us there was this scurrying and quickness of step. Glances that were more than the Black nod, more than the camp's *keep on*. A silent conspiracy. Something momentous was happening, something awesome. I gazed in wonder. And wondered.

Late afternoon, there was an air drop. Bloods' propaganda leaflets rained down, warning that the SIMs in our heads would explode if we breached the fence. The same leaflet told us:

**The Second Coming of the Messiah is Near
and Great Joy is soon to be had by all
Believers when all shall Hail Mara and be
Washed in the Newborn Blood of Jesus Returned.**

So, the Bloods were gearing up for their imminent Second Coming. No wonder they were in chaos. Second Comings were no doubt intense. We burned the leaflets in the campfires.

The Underground's drums got going and their tempo spoke. Plans were advancing at speed. Footsy took a message and when the messenger burst away, turned to me.

'This is it, the code is flying in. Right now. We need you at Runway Two. Artillery is gathering. I have to take you.'

We crossed the tent zone, heading south-west for Runway Two. We passed two children playing hopscotch. Their heads picked up, tracking us.

Magpies, perched on rubble, calling out loud enough to be mistaken for car alarms. The sky was clear, and as vast as ever.

By Runway Two, I noticed new crawl holes. They had full steel panels covering them.

The catapult squad was gathered in an open concrete culvert, shifting nervously. Haze designs patterned their faces and deflector patterns spattered their clothes. They looked jittery.

The terrain map was imprinted on my mind. The exact layout. I visualised making the run to the Resistance drone and removing its payload. Then keeping pace with Elizabeth X. Wherever she took me, when we got there, the rest was on me. The whole camp would be free if I could get my code brain working. If I could splice the hack code with the handshake code. If I could get it running so it would beam into the Bloods' night drone operating system when the Bloods' drones flew over. A long list of *ifs*. Plenty of room for things to go wrong.

I looked up and saw them now. Drone marshals. Blurred, crouching blue figures scattered around at the tent zone's southern edges, their reflective paint glinting. When next I looked up, the blue figures were gone.

I could feel my fever rising again.

By my side, Footsy nodded to me: *This is it.* Elizabeth X wasn't in the culvert. Ammunition got passed along and we armed up. Footsy gave a last briefing as we did this.

'That time we maybe never dreamed could happen? It's happening. The Bloods have been going crazy out there, chasing around. But the Resistance drone crew are in position and the drone is coming through. Our job is to keep the air channels clear so it can land. When the marshals signal it has landed, Axel is going to run to the landing spot, grab the drone's payload and get it to the Underground to do what needs to be done with it. Only Axel. Anybody else from artillery even touch the drone and they'll be killed. Understand? Runners and blockers, that includes you. Only Axel picks it up. Axel will get it safely away. Let's make this happen. Are you feeling it? We the people!'

'We the people!' came a chorus of subdued replies. We were nervous as fuck. Though under that, determined.

'All right,' Footsy said. 'Positions.'

We clambered out of the culvert, raced across the runway and climbed into our crawl holes.

Footsy was in a hole with me and we shared one last hug.

A warning whistle went. *The Resistance drone was airborne.*

The marshals began moving from the edges of Runway Two at the southern edge. They dropped flat into the grass there.

Noise from the gates. A Bloods' alarm sounding.

Footsy held up a hand and we readied catapults. I started counting down in my head, my eyes never leaving the blue marshals.

That weird feeling. A face: *Dune's.* In full detail. *Don't blub.* A breath.

Footsy, in my ear. 'Channel the energy, Ax, yeah?'

I nodded.

A flash of mirrors. Signalling.

'Fifty!' Footsy shouted out.

Due north, small dots flew up above the gatehouse. Bloods' spy drones launching. The ground shook. Scavengers behind the gates.

'Forty!'

Boosh. Red mist wrote itself across the sky, spewing from a dozen spinning canisters. They scrawled the sky scarlet. Would the Resistance's drone be able to see through that? Lidar and Terrain Relative Navigation were optical systems. Elizabeth X had not mentioned alternatives. The mist spread. The noise at the gates ramped up. Propeller hum. The jetting engines of heavy Bloods' drones. They took up a position high and too far north for our artillery to attack them. *Let them come closer.* More engine whine, high up from the north. I recognised the engines' signature. Flame drones. I saw them now. Two rows of fire, heading our way. The massed ranks of an airborne army. Had the Underground called this right? It looked like the Bloods owned these skies.

'Thirty!' called Footsy.

A drawbridge alert sounded, the Underground drums imitating the rattle of the drawbridge chains. The drumbeats scattered into a higher-pitched gate opening alert. The Scavenger squad was entering.

The blue marshals were up now, by the edge of Runway Two. They were without cover. The Bloods would see them easily if the overhead mist cleared.

Footsy jumped out of the crawl hole and I followed her. 'Runway positions!' Footsy called out. 'Load!'

Bloods' drones with large lateral fins had risen and aligned into a hawk profile. Now they burst across.

I saw now what those fins were. They sucked at the red mist, absorbing it, dispersing it.

'Shoot! Shoot!' Footsy cried.

The first rank fired too early and missed. The second rank caught the finned drones even as they twisted in avoidance manoeuvres.

Four of the nine finned drones smashed down. The other five hauled up and off. But the drones had done their job. The air above us had changed from deep red to pink and patches of sky were completely clear. Including the patch above the blue marshals.

The whine of the flamethrower drones.

'Down!' Footsy cried.

We jumped back into the crawl holes.

A whistle blew three short blasts: the firing sequence for flint volleys.

The blue marshals had dispersed. Or, at least, I couldn't see them.

Six flamethrower drones came low, flying in arrow formation through the remains of the mist, their flamethrower arms lowered. To smell petrol now would be to smell death.

'Steady!'

Footsy waited. Waited. Waited. Then called it: 'Aim and fire!'

The third artillery row hit the lead drone, rocking it off-course. It veered east, stuttering. From the second row, shards flew up that tore into drone armour. Two drones flipped, roared down into the grass verge of the runway, exploding there. I felt the heatwave roll across us. Three remaining flamethrower drones slewed south, then banked west and up.

They came again. Too high for us to reach them with catapults this time.

We heard a hiss from up there. We shot for them, but they were way out of range. *That hiss.* They were ejecting something. This stuff hung in the air above us. Tiny squares. Light as feathers. Clouds of them. Like silver confetti. Hanging up there in the air.

I turned to Footsy. '*What are they doing?*'

She didn't know either.

Maybe it was foil to disrupt the Resistance drone's lidar laser. Chaff.

The drones dropped lower.

'Load and fire bearings! All ranks!' Footsy cried.

A hail of ball bearings shot up. One drone came down vertically, without any spin. We thought maybe we had hit it, but it suddenly pulled up into a hover. Then detonated midair. Flames shot sideways. *A suicide drone.* Fire in the sky. I understood the chaff now. The little squares were plastic and the exploding drone had ignited them. Plasticky fire rained down on us. Trailing black smoke. Acrid. Impenetrable. Deadly.

The Underground Scavenger alert siren blared an octave higher. Gunshots came from straight ahead. The Scavengers were on the ground and closing in on us. Using guns for the first time.

'Load! Load!' Footsy ordered. 'Fire at will. Twenty degrees!'

We fired into the black smoke, at torso height. The limbs of Scavengers emerged from the acrid pall. An armoured arm holding a baton. A boot. An armour-clad leg. A visored helmet. All in flames. The Scavengers were burning. Set on fire by the Bloods' own flaming plastic squares. Yet still they kept closing in. One stumbled, fell. In the sky, red smoke spilled from a canister that shot across, low. Visibility hit zero.

I couldn't see any blue marshals anywhere. I couldn't see anything. Choking. I bent low. Saw gaps in the red and smoke. No sooner had the gaps opened, they closed.

Footsy nudging. Pointing.

Glimpses of blue. Running.

Footsy tapped her wrist. *Time.*

The Resistance drone was landing. I had to make the run.

'Where?' I asked her.

Her hand sliced the air, showing the route.

I glimpsed the marshal circle. Then it was gone in the smoke again.

Footsy was panicking. Pushing my shoulder. 'Go! Go! Go!'

It meant aiming straight at the Scavengers. Into the blinding red mist. Into the gunshots. I hauled myself up out of the crawl hole.

Then I was running.

Through the fire. The smoke. The bullets. The Scavengers.

Running.

For Pharaoh.

For Beta.

For Sly.

For Storm.

But most of all for Dune.

The Bloods had killed Dune. Killed even my memory of them.

And this numbness in me after Dune's death was a dangerous thing.

In Dune's name. I'd have my revenge.

I could kill anybody and not care.

I meant to break out and kill every Blood I could.

I heard a *boom* to the east, dropped, saw an eruption of flames low from that direction. Above me, Bloods' drones pivoted in a whine. Paused. Then began jetting due east. The boots of Scavengers turned too, and now pounded in the same new direction as the drones.

The Underground had promised a diversion. That must be it.

I kept going to the landing spot. Where were the marshals? I couldn't see them. Were they there? Had the Resistance drone landed intact?

Stride forty-four, I was mid-runway and hit the circle.

Five marshals. Some burned. Some bleeding. But there. Holding their ground. I burst through.

The drone was at my feet. Small as a toad. Ugly as a toad. Ugly as the diagram. Beautiful ugly. Its quad rotors were at rest. A burning plastic square had landed on it. Tiny flames lit its hood. I scooped the toad up. The red diode blinking at its underbelly. I plucked out the phone payload.

Then Elizabeth X was crashing into my side. She threw a cloth over the toad that extinguished the flames. Took the toad from me. Flipped it. Looked at its underside.

'I already got it,' I said, showing her the phone.

She clenched both fists in triumph. Then she grabbed my jacket yoke, pointed high and west. 'The old comms tower? You see it? Let's go!'

Elizabeth X led me on a run that skirted the bog zone. We dodged through broken roads, waded a sewer stream, took the camber of a rocky slope, pushed through tall grass.

I kept patting the breast pocket that held the phone, scared it might jump loose.

We had runners either side. The blockers.

I was blinking back sweat by the time we made it into the shadow of the comms tower. There was a rubble barricade blocking off the tower, topped by some kind of parapet. Elizabeth X halted. She put her fingers in her mouth and whistled. Three ascending notes. A whistle back. Movement behind the barricade. The sound of scrabbling through rubble. Bereted figures appeared at the parapet, waving us forwards. I ran for them. They caught my leap and hauled me by the jacket, flung me over the barricade. I turned and Elizabeth X had already leaped and was right at my shoulder, jumping down. Ahead, a door in the tower swung open. An arm, beckoning. My legs screamed pain. I dashed. I reached it. And Elizabeth X slammed into me.

The door swung fully back.

We were in. The door heaved closed behind us.

Inside, a long row of berets stood either side of the corridor walls, and as we moved through them, they high-fived Elizabeth

X, and bumped my fist. We took concrete steps that corkscrewed down into in a basement room.

A laptop was set up there, its innards on a bench separated from the screen, cables coiling from it.

On the screen, I could see the handshake protocol code.

Elizabeth X signalled I should connect the phone to the laptop. I fingered the micro-USB cable that was already hooked up to the laptop.

A detonation sounded above us that shook the basement.

My hands were hot and wet. The laptop screen flickered.

At least ten Underground members were in the room. And all eyes were on me. *No pressure then.*

I felt my pocket. It was there. I held the phone in my fingers. Checked which way up the wire would plug in. Then slotted the cable into the phone. The laptop responded. A song came through the laptop speakers. Elizabeth stared at me, her *whatthefuckisthat?* face on.

'Sylvester's "You Make Me Feel",' I said. 'The hack code is hidden in a song.'

It was a neat camouflage manoeuvre by the original coders.

I routed the pathway to the hidden hack code folder. The song cut out. I found the exec file.

The berets were talking among themselves quietly:

'Traffic flow?'

'No increase.'

'Airwave chatter?'

'Civilian quiet. Bloods' networks suppressed.'

The exec file ran. The laptop acknowledged the phone's SSD drive's hidden files and its code began scrolling on the screen. I froze it.

The tingle was in me again. I examined the screen. It was Breeze software, coded in JavaScript with short Python extensions. It was tight, elegant code.

I spliced the handshake protocol to the hack code's bootup subroutine then made it rerun from boot.

'Good?' Elizabeth X asked.

I nodded.

'What's it saying?'

'It's all good. It's hack code. Looks like AI driven.'

There was quiet now. I checked the output cable for the comms tower.

'You want me to press *Upload*?' I asked. 'Or you want to do it?'

Once we pressed *Upload*, the accuracy of the handshake protocol would be tested. It would be like turning the key in a door. Would it unlock access to the Bloods' drones? Or would it be a dud key: the wrong code?

She nodded. 'Go ahead. It's on you.'

A couple of people in here besides me needed a shower.

'What are you murmuring?' I asked Elizabeth X as my finger hovered by the *Upload* key.

'Names of the ancestors,' she said.

I pressed.

The handshake worked without a glitch. Then the code itself.

Elizabeth X continued murmuring as the upload ran. I watched it fly. It was the real thing. A beaut. Every subroutine flew neat and tight. No debug error lines at all. Whoever wrote this had a beautiful mind.

In little more than two minutes it was done. *Upload complete.*

The first high five. Just me and Elizabeth X. Everyone else hoping, holding their breath.

'What now?' asked Elizabeth X.

'We wait for the night drones to suck it up when they fly over tonight. Only takes one drone to take it up, and the code will rip through their cloud servers and run across all their drones. Then their drones download the code to us. When that happens, this hack code bricks our SIMs, frees our blocked memories, and shuts down the explosives triggers.'

'So it's all on the Bloods' night drones now, to suck it up?'

'Yup. Not gonna lie. Nothing more we can do.'

'We good?' a beret called out to Elizabeth X.

There had been more blasts outside. The tower basement floor was shaking.

'Yes,' Elizabeth X said. 'Stand down to amber alert.' She turned to me. 'We go now. Quit from here fast. Artillery is meeting at the tent zone for debrief. It's best for you to be there with me to explain what we've done, and the need to now wait.'

'OK.'

We ran from the comms tower, clambered over the barricade. Berets ran alongside us till we were at the perimeter of the tent zone. As we ran, I checked the skies. The battle was over, the skies clear. Flames still burned over by Runway Two. No sound or sight of Scavengers.

There were nods from more berets when we pulled up at the tents. They took Elizabeth X to one side and briefed her in whispers. From her reaction, it was looking good.

They left and it was suddenly only me and Elizabeth X.

It was the first time I'd walked through the tent zone with Elizabeth X, just the two of us, side by side. The camp was in high fever. Messengers came at her from all sides. I caught a couple of them. The Peace Committee had disbanded. The electric fence was still powered up and guards remained at the gates. There were two dead from artillery, many wounded, especially burns. There were no signs of Bloods' reinforcements on ERAC camp approach roads. There were rumours that a platoon of Bloods had been recalled from outside Leicester where they'd been shelling, and were heading to Huntingdon.

In the main standpipe square, the artillery squad was gathered. There were burns to shoulders, arms, hands. Blood seeped through bandages. Blisters swelled and skin peeled. There were sobs from the pain and shock. First aid teams were busy.

'We lost two,' said Footsy to Elizabeth X. She was kneeling by a standpipe, bandaging someone. 'Both to burns.'

Elizabeth X muttered something under her breath. Then, 'OK.'

'What now?' Footsy was terse. I could see small rectangles of charred skin on her arms. From the plastic. We all had them.

People were gathering round us and pointing to Elizabeth X. Even the medics looked up. The air filled with expectation.

'The news is good,' Elizabeth X said. She looked to me. 'Axel, please explain.'

'We did it,' I said. 'The code that will shut down these head SIMs and free us from them, went through fine. But we need to wait now. That code has to upload to the night drones when they fly over. By tomorrow morning, it'll be uploaded and done, and then we can break free.'

'You mean we're still not breaking out yet?' It was Wires. His forehead was bandaged. Blood trickled through the bandage's underside. 'We're always waiting,' he continued. 'Why not break out now? The guards are all over the place, yelling at one another. We took all their fire drones down. Let's break out now before they get reinforcements.'

Elizabeth X intervened. 'Trust me,' she said. 'We can't break out yet. The Bloods can still detonate our SIMs. The new code must upload and install first, to stop that happening.' She held her hands above her head and spread her fingers out. It was part prayer, part appeal. 'We are so close. Be patient. Keep the faith.'

There were mutterings. Some open shouts of rebellion.

I spoke up. 'I'm feeling what Wires feels,' I said, to Elizabeth X, and to everyone. 'I'm feeling what all of you feel. We've been waiting so long. Too long. I'm with you. This is my last night. I leave tomorrow morning, whatever happens. Download or no download. Chip deactivated or not. Tomorrow, I'm leaving. Or I'll die trying. But let's give it time. Let's find the strength to wait out this last phase. We can do it.'

I held my breath. There was talk. Quiet groans. Whispered exchanges. Slowly, the crowd swung round.

I nodded in thanks to them. I'd defied Elizabeth X. But I'd won time for us with the crowd. I looked over to Elizabeth X, lifted my chin with the question.

Elizabeth X conceded. 'Tomorrow's all I ask. We break out tomorrow.'

She smiled briefly to me, nodded to the crowd, but I could see she was disappointed in me. She glanced at me one final time, then turned and walked away.

I tried to make myself useful with the medics but my first aid skills were scratchy, and I could feel fever creeping up again on me. The medics had it all covered anyway. So I took back to my tent, lay down and fought the fever.

*

For the first time ever, as the evening dragged on, I wanted to hear the night drones coming over.

The wait wasn't long.

Darkness fell. The curfew wail went off.

From the sound of the motors in the sky, a full fleet of night drones was coming.

The whistling peaked.

I felt a surge of heat at the SIM side of my head. Then a background hum, a hum that I'd never noticed before, suddenly clicked off in my head. And I heard the night in pristine clarity.

The drip of a raindrop.

The shuffle of a leaf in the soft wind.

The night drones' high whistle shifted up a note. Then *whoosh*. Something happened in my head. It was like a six-screen, surround-sound cinema of my life started playing. It flowed and flowed: stuff that had been erased from me, everything I thought I had lost, came zooming back.

I lay there and let the images roll.

Mum.

Mum trimming my Afro with tiny scissors. *Mum's face. I was seeing Mum's face once more.*

Dune.

Dune throwing up in the car as Dad drove us up Stukeley Hill.

Dune, neck rolling, finger-clicking, singing, *Under the Heavenly Sky.*

Dune, dropping and laughing into my chest.

Dune, the full, glorious scent of them.

Dune and me, riding a plume at the indoor water park, both of us screaming and clinging to each other.

Dune keeling into me, laughing till their mouth frothed because of when we had that fish barbecue and Dad took a fish out of the ice and it started flipping and Dad yelped.

Dad, ploughing through his organic chicken-shit pile to rescue Dune, who had fallen into it.

I was bathed in a glow of remembering. Other things came. Images of Stukeley.

The turret of a blasted mosque, its mashed steel skeleton twisted up into the sky.

The church bells peeling at Stukeley's church. The bell ropes flying up and down in the belfry.

A lime dot that became a button that became a cuff that became the left sleeve of my fave Givenchy jacket that became my wardrobe that became my bedroom. I thought, *Yay. Nice camera work, Memory.*

Me and Dune getting locked in the fairground Cage of Doom. Its lurch. Flying up. The spin. Dune throwing up hot dog on me. They were always throwing up on me. That and the kissing.

A to-die-for close-up of Dune's lips.

The images kept rolling.

And my tears of bliss fell.

I woke in the morning refreshed.

I was Axel.

Was I free?

31

Everything and All

Klaxons. Whistles. Alarms. Cries. Whooping. The scatter of feet.
It was all sounding at once. I scrambled out of my tent.

Nobody stood around at the standpipes, disturbed, rocking, or
listless. No Blanked people shouted *'Holy! Holy!'*

The blur of running bodies. The tumble of collapsing tents.
People openly cursing the Bloods.

The Underground drums kicked in over it all, beating a message
loud and clear: *Rise up!* There was a charge of people to the gates
that was on the cusp of becoming a stampede. People with babies
at their hips. Herding children between their legs. People in filthy
rags. In patchwork dungarees. In bandanas and hijabs and shawls
and blankets. They flowed to the camp gates. Their hands full with
rocks. With catapults. Knives. Concrete lumps. Crossbows. Spears.
I ducked inside my tent, found my catapult and ammunition bag.
Shoved my knife into my trouser pocket. Then rushed back out
into the throng.

'I see you! I see you!' Someone shouted to everybody and nobody,
waving a metal tent pole.

'Freedom now!' a woman cried, her one hand clenching a book
with a black X on its cover, her other a lump of concrete.

'Free! Free we shall be!' A rhyming cry rang out amidst the
crowd from a choir group, in flowing purple gowns, accelerating

through the crowd in unison, their palms held up to the sky as they sped. 'Free! Free! Free! Free we shall be!'

Hemmed in by the crowd, I surged past static Scavengers at the north edge of the tent zone. They were in squad formation, but frozen; their batons were raised but their eyes dead. Like tinplate soldiers. We toppled them, beat them with tent poles till we heard bones break, then swept on.

Yes, read that again. We. I was part of the mob. A bloodlust was running through me. I could taste it on my lips and feel it in my heartbeat. And yes, those Scavs had once been human and maybe some pity should be afforded them. But no, I didn't feel it, no, I didn't care. That was how bloodlust worked.

Tents were going up in flames, the Peace Committee tent the biggest among them. Two ex-Committee members went running up and down alongside us in their white robes, holding up Bloods' leaflets, telling us not to bring down the wrath of the Bloods, especially now the Second Coming was imminent. A thought struck me. Others squinted at them too. *How had they remained aligned with the Bloods now their SIMs were shut down? Did their actual minds really believe the Bloods' propaganda?* Nobody paused to debate this. Two purple-robed church singers cracked the ex-Committee heads with bricks, and the Bloods' leafleteers dropped into the dust and mud.

We crossed Runway One and merged with two other crowds coming from the tents. The chant went up: *'The time is now! Freedom now!'* Clenched fists shot into the air in unison. A memory of a march with Mum and Dad in Stukeley stole into my mind. Another chant rose up. *'We the people! We the people!'*

We knocked tent poles together in the air. The sound soared into the sky.

315

The robed choir began a stomp march. 'To the gates!'

As we neared the perimeter of the tent zone in the north, the Interrogation and Reception centre hove into view. The boom of the Bloods' crane remained high and bodies were still swinging from it. Guards were black dots on the white concrete forecourt of the centre. There were not more than twenty dots there, a handful more were closer to the gates. The grey cubes of four trucks were outside the centre, and two vans. No tanks were parked up by the centre. Or on the approach road. No rocket launchers. No grey Bloods' jets circled above.

A frightened roar rose from the crowd ahead of us and the crowd split, as if gouged. Frenzied barking. A flash of bared fangs. Dogs bounding into us. The moat dogs. Dobermans. A low growl. The lead dog neared. Leaped. Screams. Running. It caught the arm of a toddler in its jaws, wrestling the child from her parent, shaking the child this way and that. A single machete blow decapitated the dog and blood spurted from its neck. The machete bearer scooped up the toddler and passed her to the man who had been carrying her. The child was smeared in blood, both the dog's and her own and her broken arm was lifeless, the child herself howling. The crowd beat the dead dog until its blood and bone and brains and fur were spattered over us all.

The entire camp population was at the gates now. Elizabeth X was in the eye of it all, guarded by a phalanx of camouflaged berets. I pushed through to them. Footsy was in the phalanx and spotted me. She fought through the crowd to get to me, pulled me to her. She was crying with joy. 'It's almost done,' she breathed, 'we're gonna be free.'

Wires was in the phalanx, looking blissful. We knocked fists.

There was a flurry of whistling from the berets around Elizabeth X, sending orders.

'How? How?' I asked Footsy over the whistles. 'All this?'

'We got confirmation from the Resistance,' Footsy shouted over the crowd's noise. 'The upload worked. Our SIMs are bricked. They can't be detonated. Our minds are free. Bloods' troops are still outside Leicester, bogged down. Resistance are hitting them with mortars, bombing roads, blocking reinforcements arriving at Huntingdon. We break out now. Escape before they can regroup. One of the Bloods' guards is working for us at the I and R centre. He's going to open the gates. Or else, drive the crane through them. And we've got cutters for the fences. Any which way, we'll get out. We've got crossbows. Smoke bombs. Fire bombs. Every Underground cell in the camp is activated. This is going off, Ax. This is it. Finally, we're gonna be free.'

I looked around and took in the scale of it. The size of the Underground forces. So many units. Most of them I hadn't known about. And I thought of the discipline the Underground had imposed, which meant no unit ever knew any other till now. None of us had known the full scale of it.

'I . . . I underestimated them,' I said. 'I mean the Underground.'

'We all did.'

I felt a pang. Dune would have loved this moment. Then I got mad. Dune *should* have been around to see this moment.

The carcass of one of the Bloods' dogs was being thrown at the gates. There were cheers. Then the crowd at the gates shuffled and transformed into an army, with ranks and divisions, massed in formations according to their weapons.

'You like it?' said Footsy, seeing it happen. She was proud. 'At the rear is the artillery squad, ready in case of drones or Scavengers. We've got bullet shields. Crossbow archers have killed all the dogs guarding the moat. It's only the gates and those guards holding us now. Look at those guards. Look at them shaking.'

'Are we getting the bodies down from the crane?' I asked.

'No. Elizabeth X says our business is the living, not the dead. We leave them there.'

Across the gates, beyond the moat, the Bloods' guards sheltered behind plastic riot shields. Their guns were unholstered. I wondered why the crossbow archers hadn't shot them already. What were they waiting for? The insider, I assumed, to open the gates.

A Bloods' klaxon started up.

A chant got up from the crowd: 'Force the gates! Force the gates!'

The metal drawbridge began lowering, to cheers. *The insider, coming good.* It caused panic among the guards. Some fled for the grey trucks. The trucks fishtailed away along the camp's approach road. There were shouts among the remaining guards. Threats. An officer rallied them and the remaining guards retreated into the I and R centre building.

I expected the gates to open after that, or the crane to move, but instead there was a spark from the electricity substation behind the reception centre and the yellow beacon lights on the gates went out. The electricity had been cut. The gates wouldn't be opened by anybody throwing a switch.

More whistled commands flew from the phalanx of berets. Three steel bars, each the length of a railway sleeper, passed over our heads. Berets wedged the ends of the bars into the gates. The entire crowd surged forward and those closest took the bars into their midriffs and onto their shoulders and began to heave. Grunts rose up at every heave, each heave ending in a cheer as the gap between the camp gates inched wider and wider.

Thup, thup.

Gunshots.

From the I and R centre's upper windows.

Screams.

We ducked down and scattered. The bars were abandoned, still wedged in the gates.

The air above us thickened with crossbow bolts that flew up to the centre's windows. Glass shattered.

Thupthup. Thupthup. Thupthupthup.

Bullets. Raking across those at the front of the crowd. I felt a brush across my forehead. *Death passing by.* I dropped down to my knees.

Blood. Screams. A whistle.

A cry from one of berets, down on the ground: 'Elizabeth X's down! Medics! She's down! She's hit!'

A barrage of crossbow bolts flew up at the reception centre. Not a metre away from me, Elizabeth X lay on her chest. Footsy had dropped low to her. I crawled over and joined them. A row of berets rushed across in a clatter of steel shields. I heard the *whup* of more crossbow bolts. The clatter of the shields forming a canopy around us. Bullets ricocheting.

Footsy had cupped Elizabeth X's head. I was down by Elizabeth X's other side. 'We'll get you out,' I said. *Where were the medics?*

The hail of bullets stopped. Either the crossbow archers' covering fire was working, or the Bloods' snipers were lying dead or wounded up there.

Elizabeth X had a thin line of blood trickling from her nose. She beckoned to me with a hand.

Whistles. I could hear the crowd at the gates. I heard the heaving restart. A great roar rose up.

'Through! Through! We're through!'

I lay my head down next to Elizabeth X's, close enough to see particles of dust lift as Elizabeth X breathed in through her mouth in small gulps. She wanted me even nearer.

We had to get Elizabeth X out now, while we could. I lifted her arm to put across my shoulder so I could move her.

'No,' Elizabeth X gasped, withholding her arm.

Blood was trickling across her upper lip. 'Here, Axel. Take this and get out.' She fumbled at her neck with a gloved hand. There was a locket on a necklace there. She pulled it off. 'Look inside,' she said. She took another breath. 'This is all the code you'll need. In the locket. On the micro-card inside. The Underground's store of code. The Resistance's store of code. All of it. Keep it safe.' She pushed the locket into my hand.

I popped it and looked. A tiny, rectangular, silver sliver.

She placed her hand over mine, sealing the locket shut. 'Take it and go. Leave me. I . . . I got this. Get out. That's an order.'

I looked around, called out. 'Footsy! Where are you? Footsy!'

Elizabeth X cursed through red teeth. 'No! You and Footsy go! I said I got this. The medics will patch me. Go now. Break free! That's a command. We need you on the outside. Carry the code. This is your moment. Go!'

I cradled Elizabeth X's head in my hand. A sac of blood burst somewhere inside her and blood gushed out of her nose and mouth.

Shit.

I kissed her forehead and her head dropped and the full weight of it fell into my palms and I knew she was dead.

There were screams behind us. Frozen Scavengers had blinked back alive inside the camp.

I let Elizabeth X go. I couldn't see Footsy anywhere. The gates were wedged open. I ran into the maw of the crowd and clambered through the gap in the gates with them.

Dust and smoke. More screams. Thuds. The *whoosh* of crossbow bolts again. A gunshot. Another fusillade of bolts. I ran across the lowered drawbridge. Made it to the I and R centre. An angry camp mob was swarming there. I heard a gunshot from inside, but nobody fell, nobody moved back, the cries of rage only got louder. Bolts whizzed above our heads. The crowd was smashing the lower windows with bricks and rubble, climbing in through them, climbing up the walls, clambering onto the roof, pulling tiles off there. I went inside the centre with the crowd through the smashed-off door. I drew my knife and slashed a guard lying on the floor, butchered him across the face. Yeah, I was going psycho. I had that in me. You'd always seen it? Thanks. I pushed the same knife deep into another fallen guard's guts. *For Dune.* I was only getting started.

I saw a guard face down in an office room. Turned him over, ready to stab him too. He was dead. I stabbed him anyway.

Sirens and caterwauls and screaming. Yells. Thuds. Gunshots.

Suddenly, the madness all around me muted. I looked around and realised there was nothing for me inside here.

I left. Even as the mayhem continued. I didn't look back. Didn't flinch at the cries and shots and yells behind me.

I know you're thinking the ending of a story like this should have bombs going off, maybe a tank firing and a big building blown up. OK, there were more shots fired. The crossbows replied, the spears were thrown. But I didn't hang around to see who had shot whom. It just didn't seem like good life skills. That was one of Dune's phrases, I bet you spotted it. *Good life skills*. If I had bullets and a decent gun and those dogs that tore Dune apart in the moat were still around, I would have shot them for sure. I still presumed Dune was dead. From the noise the dogs had made ripping into Dune, it was a fairly safe bet. So I didn't dawdle, like, stay in the reception and find a filing cabinet or Bloods' laptop and go through guardhouse records, trying to discover if they found Dune's body in the moat and if they did, where they took it. Or try to find out which Bloods' roadblock crew had shot my mum and dad dead and raped Dune. I didn't do anything organised and stupid like that. I didn't need proof that Dune was dead. OK, maybe I liked carrying that little bit of uncertainty about it, not knowing for sure. Or maybe I got out fast because I was more attached to staying alive than finding out about Dune, which I guess makes me a bit of a coward in your eyes. Hey ho. I can live with that.

I knew from what Footsy had told me that the victory at the camp was going to be temporary. There was no way the Bloods were going to let that camp go, they were having too much fun in there. Their tanks up north would be turning around. Their fighter jets would come back and strafe the place, and they'd get the fence and the gates working again and try to round everyone up, maybe even send their drones out, looking for escapees. I had to get away from here. My head hadn't blown up. I guessed the Resistance's hack code had saved me from that fate, saved us all, though of course, we all still had a SIM in our heads. And for some perverse reason, hack code effective or not, it wasn't a feeling

I enjoyed, carrying a small unexploded bomb in my head. Elizabeth X's locket containing the micro-card was in my trouser pocket. And I had a bag on my back with some other stuff.

I could hear the whirr of drones nearing. Were they ours or the Bloods'? If they were the Bloods', then the beret and the gunk might give me some protection from their sensors. But I got off the road. My goal was to get to a Resistance SIM removal centre and have the SIM lifted out. It was the only way to know for sure you were free. Getting to a removal centre meant heading north. That meant dodging the Bloods along the east coast, the ones who had been heading north but were now, from what Footsy had said, doing an about-turn. Dodging the equally shitty White Army who were dug in around Leicester. Dodging the British National Liberation Front who were scattered everywhere around the north. Dodging the Pure English Army who were camped outside Birmingham. A lot of dodging. The people who wanted me dead had tanks and rocket launchers and bullets and flamethrower drones and trackers. I had a pocket catapult. No problem then, right?

I didn't try to team up with anyone. Truth was, I didn't really know where Wires or Footsy or any of the others were. I'd lost them in the mayhem at the gates. And I didn't fancy waiting around to see if we could reunite, sing *kum ba yah* together.

Instead, I did what my dad said I should always do in these situations. I put one foot in front of the other. I walked down that road and away from the camp. I took the smallest lanes, to avoid Bloods' reinforcements. If I heard an engine, I threw myself into the hedgerow. I kept walking for hours.

I came across a wind turbine on a small farm. It was knocked over, its propellors gone. I saw car wash equipment set up on the forecourt of an abandoned petrol station and four bloody corpses scattered around. By an old road sign pointing to London, I saw a huge steel pipe butt, with a colossal tap structure welded to it, wrapped in oil cloth, dripping a clear fluid. It could have been water, but I didn't risk it.

I was heading north, away from London, away from Huntingdon. I kept listening and checking the sky for planes and drones. If I spotted one, I made myself small.

Everything looked new after so many weeks in the prison camp. And small things looked beautiful. Mist. Soft rolling fields. Sheep. Telegraph poles carrying cables. Three small birds flying low in a straggly line. Sweeps of brown heather. A line of bare trees on a hill, looking like Arabic writing. Stone walls. The rusted, zinc roof of a storage barn half full of straw. The grey stump of a dead tree. A dead cow in a field. An old ironwork bridge painted red and full of rivets, bolts and intricate patterns and shadows.

Yes, the bridge looked pretty. It had grown dark, and I had grown tired. I slipped down the banks of the road and went along the riverside grass and nettles, walked a few metres until I was under the bridge. I clipped Elizabeth X's Afro comb earring onto my earlobe, and I curled up under that old bridge. And in the darkness, under the cover of the bridge, I cried softly into my hands. For everything and all. For Dune.

Acknowledgements

This novel couldn't have been written without the help of so many others. First, the two *amigos*. Tariq Mehmood was the prime instigator – the one who asked that key question 'What if?' and got us enthused about creating the world. Melvin was assiduous in going through every detail to ensure that this was no pipe dream, that we could actually do this. Both were an endless source of inspiration and speculation.

Then, more widely within the writing community, thanks to Clare Weze, Muli Amaye and Desiree Reynolds, for reading drafts and just plain keeping me going as a writer during this period, by expressing love for my work and reviving my faith when it flagged. Thanks also to the writing community at Cultureword, especially Identity black writers group, a wellspring of inspiration and encouragement.

And my coding friends. Thanks to the mercurial Manchester Coding Club, and to Florence Okoye, organiser of Manchester's first and highly influential Afrofuturist Festival. Thanks also to Maya Chowdhry, Femi Taylor and Dr Duddell. And, in the latter stages of the writing, to Michael at CERN.

For all the songs along the way, thanks to my musician-daughter, Naomi Kalu: we will record them, for sure!

Finally, to Andersen Press: thanks to Charlie Sheppard for her leap of faith and her thoughtful editorial creativity, and to Chloe for her gimlet eye.

Three Bullets

MELVIN BURGESS

My name is Martina.
You won't like me, not many people do.

While the big powers fight for the future of a war-torn England, all Marti wants is to escape. Just by being herself, she is everything that the ruling religious white supremacist government – the Bloods – hate.

With her friend Maude and baby brother Rowan, Marti heads out to find a new life away from falling bombs, fleeing refugees and brainwashing by the Bloods. All she thinks about is herself. But will her enemies – or her friends – stop her from finding her freedom?

'Funny, rude and violently enjoyable'
New Statesman